T0209263

Dawn of the Hunters

The Hunters of Infinity Series by Ryan Wieser

The Glass Blade

The Shadow City

Dawn of the Hunters

Dawn of the Hunters

Hunters of Infinity

Ryan Wieser

REBEL BASE BOOKS
Kensington Publishing Corp.
www.kensingtonbooks.com

REBEL BASE BOOKS are published by

Kensington Publishing Corp.
119 West 40th Street
New York, NY 10018

All Kensington titles, imprints, and distributed lines are available at special quantity discounts for bulk purchases for sales promotion, premiums, fund-raising, educational, or institutional use.

Special book excerpts or customized printings can also be created to fit specific needs. For details, write or phone the office of the Kensington Sales Manager: Kensington Publishing Corp., 119 West 40th Street, New York, NY 10018. Attn. Sales Department. Phone: 1-800-221-2647.

Rebel Base and Rebel Base logo Reg. US Pat. & TM Off.

First Electronic Edition: May 2019
ISBN-13: 978-1-63573-028-9 (ebook)

First Print Edition: May 2019
ISBN-13: 978-1-63573-031-9

Printed in the United States of America

My loves, they're all for you. My sunshine, my comet, thank you for our perfect world.

Prologue

He had become certain of one thing, and one thing only: Fire-Wielders were not to be found in Daharia. He had searched, traveling as far as he could during the brief time Lord Gredoria allowed him leave from the Blade, with the hope of finding more. In part, he knew it was because Gredoria was as fascinated by the idea of Fire-Wielders as he was, but it was also simply a luxury afforded to him for his superior abilities. He didn't need to train as hard, as fast, as long as his brethren. Hanson, Urdo, their masters—all of them knew he was going to be the next Lord Protector.

He leapt from his docked Soar-Craft, his boots landing softly on the lush ground underfoot. He had one night in Haycith before having to return to Azgul. He removed his dark gloves and ran a hand through his mess of brown hair. "You must learn to plait it," Hanson had told him. Hanson kept his golden locks in pristine order. "Or cut it," Urdo had quipped. He had laughed at his friends' suggestions. "When you shear those whiskers, Urdo, I'll cut it." He was close with his brothers, though inexplicably different from them.

He let his eyes trail up the path to his family home—an expansive manor, built from the smoothest of dark stones, melded together to form perfect lines. It was the largest, and grandest, of homes in Haycith. He was quite certain there was no place in the world he preferred more. Not even the Blade. He pushed open the heavy black door and entered the cool corridor. "Mother, Father." He bowed his head at the black stone busts lining the entryway. His family had long since passed away, a terrible accident claiming his parents' lives many years ago. The home was maintained by workers in his family's employ and whenever he had a chance, he would return to oversee the estate.

He crossed the dark hall, briskly leaping onto the smooth black stone stairs that led up to his chambers. He cleared several at a time, light on his feet, wondering—

He froze. He had heard the movement beneath him, still in the foyer. It was the softest sound of leather brushing against stone. He had been certain of it. He knew when he was alone and he knew when he was being watched. Someone was in his home. With his hand lightly poised on the black railing, he flung his body back over the side, twisting in the air. He landed on the ground below in near-perfect silence, appearing behind the cloaked intruder. He struck quickly, locking his forearm around the hooded neck of his assailant.

"Big mistake," he hissed, shifting his position ever so slightly, ready to snap the intruder's neck.

"*Wait!*"

The woman's voice startled him, forcing him to loosen his grip. She spun about in his arms.

"Let me go." Her voice was deep, her eyes angry, her words an order. She had the longest fair hair he had ever seen; it trailed around her face, down her chest. She was young and she was beautiful. Despite trespassing in his home, she had barked at him with aggression, possessing a natural authority Hydo hadn't seen in many.

She wasn't the only one of them accustomed to snapping orders though, and while he refrained from harming her, he did not let her go. "Who are you?"

As she stared at him, her fiery gaze softened, the tension in her body lessening. "I heard you were looking for someone like me."

He finally loosened his grip on her. "I don't know who you are or what you've heard, and clearly you don't know who I—"

"You're Hydo, the greatest Hunter since Gredoria Vane himself. You're the next Lord Protector," she smiled, though there was a mocking tone in her voice.

"Aren't you clever. Then you know I can enter your mind and find out just as much about *you*," he threatened.

"No one's stopping you," she whispered, leaning into him, tilting her head up to his.

She was so close to him, he could have closed the distance with a kiss. He held her stare, wondering for a moment if that was what she wanted—if it was what *he* wanted. She was beautiful, but she was an intruder. She was a total stranger who had broken into his home to find him. He wondered who she was and why he hadn't already entered her mind to find out.

Suddenly, flames erupted around his hands. They were enormous, wild and crimson, and they laced over their interlocked hands, up his arms, circling about their embrace. At first, he feared that he had lost focus—that he had been so enamored by the woman he had started the fire without intent. With all his energy he concentrated on extinguishing the fire before he harmed her. Only when he couldn't did he realize the flames were not his own.

She held his gaze with a wicked smile painted across her perfect face. She kept her eyes locked on him and with her mind she willed the flames higher around them, building them up before extinguishing them instantly. She was a Fire-Wielder. He had crossed the greatest of territories in search ...and here she was.

"I told you, I heard you were looking for someone like me."

He didn't know what to say. He had never seen another with the power he alone had seemed to possess. He knew, logically, that there were others. He had grown disheartened with every futile search though. He shook his head at her slowly.

She continued to smile up at him. "You have the darkest eyes I've ever seen."

"And you have the greenest." He flicked his gaze over her once more. She was like him. *Truly* like him.

"Who are you?"

"You can call me Octayn."

Chapter 1

The Soar-Craft jerked violently, sending crates and weapons along with bedding and provisions flying about. Jessop and Falco gripped one another tighter. There was a deafening sound of wind blowing through the vessel. They were under attack.

"Falco—we're crashing!"

They fell faster and faster, and all she could think of was their son. They couldn't die in a Soar-Craft crash, not when they still needed to rescue Jeco from Hanson Knell and Hydo Jesuin. Jessop looked around the vessel, her eyes darting over panicked faces. She knew what she needed to do. "I need you to let go, Falco!"

"Never!"

Jessop gripped Falco tightly. "Do you trust me?"

The way he looked at her, amidst chaos, was with a perfect stillness. "Of course."

She kissed him, deeply, with all of her love. As their kiss ended he rested his forehead against hers. She slowly pulled away. "Then let go."

Falco stared at her with his concerned gray eyes, ignoring the surrounding panic, and finally let her go. She nearly fell, but her superior balance helped her regain her footing quickly. She turned, facing the control panel at the front of the Soar-Craft. She crouched low down in the aisle, and allowed for the force of the fall to move her down the vessel. She used her Sentio to throw items and falling men out of her path. She braced herself as she fell against the control seat. The vessel was falling nose-first. With a quick tumble, she leapt over the seat and fell against the glass window.

She could not deny that the sight of the desert ground, nearing so quickly, didn't concern her. She already disliked flying. She couldn't focus on the danger, though. She took a deep breath and laid both her hands against the glass, closing her eyes, and focusing with all her might. She knew they fell still. She breathed more deeply, and thought of Urdo and all he had shown her during their siege on Aranthol. She envisioned her abilities like a wave of light, traveling through her body, out her fingertips. She imagined the light clearly, and this time, it was a crimson red. It trailed from her hands, through the vessel, snaking around the Soar-Craft.

She thought perhaps the vessel was slowing, when the sensation of blood trickling from her nose distracted her. It wasn't working. She pushed the light further from her, focusing with all her might on catching the falling ship, yet it still fell. She didn't have much longer. She tried to regain her focus when his face appeared in her mind: Jeco. A perfect son, the exact image of his father with the same dark hair and gray eyes. He needed her. He needed her more than ever.

And if she were going to save him from Hanson and Hydo, she would need to survive this crash. She would need help.

"Falco!"

Instantly, she felt him at her side. He tumbled over the control seat and, realizing her plan, thrust his hands against the glass. "Urdo—push the plan to the others!" He shouted over his shoulder. Jessop couldn't think about the two other Soar-Craft traveling alongside them—*crashing* alongside them. She couldn't think about Urdo using Sentio to tell the Hunters on board the other vessels to attempt to copy her plan, to use their abilities to slow the vessels to a safe landing.

She couldn't think about anything other than—*crash!*

Jessop didn't need to open her eyes to know what had happened. The explosion, the instant smell of smoke. One vessel had already hit the ground. Suddenly, she felt Falco's fingers lock around hers. He held her hand and she could see his face when they were children, she could feel his kiss when they were youth, she could hear his vows the day they married, and with an unexplainable, violent jolt, their vessel froze in the air. The sound of men falling, yelling, boxes breaking, and weapons clashing into the metal walls in a cacophony of noise surrounded her. And then everything was silent.

Slowly, she opened her eyes, fearful that if she broke concentration for just one second, the vessel would smash into the ground below.

Jessop's stomach turned at the sight of the sandy ground not twenty paces below the glass she and Falco leaned against. There were thick, billowing clouds of black smoke racing across the window from the Soar-Craft that had crashed. She thought of Falco and Dezane's soldiers and felt more than sorrow. She felt rage. "Let's bring it down slowly," Falco whispered to her.

He held her stare and together, with their combined Sentio, they brought the vessel parallel to the sandy terrain, before focusing on lowering it slowly. She was thankful that whoever had shot them in the first place had ceased their attack, even if it were only temporary. Jessop could feel the blood drying on her face, the sweat dripping down her temple as she pushed herself, forcing all her attention onto the vessel. A deafening nearby *thud* distracted her, and instantly the Soar-Craft fell several feet.

"Easy! Easy!" Urdo's voice filled the cabin, calming those around him. Jessop kept her eyes on Falco. He nodded at her slowly. A bead of sweat hung on his brow. His fingers locked tighter around hers. She envisioned the red light gently lowering the vessel to the ground, and just like that, the Soar-Craft found a place on the soft sand. They had landed.

Jessop slowly released Falco's hand, turning to see the ransacked cabin, the eyes of all the men on her and Falco. Urdo nodded to her approvingly, "Hode Avay managed to land his vessel—though somewhat less slowly." She thought of the young Hunter Urdo had introduced her to back in the Blade and was instantly impressed. "Teck was with him," he added, and Jessop nodded slowly, knowing the Oren had many remarkable abilities.

She let her gaze move from Urdo, to Dezane, over the stunned faces of the many warriors they traveled with, to Kohl. He had a cut on his face, and Jessop knew he must have been struck during the fall, but otherwise he seemed fine.

Their vessel shuddered violently as they were struck again. The metal rung all around them, aching her ears. She grabbed Falco to steady herself. The Hara'agul assailants were shooting at them. Jessop thought of the fallen vessel, of Hanson traveling through these lands with her son. And she felt the fire burning inside her—the rage coming forth. She leapt over the control seat, moving around fallen items and men, making her way for the door.

Kohl immediately leapt in her way, and she could feel Falco following her. "Jessop—these aren't raiders, they are Soren—desert brigands—and they have a Bakunawa!" He referred to the giant canon they were using to shoot scrap metal at the Soar-Craft.

She didn't care if they were mercenaries or Soren or anything else. She didn't care what weapons they possessed. She side-stepped Kohl with ease.

"Not for much longer they don't." With a heavy slam of the release button, the door began to open, lowering down to the sand.

"Jessop—*Jessop*! You need to recuperate," Falco urged, appearing at her side.

"I'm fine."

She shrugged off his concern and ignored Kohl as he came up on her other side. She *did* feel fine. She had exerted herself greatly, but she did not feel faint or weakened by her feat.

As soon as the door was low enough, thick black smoke filled the cabin. The smell of burning flesh settled in her nostrils, reigniting her anger. Men who had followed them into battle, who had trusted her, were now dead. She immediately felt as though she were standing in the Gahaza Square of Aranthol once more, leading her men into Kohl's ambush. She knew her weakness. She was no leader. But that didn't change the fact that she was an excellent fighter.

She leapt from the doorway, her boots finding the soft sand with a firm landing. Through the smoke and hazy sky, she could make out the hordes of Soren from Hara'agul—and their Bakunawa. The Soren were unlike any Jessop had ever seen before. Their bodies were made up of metal scraps and exposed bone, flesh covering bits and pieces of their faces and trunk, a mess of wires and veins crossing over and under steel and cartilage. They wore red tunics and half of them had makeshift caps on, as if the skull bone and metal needed protection from the desert heat.

Centered within the group was the massive cannon. A giant rusted-red barrel, large enough for chunks of scrap metal to be stuffed into and shot back out. With a flick of her hand, Jessop sent the Bakunawa across the desert terrain, with such force that the barrel came loose from the wheelie-stand, rolling off into a dune.

A man with two silver eyes, wild black hair growing straight out of exposed bone, and a shining, metal jaw, shot his arms up, as if to guard himself from the flying, crumbling weapon. He turned, locking his eyes on Jessop, his metal jaw grinding in anger. He was their obvious leader. Jessop was certain that if any of the machine-men Soren knew whether her son had passed these lands, it would be him.

He pointed a boney hand at her, the sleeve from his crimson tunic falling back to expose a forearm made of shimmering copper.

"*Attack!*"

Jessop drew her daggers and flung them out before her, instantly striking two oncoming attackers in their fleshy trunks. With Sentio, she called the blades back to her, ducking under swords and metallic, skinless fists, incapacitating any who came before her. However many there were, they were no match for Falco, Kohl, and Urdo, who fought in a circle around her, keeping many at bay as she made her way for the silver eyed leader. Falco spun about her path. He moved his sword with such speed she could only make out a shimmering glint of its path. His lips remained tightly pressed together, his gray eyes dancing about his opponents with a sense of disinterest. What she had said aboard the vessel to him may have been true—perhaps she *was* surpassing his abilities of the mind—but that did not by any means diminish his vast skills with a weapon. He was unstoppable with a blade.

Jessop threw her arms out with carelessness, unconcerned by how much damage she inflicted and upon whom. The man with the silver eyes watched as his brigands fell at her feet, helpless against her and so many Hunters.

"Jessop, *duck!*"

At Kohl's instruction she dropped to her knees, sliding across several feet of silky sand, her body leaning so far back she could feel the trail her braid left in the granules. She saw as Kohl flipped over her, his sword spiraling about him, his blond hair whipping about his face. He landed with grace on her opposite side, cutting down a man with a metal bow and arrow trained on her.

She leapt back to her feet, appearing just before the Hara'agul leader. He reached for his hilt, but Jessop was much faster. She locked her hand around the metal and bone of his wrist and violently twisted it outward, forcing him to release the hilt with a sickening crunching of bone. With a forceful kick to the side of his knee, he fell before her and with all her might, she locked her fingers around his throat, only partially covered in skin. Her fingers were slick around exposed veins, her thumb futilely pushing against a sheet of metal leading up to his jaw. Nonetheless, she squeezed, knowing she could kill him regardless of his metal makings.

"We did not know you traveled with Falco Bane." He choked out the words, glancing over Jessop's shoulder. The ruckus had died out; she felt Urdo, Kohl, and Falco take their places at her side.

Jessop ignored his explanation for the attack. "Do you know Hanson Knell? The Hunter—he's been reported traveling this way with a boy." She could not control the speed at which her heart beat, the sweat appearing on her lip. She knew whatever information this man had could change her entire life.

His strong, boney hands found her wrist, trying to pry her fingers off of him, to no avail. She forced her fingers tighter into the mess of wires and bloody veins.

"We—*argh*—we all—*cahh*—kn—know—"

"He can't breathe, Jessop."

She ignored Urdo's words. "Answer me or die here."

She could see, in her periphery, some of his Soren army approaching once more. They were hesitant to reengage with the Hunters, but she did not question the depths of their loyalty. If they needed to, they would come to his aid. She refocused, clamping down with her strong fingers.

"*Answer me.*"

"He came through last night with a boy, a dark-haired, small thing."

Jessop released her grip on him. He coughed violently at her feet, blood dripping from his throat to the hot sand.

"Was the boy harmed?"

"No, he seemed fine. They didn't stay long, just refueled their vessel and left."

"He *seemed* fine?" Jessop spoke, her heart racing, her fists tensing.

Falco moved closer to her. "Jessop."

"That boy is *our* son, you fool. My son. Falco Bane's son!" Her voice traveled far, ringing about the dunes.

"We didn't know. I swear it." His voice was loud and desperate, his silver gaze turning from her to Falco.

"Jessop," Falco spoke her name once more, but it sounded so faint.

Blood was rushing to her head and she felt dizzy. White spots appeared before his silver eyes, down his metal and bone and flesh, over his red tunic, dancing across the sand all around him.

Mama.

She could hear him. She could hear her son. She spun around but saw no one—Jeco was not there.

Mama!

She blinked, and the Soren leader once again was in her sight, but no Jeco. She fell to her knees and grabbed his tunic.

"Where is he? Where is my son?"

She shook him with all her might. Jessop could see his mouth moving but she heard nothing. She shook him harder, and harder. She could see all of the exposed bones of his hands as he locked them onto hers, trying to push her off him, but she could not feel his touch. She could hear nothing but a distinct ringing. White spots clouded her vision. Blood thumped against her temples. She could taste blood—was she bleeding? She didn't know.

She closed her eyes and tried to focus. Someone was screaming. Was it her? She could feel the heat. She could smell the burning skin and charring bone. Fire. There was so much fire. Just as there had been when she was a child. The smell of burning flesh ...She had been so young then. She had come home to the small cottage her family had lived in Beyond the Grey to find Hydo Jesuin, Lord Protector of the Blade of Light, leader of the Hunters who patrolled Daharia, attacking her parents. Her father was dead on the floor. There had been so much blood. Falco had saved her. He had fought Hydo and forced her from the home. He had saved her before the flames could take her.

She could never forget the smell of the burning skin.

Strong hands pulled her to her feet, wrenching her back. The ringing was gone. The screaming had stopped. She could no longer hear Jeco. There were no white spots. There was just the Soren leader, his charred remains smoking in the sand. Jessop had burned him alive.

* * * *

The Soren had retreated at the sight of their dead leader, but not disappeared. They waited on the desert periphery, metallic skeletons whispering and watching, staring down at Jessop. She closed her eyes as the winds picked up the sand, forcing the smoke from the crashed Soar-Craft and the smell of the burned Soren into her nostrils. It was enough to make her want to wretch, but she resisted.

As the breeze calmed, she looked down on the charred remains of the Soren leader. She felt Falco's eyes on her, she could hear Kohl's unvoiced concerns in his mind, she could sense Urdo's alarm. She had killed with fire, without control, without true awareness. Slowly, she rose from her knees, her boots pushing softly into the sand. She knew she had scared them all and yet ...she did not care. Soldiers were dead. Brigands were dead. Jeco was still missing.

"Jessop."

She felt Falco's strong fingers coil around her elbow, willing her closer to him. She knew his thoughts. She was not controlling the fire—it was controlling her. It was true. The flames were unstoppable. She could not control the newfound ability and she did not care to. She was more powerful than ever, and power was what she needed in order to get Jeco back.

If it brings down any who stand between my son and me, what does it matter?

She pushed the thought not just to Falco—but to all of them. To Kohl and Urdo, to Teck and Hode Avay, who had since exited their Soar-Craft, joined by their surviving soldiers, to stare at her in shock, to all of the

Kuroi and all of Falco's army. She forced her thoughts into their minds without hesitation or apology.

She had horrified them—she could see it in their faces. None spoke. She jerked her arm free from Falco. She studied their expressions, the fear in their eyes, the uncertainty as they looked between her and Falco.

"Tell me! What does it matter?"

Several startled at her anger—obviously fearful of the flames she could reignite.

"We don't kill indiscriminately, Jessop."

The soft words were spoken by Kohl. She locked her green gaze on his hazel eyes, large and filled with concern.

She took a step towards him. "Any who stand between my son and me—any who align with Hydo Jesuin—I will kill."

"I know…" he began, taking a cautious step towards her. "We'll get your son back. But we can't kill *everyone*. We aren't monsters."

He held his hand out to her, as though offering peace, or companionship. She stared at his fingers—at his sword-wielding hand. It was the same hand he had used to cut down her enemies, the same hand he had once wrapped around hers in affection. He had fallen in love with her the instant they had met. She was never supposed to feel anything for him, he had merely been a part of a greater plan. It would be a lie to insist that things had played out that way. She had cared. She had cared so much she'd thought of killing him, to hide their bond, and she had cared so much she had also thought of saving him from Falco's wrath.

She thought of the day she let Falco into the Blade. She thought of all Kohl had said to her then. She had offered him the opportunity to return to his family, and he had spat it back in her face. *How could they ever be safe when a monster like you knows where they are?* His words had hurt. As most honest words tended to. She pushed the memory into Kohl's mind, letting him recall his own sentiment.

She looked away from his hand, returning her gaze to his big, dark eyes. "Speak for yourself."

Chapter 2

Twenty-five years ago

He watched her with narrowed eyes, his arms crossed tightly over his chest, leaning against the onyx wall of his family home. She walked about the room, admiring the books and artwork his parents had collected during their lifetime. She seemed enamored by his family's books. He wondered if she had almost forgotten he was standing there. "Where are you from, Octayn?"

"All of these tomes, sitting here, gathering dust. It's such a waste."

He flicked his dark hair out of his eyes, trying to hide his annoyance. She was truly stunning. Beautiful in a way that made him feel like he needed to be near her. She seemed familiar to him and he wondered if it were simply their shared ability that made him feel that way.

"What about your family? Who are they?"

She turned from the bookshelf. "You ask a lot of questions, Hydo Jesuin."

"I feel like this is a rather pleasant interrogation for an intruder."

She crossed the large room quickly. He studied her step, her movements, her voice—her imperious nature let him know that a family with substantial means had raised her. She held her shoulders back tightly, her chin just slightly higher than necessary. But it wasn't just her confident stride that struck him. It was her stare. She had such clear green eyes, unblinking, and they held him with such a seizing force—as though by look alone she could make him do anything. She stopped just short of him, her body grazing his forearms. "I've heard all about you, Hydo. The strongest, the fastest, the keenest mind ...People fear you in many parts of Daharia. You

Hunters. You know what makes you lot different than those you hunt and drag back to Azgul?"

He bit the inside of his cheek. "What's that?"

"You've just been trained to fight better. It's that training that makes everyone fear you."

He uncrossed his arms. He knew his own reputation. He knew the reputation of his brethren. The Hunters weren't necessarily there for the greater good of all. They were there for the greater good of Azgul. They were there to guard the Blade of Light. They kept the Soren, the mercenaries, the Bakora, the Kuroi, and the Oren mages all in check because at any moment, if any of them got too strong, they could take the Blade. Daharia feared the Hunters. Daharia feared *him.*

"You clearly don't fear me."

She kept her piercing stare on him. "Do you want me to?"

He stared back at her. Her beauty was captivating, her eyes mesmerizing, but it was *more* than aesthetics. She had shown him what mattered most— she, too, had the fire. He knew that if she feared him, she might leave. If she left, would he ever find another?

"No. Of course not."

She offered him the faintest smile. "You don't seem as bad as they say you are."

"You don't know me that well."

* * * *

Her'ay was the woman who took care of the family home. Hydo had known the older woman all his life. Returning from his training at the Blade whenever Gredoria allowed, he would spend the days with Her'ay and the evenings with his parents. When they had died, he spent the evenings with Her'ay too. In his mind, she had always been the oldest woman he had ever known. A mute, with a fiery temper and long silver hair. He knew she had been a soldier for her own people many years before, which was why she could fly his Soar-Craft better than him. She had been the one to tell him about his parents. She had commandeered their vessel, knowing she needed to get to Azgul to break the news to him before any other could. She had written a note and ensured it reached Gredoria, instructing the Lord Protector himself to let her see Hydo. She had communicated it the way she had communicated everything else all his life—with her hands and a somber expression.

She hugged him tightly, eyeing Octayn with a critical stare. *Who is she?* she signed. Hydo shrugged. *I don't really know.* He pushed his answer into her mind. Suddenly, Octayn lowered the book she had been reading and crossed the large room, offering Her'ay a warm smile. She bowed her head slightly to the older woman, and then began to sign a greeting. Hydo watched with shock as the young woman perfectly signed her name and a warm salutation, then an explanation that she had been told to find Hydo to discuss Hunter business. Her'ay signed back that she would want to know more soon.

Octayn's ability to communicate with Her'ay seemed to instantly put the older woman at ease, and as Her'ay communicated that she would be back soon with supper, Hydo felt once again completely taken aback by the young woman who had broken into his home.

He shook his head at her, baffled. "Where did you learn to sign that well?"

"I believe it's important to be able to communicate to as many people as you can."

"That's not an answer."

"Don't take that tone with me."

Her voice was sharp and her eyes instantly narrowed on him. It was an order. Everything the young, beautiful woman said was said as an order.

"I'm sorry. It's just, you've been here all day, and you've yet to answer any of my questions directly—aside from telling me your name. If you were even being honest."

"We both know you can find all the answers you wish, all on your own."

"Why does it seem like you *want* me to search your mind?"

"Maybe I do."

"Nobody wants their secrets forced from them."

"Maybe I don't have any secrets."

He studied her perfect, pale face by the light of the fire burning in the hearth, a pang of anger striking him. "Don't lie. Secrets are one thing. But never lie to me."

She wasn't the only one with a sharp tongue for orders. She wasn't the only one with any power. Hydo would not tolerate lying.

"You don't know if it's a lie. You don't know me, Hunter."

She began to turn from him when he grabbed her quickly. He didn't want to hurt her, but he knew his grip was firm. "But I want to."

She looked up to him, her green eyes wild. "Want to what?"

Hydo could see the fire from the hearth reflected in them, the red flames dancing in her gaze. "Know you."

* * * *

He tried to refrain from rushing his goodbye with Her'ay, but he felt nervous. He knew how he had been with women in the past; he had, at times, been told he was too invested too early. He didn't like to be alone. He didn't want to scare her. He couldn't risk the only Fire-Wielder he had ever found leaving him.

She had asked to bathe and he had acquiesced. He told himself over and over that she was upstairs bathing. He could still hear the water running and he could still sense her presence. But he knew that at any minute, she could pry open a window, duck out into the night, and leave him behind to once again wonder if he would ever find another like him.

He felt odd for fearing that she may "escape." She was free to leave of course ...*escaping* implied he was keeping her there. He suppressed the thought, always critical of his own words, and hugged Her'ay once more. Octayn wouldn't leave; *she* had come to *him*. She had broken into his home just to find him and show him how they shared the same Fire-Wielding abilities. Leaving simply made no sense. She wanted to be with him.

I'll return home soon. He pushed the thought into Her'ay's mind as she waved to him once more before disappearing from the room. He paced. He drummed his fingertips against one another. It really had nothing to do with her beauty, even though her beauty was abundant. It was what they shared. Of course, they barely knew one another, but they were both Fire-Wielders. Their bond was instantaneous, and she surely felt it too?

He knew he should speak to her about it. She would likely be done bathing. He ran up the black staircase, rounding the corners tightly, until he stood outside the chamber door. His hand froze over the handle as he heard the splash of water. He retracted, crossing his arms and leaning against the corridor wall. He would simply wait. He could wait for her to finish. They would speak when she was done.

He resumed his pacing, his heart quickening minute by minute. He wondered what he would do if she had left—if she had leapt out a window. Perhaps he had pressed her too hard with his questions and she would search for another. He needed to know if she had gone. As he turned for the door, it suddenly opened. Octayn leapt back, clearly startled to find him there.

"What are you doing, Hydo?"

He lowered his outstretched hand. "I—err—I was waiting for you."

"Outside the door? The whole time?"

"I thought you might have left."

Her long hair was wet and brushed back severely. He knew she must have used his mother's comb. She wore the same clothes she had been wearing before.

"Am I not allowed to leave?"

He forced himself to look into her pale green eyes. "I don't want you to."

At his words, her face softened, and she offered him her wide smile. "I would never just leave without saying goodbye."

"Promise?"

"What?"

"I need you to promise. Promise you won't just leave. I know how I sound ...it's just I've never found another Fire-Wielder. I need you to stay with me."

She looked at him with a sense of deep understanding. Slowly, she reached for his hand, holding it tightly. "Of course. Never."

* * * *

Octayn had agreed to return to Azgul with him. He hadn't thought out all of the details but he knew he needed her to be near him. His family, like many prominent Daharian families, kept a home in Azgul. After his parents' deaths, Hydo had kept it, sometimes taking Urdo or Hanson there for a break from training, to exist in the real world for a night. He knew Octayn staying there wasn't perhaps a perfect plan, but he couldn't take her to the Blade. Gredoria wouldn't hear of it, even if Hydo explained that he had finally found another Fire-Wielder. Women weren't allowed. They said it was because they didn't have what it took to master Sentio, but Hydo sensed the truth. In Daharia, women didn't have a history of suppressing others for their own gain.

She sat behind him in the Soar-Craft, and as they traveled in silence, he thought only of the night they had shared. They had stayed up talking for many hours—or rather he had talked and she had listened. She would speak about books and travel, the ways of Daharia, the things she had seen, but she would never mention family or friends. She spoke as though Daharia were not her home, but he had refused to press the matter.

They had slept next to one another. She had fallen asleep listening to him speak about life in the Blade. He hadn't taken offense—it was nearly dawn. He had draped a blanket over her and was crossing the room when she woke up.

"Stay."

She had whispered the order so softly, he could have imagined it, but the slightest inkling was enough to convince him to lie down beside her. He had watched her sleep, finding it near impossible to look away from her beautiful face. At some point, he too had fallen asleep.

He wondered about her. He had known many women. While Hunters weren't encouraged to marry, they were not banned from forming such relationships. Himself, Urdo—even Hanson—had all carried on relationships with women. He had seen beautiful women, women from all across Daharia. But none had captured him the way Octayn had.

He knew the way she slept, he knew the way her mouth pulled when she spoke, he knew the way her own fire illuminated her eyes. Yet, he did not know her. He knew her power, he had felt it, and he knew her authoritative nature. His own abilities were immense; if he acquiesced to her it wasn't out of fear. Skills aside, he did not fear her because of the way she looked at him. He found something in her gaze that he had maybe only ever seen matched in his own dark stare—true loneliness. Not simply the loneliness of love lost, or abandonment. Not just the loneliness one experiences when travelling through the darkest skies with no one at your side. Not even the extreme loneliness his brethren had all come to know so well, the loneliness they masked with their augmented kinships within the Blade. It was the loneliness of nature. The loneliness one could only know when they lived without equal for so many years. The loneliness one felt when they realized they had no one who could ever truly know them, for they were not *like* them. Like realizing you were the last of your species. He had heard of creatures living out similar fates—when their species became hunted, endangered, decimated. When there was only one left, waiting for the end.

Hydo felt her hand run over the back of his neck, finding a resting spot on his shoulder. He glanced down to her fingers and saw the small, blue flames running over her fingers. The fire disappeared as quickly as it had materialized. "You're not alone anymore, Hydo."

Her words were intoxicating, her voice trailing about them on the scent of fire. She spoke more than words of comfort—they were a *promise*. She was with him. She was *like* him. And he suddenly realized she had spoken an answer to his unspoken thoughts. He did not know if he was surprised. A woman had never grasped Sentio, though many had spoken of the Kuroi people and the Oren—all desert tribes had an advanced grasp of the human mind. There had even been rumors about Gredoria Vane's own wife, Hadonia, having learnt the ways from her husband. But those had never been confirmed.

He flicked several switches on the panel of his Soar-Craft, ordering the vessel to command its own flight and quickly turned in his seat to face her, flicking his dark hair out of his eyes, reminding himself to regard her with affection and not intimidation—to inquire and not interrogate. He did not want to scare her. Not even if it turned out she had secrets perhaps too great to keep.

He held her green eyes and took a deep breath before speaking. "Can you read my thoughts?"

"No better than you can read mine." Her smile, as always, appeared wicked. She teased him with her ambiguous answers.

He had to force himself to remain calm. He didn't understand why she hid from him the way she did. "Why won't you answer me on anything? Why can't you tell me who you are?"

She leaned forward and grabbed his hands. Immediately, she ignited a fire around their skin. He responded in equal measure, his own flames traveling over their forearms. He had the control over his own fire, he could determine if the flames burned, if they smoked, if they did any damage at all. If he wished it, the flames could simply dance like cold air upon the skin of another. If he wished it, he could build an inferno that could bring down an entire home.

She narrowed her green eyes on him. "But don't you know me? As I know you. I don't need to be a mind reader to know you, to know your thoughts. What we have ...does it require a history?"

Her words excited him. What *they* had. They did have something. She sensed it too. He knew it. They were meant to be with one another. Did he need to know her past or know everything she was capable of? No, not if it meant she might leave him.

"Your history means nothing to me ...as long as you swear your future is mine," he spoke softly. He was cautious of his own words, afraid of the potential they had, especially spoken so soon. She could deny him. She could leave. He had finally found another and he could lose her so quickly. Like their flames, she could vanish as quickly as she had appeared.

"You've known me a day and you would ask me to commit to you?"

"This isn't lust. It isn't love. It's something *else*. I don't know how to describe it, but I feel as though we share something."

"And you'd forsake all others, if I swore my future to you?"

Her brow was arched high. Though it was he who had asked the question, it felt like he was the one swearing fealty.

"I'd do anything to not lose the only other Fire-Wielder I'd ever met."

"It's just about the Fire then?"

"No. It's about you."

"Then you admit its lust."

"*No.*"

"I long for you, as well, Hunter. Your reputation and appearance, your control of the Fire, it all has made me want you. I came to your home prepared to commit myself to you, but not out of desire."

He waited, silent, hopeful.

"We don't share a history. I sought you out because I knew we could share a future. I have a plan for my life, Hydo. I would very much like you to be involved."

Before he could say anything, she pushed forward in her seat and kissed him. He was surprised at first—but the surprise was quickly surpassed by elation. It was an agreement. He kissed her back, finding her lips to be as sweet as he had imagined. He knew her kiss was a promise. As was his own.

* * * *

They landed in Azgul late, the crimson sky thick with red dust clouds in the evening. He brought the Soar-Craft down slowly on the landing dock of his family's home. The dock was situated on the rooftop of the large building. The rooftop was entirely flat, with a small glass box protruding from the far corner—the travel pod. Hydo was the only one who could gain entry to the pod—the doors were fixed to open for a scan of his handprint alone. In time, he would need to add Octayn's, so that she could come and go as she pleased. There was no reason, he saw, to do that right away.

He helped her out of the Soar-Craft and held her hand tightly as they crossed the rooftop. On the second attempt, once he had dusted the pad off, the doors opened. Octayn walked in first, confident and poised as ever, regardless of their long trip or it being *his* home that she once again simply entered. He smiled at her. She was self-assured. And after their kiss and all they had spoken of, he was fairly certain he would do anything for her. Whatever her plan for her future was, he did want to be involved.

They traveled down the glass chute in silence, lights igniting as they passed through each level of the house, revealing pristine floors—glass walls, white tables and seats and beds, pearl floors. He watched Octayn's face, pleased to see she approved, even if she only smiled just slightly. When the pod stopped, the glass doors whirring open, they stepped into the living area. The room was large and immaculate, entirely white in décor, with glass and silver fixtures. It was designed to completely contrast the dusty, red city that his mother had so often complained of during his childhood.

He took her hand in his. "Welcome home. Everything you could need is already here and I will return tomorrow, as soon as I can."

She regarded the room slowly, before turning into his arms. "Stay the night with me." Once again, the sense of authority in her voice roused him. She commanded his attention. She determined her own path. She was a master of her fate—and his, it felt.

"I need to return to the Blade tonight. Gredoria wishes me to be there."

She cocked her head at him. "And what of what I wish, Hydo?"

"I suppose if I return to him with the news that I have found another Fire-Wielder, he will be forgiving."

"No. I do not want your brethren to know me. Not yet."

He took a step back from her. He kept nothing from Gredoria, or from Hanson and Urdo. They were his brothers. His kin. "Octayn, I cannot keep such secrets."

Her eyes widened and then narrowed on him quickly. "You would deny me such a small request?"

It felt as though her hands were slipping away. He gripped them tighter. "Ok. We can wait to tell them."

She smiled at him and any uncertainty he felt disappeared. She was not the first beautiful woman to smile at him. He was handsome and well-known as a great Hunter; many women approached him. But they weren't like her. They were not bold Fire-Wielders who knew his mind and would do anything, however extreme, to meet him. She pushed her small body closer to his, holding his stare with his green eyes. "You know Fire-Wielders are not taught—we are *born* this way? None can learn the abilities if not born with them."

He thought of his mother. He had been so young when she died. He thought of her long, black hair, of her sad smile and the accident that had claimed his parents' lives. She had been the only one like him. "Of course."

"Both of my parents have the gift of Fire."

She ran her hands up his chest and loosened his vest. He shirked back knowing he needed to warn her. The life of a Hunter had left him marked. "I have many, *many* scars."

She ignored him, her hands pulling at his tunic.

He stopped her. "You needn't rush anything. I will want you tomorrow or the next day as greatly as I do now."

"Rush? *Rush* ...I have been looking for a Fire-Wielder who is not of my kin for several years, Hydo. Why do you think it's so important that Fire-Wielders find one another?"

He stared down at her, but he did not voice his answer: *To not be alone.*

She shook her head up at him, her expression softening, her smile sympathetic. "To have a family of Fire-Wielders. When only one parent has the ability, there is no guaranteeing any child will inherit it, a fact that leads to a suffering patience for me now. But when both have it, as my own, the fate of the child is certain."

He was absorbed by her words, however confusing and provocative they were. He felt foolish for not knowing sooner—for not realizing. He had searched for another Fire-Wielder for answers, perhaps companionship, someone to train with and learn from. He had never thought about an alternative future ...He had never thought about what power ran through him, what power he could pass on. He rested his hands on her small hips.

"You found me because you want a family of Fire-Wielders?"

She smiled her familiar, incendiary smile—daring him to imagine more than he had ever imagined. "Oh, I want much more than that."

Chapter 3

Hara'agul

Present Day

Teck made their camp for them. With waves of his cloaked arms, tents unfolded from their closings, canvas and wooden poles bound together, linens escaped their packaging and tightened around bedrolls. Jessop stood high on the lip of a sand dune, watching him use his mystical abilities, building their lodgings with ease. Hode Avay stood near him, watching with amazement. Teck was amazing, likely the strongest of them all, barring herself, Falco, and Dezane. He had untold abilities.

He certainly captivated Hode Avay. The young Hunter with short auburn hair had a shadow of a beard across his pristine face. She knew his body would be as scarred as Falco's and Kohl's, but he was young and had fewer battle wounds than the others. He was good though, according to Urdo. He and Teck had saved their vessel from the Soren attack. Mar'e had been with them. Had they failed, she would have died. Jessop had nearly killed Mar'e herself, stabbing the woman who had let Jeco get abducted. She'd survived the assault, thanks to Falco.

The Soar-Craft that the Soren had brought down had killed many—dozens of members of Falco's army and two young Hunters manning the vessel. Jessop wondered what their names had been, certain that Urdo had told her. She couldn't recall. She didn't try very hard to. She couldn't do anything but focus on Jeco. Her son. She had been so certain he was calling her name before. So certain he had been near her.

"I feel my mind descending into madness," she spoke aloud. She could sense Falco standing behind her.

His strong hand wrapped around hers as he appeared at her side. "You are not alone. He is all I think of."

Jessop's eyes stung, the wind and sand and despair willing her to cry. But she contained her tears. "I cannot stay the night here, Falco. I understand the men may need to, but I cannot. I need to go for him."

"One Soar-Craft needs to return to Azgul with the remains ...Several warriors accompany it, one to explain what happened to Trax, who will then be able to send us more soldiers and supplies, and a handful of others to ensure safe passage. We cannot abandon the remaining warriors here without a vessel."

Whoever manned the Soar-Craft that would return to Azgul would only know how to come back to Hara'agul. It would not know where to find them if they carried on into the Golden Death Valley. Jessop knew if they left, the Soren would return. If the Soar-Craft flew over once again, with new supplies and new soldiers, the same brigands might attempt to bring it down again. The soldiers Trax would send would be relying on the men on the ground to keep them safe.

She knew all of this. She heard Falco's words and yet, they meant nothing to her. She felt all the love she had always felt for him, still residing within her. But she also felt more ...She felt anger. Anger at his plan, anger at his support of her vengeance against Hydo, anger at his level-headedness since their son had gone missing. She was angry he could handle the despair of their loss.

He moved in front of her, blocking her view of the camp and the men below. "I am not handling the despair of our loss, Jessop. I simply don't want the men who will help us get Jeco back to die in Hara'agul."

"Then stay with them. I will go on foot."

"*What*? We know nothing of this part of Daharia. We don't even know how long it would take to—"

"Help me find him then."

"What?"

"Help me find him. We can sense another Hunter. Urdo showed me."

"Of course. That might just work."

"Let me help."

Kohl's voice surprised them both. She and Falco turned, finding the blond Hunter standing several feet behind them. "All of us can help. If we all search for him, it will be better, faster."

Jessop eyed him slowly, and then nodded.

* * * *

Falco's soldiers and the Kuroi warriors formed a circle around the Hunters, offering protection to them during their quest to find Jeco by sensing Hanson Knell. Dezane and Mar'e stood on either side of the wide circle, keeping their unblinking eyes on the Hunters. Urdo, Hode Avay, Kohl, and Teck formed a smaller circle with Jessop and Falco.

Urdo cleared his throat and trailed his intense gaze over the small group. "The desert is vast, we will need to search quickly and thoroughly. Searching like this is not intended to last for long periods of time—it is an exhausting measure. We must be quick."

"How will we know which way to start?" Hode Avay asked.

They were all silent for a moment. Jessop didn't know. None of them knew much about this territory, further out from the lands Hunters regularly patrolled.

"East, Hunters. The Golden Death Valley is east of here." Dezane DeHawn spoke, his soft voice circling them with a supernatural ability. Jessop nodded to him with appreciation and he regarded her with a slight incline of his head.

"East it is then," Urdo spoke. Jessop took Falco's hand in her own, he grabbed Teck's, Teck took Urdo's, who took Hode Avay's, who latched on to Kohl's. The circle would only be complete once Kohl used his spare hand to hold hers, connecting to Falco and the others. Without looking at her, he locked his fingers around hers. She hadn't realized she stood between him and Falco until that moment.

The energy that ran through their circle was electric, pulsating from one to the next. No one spoke. No instruction was required. They all felt it. The search began unanimously, their shared abilities escaping them like a wave of light shooting straight up into the sky before jetting east.

They breathed in unison. Their hearts beat as one. They searched from the sky like a bird of prey, flying on the breeze, eyeing the sandy dunes below. They soared above sand walls and dipped into gorges. They moved quickly, gaining pace, searching more thoroughly, no single Hunter pulling in the wrong direction. And Jessop felt what they all felt—that guiding them was Falco. He forced them forward and drew their shared eye over each potential movement below, determining their course. He was their leader.

Jessop found herself squeezing his hand tighter, offering all of her abilities to him, all of her power and all of her faith. She was a vessel for strength and destruction. Her power was without compare, but she knew her faults. Falco was a leader. She searched over the sand, over the miles of glistening golden desert. They traveled far—further than she had thought they would need to. They passed over more Soren and groups of nomadic travelers. They passed the last source of water for what would have been miles and miles. They flew low to an adjacent cave and ducked under—

His laugh. Jessop heard Jeco's laugh.

"Jeco!" She screamed for him, and as she opened her eyes, believing for just a moment that she truly was at the caves, she accidentally wrenched free from the search and fell back into the present, surrounded by warriors and soldiers, many miles away from her son. She had broken their connection.

"Jeco, Jeco!" She shrieked, but it was pointless. She was standing in the circle of disoriented Hunters. She pulled her hand from Kohl and grabbed onto Falco. "He was *there*! He was at those caves! We need to go."

He nodded quickly. "I know. I heard him too."

"Let's g—"

Jessop's words died out under the sound of drums—a loud beating, shaking the sands, echoing around them. "What is that?"

Falco did not answer. He did not know. They all looked around, as the beating grew louder and louder.

"The Soren!" Kohl was the first to realize, his voice ringing out between booming drum beats.

Jessop unsheathed her sword. "They're back?" The drums grew louder and louder. The brigands were close. The sound was coming from just beyond the dune wall, where the remaining Soren had watched her warily.

"Apparently they didn't take well to you cooking their leader," Kohl snapped, removing his own sword.

"Imagine that," Falco scoffed, shaking his shoulders loose before drawing his weapon.

Jessop flicked her gaze between the two men, watching as they amped up for battle. Falco had been planning on killing Kohl, and here they were, ready to fight together once more, exchanging quick quips. She had no interest in the state of their relationship—their brotherly banter contrasting with every time one had tried to kill the other. She needed to get to those caves. She needed to get to Jeco.

Urdo turned to face her. "We will hold them off—you get to your son."

She could see the throngs of Soren coming over the rise. "You need me." She was prepared to run off into the desert, but some part of her faltered. She didn't want to leave them to die. She had never felt loyalty to any other than Falco and yet, she hesitated at Urdo's side.

"They're desert bandits, Jessop—nothing we can't handle. Just go!"

They might have just been desert bandits, but there were many of them, perhaps near one hundred. Dressed all in red tunics, armed with crude weapons, they stared down on the Hunters and warriors with a steely determination, their metal and bone forms ready to avenge their leader.

"Jessop, *go!*"

She turned to Falco when all of the sudden a large bag was being thrust into her arms. She wrapped an arm around the parcel, looking into the inky blue eyes of Teck Fay. *Go, Jessop,* he whispered into her mind. With a twirl of his cloak, he spun away from her, vanishing.

"Ready yourselves, Kuroi! *Far'a harana!* *Far'a harana!*" Dezane's voice called out and immediately the Kuroi warriors moved into a formation, spears and shields at the ready, short swords drawn.

"At the ready!" Mar'e yelled from her place near Dezane, as she drew her own blade. Jessop watched as the Kuroi woman shifted her gaze to Kohl. She held him in her stare for a long moment and then readied her stance beside Dezane and her warriors.

"Wait!" Jessop yelled, urging them not to charge the brigands.

Her eyes had fallen to the still smoking wreckage, the vessel that the Soren had brought down. Heaps of metal were strewn all about, ripped from the Soar-Craft when it crashed. She focused on the great body of the destroyed machine. She threw her hands out and the heap began to shake. She had used much of her energy already on preventing the vessel she had traveled on from crashing and searching for Jeco in the caves. She needed help.

Falco saw her intentions and joined her effort. He hit Kohl in the arm to get his attention. Kohl looked from the wreckage to Jessop and focused his energy. With the three of them sharing a common goal, the smoking metal body levitated high above the ground. They held it for a second, as if getting a stronger grip, before lobbing it over the surviving Soar-Craft, over the heads of the Kuroi warriors and Falco's army, towards the Soren.

Many leapt out of the way—but they also struck many. Urdo and Dezane didn't wait any longer, seeing the opportune moment to strike. They charged, leading their soldiers forward without looking back to her. She wished she could help them. She reminded herself, as she watched them run towards the Soren, that they were some of the greatest warriors she'd ever met. She told herself, as she turned and began to run into the desert, that if any could survive, it was them.

* * * *

Falco ran at her side. They sprinted, zipping up sand walls, sliding down dunes, making their way blindly towards the caves they had seen earlier.

It had taken her a near minute to realize Kohl had run with them. She couldn't stop to question him; they needed to put enough distance between themselves and the Soren first. They sprinted silently; their strong bodies were built for endurance.

As she ran, her sword sheathed on her hip, the bag Teck had given her tight under her embrace, she thought of more than just Jeco. She thought of Urdo and Dezane. She thought of the Soren. She thought of them running, weapons drawn. They had sacrificed so much for her. She hoped that their lives wouldn't be added onto that debt.

As the three of them slid down a near-vertical drop into a dune, Falco grabbed her arm. The ground began to level out and he pulled her to a slow stop. "Stop for a minute —we can stop."

She pulled free from him and rounded on Kohl. "Why did you follow us?"

Sweat dripped down his brow as he tried to regain his breath. "I ...Because I can help you."

She narrowed her eyes on him. "You could have helped *them*! They need you—not Falco and I."

"I just figured..." he began, looking from her to Falco, back to her.

"What? You figured what?"

Falco grabbed her hand, urging her to calm herself.

"It just seemed like the right thing to do."

She couldn't help but roll her eyes at him. "Yeah, follow the two people you've most recently been at war with. *Sure*, that seems like the right thing to do."

Falco shook his head at her. "It does feel right, Jessop."

"What?"

"The others will be fine and Urdo will search for us when he's ready. They face common brigands. *We* are going after Hydo Jesuin. Kohl made the right choice in coming to help us."

She stared at him with disbelief. She had ruined Kohl's life for Falco and now she was tormented by her actions, and they had reignited their brotherly relationship. "You were planning on killing him just days ago."

"That was then."

"You've only just been reunited and instantly the brethren bond appears once again, strong as ever."

He reached for her hand once more, but she ripped out of his reach. "Don't. Just don't, Falco."

Kohl cleared his throat. "There's more, Jessop. There are things I haven't told you. Things I need to tell you."

"Such as?"

"Things I found out when I was with Hydo and Hanson. Things that I do not know much of, but what I do know, you should know."

She stared at him with anger and suspicion. She had been terrified of him dying, despite at times wanting to kill him. She had mourned the relationship they'd once had. She had cared for him and he had loved her. And now, it seemed as though he loved Falco more, despite their years of mutual hatred. She wasn't jealous ...She was mad.

"You are bringing this up with me now?"

"At first, I wasn't going to tell you. Then I didn't want the last words between us, if Falco had killed me, to be hearsay from Hydo. When Jeco went missing, I thought I could find a time to bring up what I had learned ...Either way, now might be the only time we have."

She was impatient with him. Impatient with both of them, impatient with waiting in the bottom of a dune for a battle to finish behind them and one to start ahead of them. "And what did you learn, Kohl, that is so important?"

He held her with his hazel eyes in a way that seized her heart. It was the way he had regarded her so long ago, when he had first loved her. She had been so certain he would never look upon her with that gaze ever again. She knew, instantly, that whatever he had to say was actually important.

"Kohl, what is it?"

He took a deep breath. "It's about your mother."

Chapter 4

Azgul

Twenty-five years ago

Hydo ran his hand gently over the smooth skin of Octayn's back. It was milky and taut, pulled tightly around her rib cage. Her mess of pale blonde hair trailed over her shoulders and spread out around the bed. "You're stunning."

She rolled over and propped herself up on one elbow. He watched the way she regarded his scarred body. Without hesitation, she reached out and traced one of his many scars, running the silver line from breastbone to hip. "Tell me about this."

She touched him like he belonged to her. She spoke to him like he was hers alone to speak to. And as far as he was concerned, he was.

"It's a final test, so to say."

She stared at him, expectant.

He took a deep breath. They were not meant to tell. They were not meant to tell many of the things he had told her. "Every day for a year, in our thirteenth year, we submerge into a pool. It's difficult to explain, but it's not a normal pool. Each time, our mind gets searched, and the pool does something—to say it cuts you would be the easiest way to explain it."

While her dispassionate exterior remained unmoved, Hydo could see her pupils widen. He rolled onto his back, regarding the white ceiling above. "They want to know if you would defect, if you ever think about leaving the Blade, if you're truly loyal ...They want to know everything. By the end, you have no secrets and no will to hide them even if you did. And that's when the fight happens."

Octayn inched closer to him, as though concerned he might not continue. He waited a long moment, enjoying her undivided attention. He had never said these things to anyone. He had never needed to. Had he ever considered it before, it would have felt like a betrayal. But he'd also never had anyone to tell it to who hadn't also endured it.

"We fight our mentors. The pool weakens us; exhausted, already wounded ...we never win. We aren't meant to. We are meant to quit."

"This is vile. It's treacherous."

He jolted at her words. "Wh—"

"They train you, nurture you, bond with you and then they try to break you—all to test your loyalty to a regime that was only established to maintain power for a handful, and control the rest."

"I've never thought about it like that. It's just how it's always been done."

"You think that that makes it okay?"

"I don't know. It's just the Hunter's life."

* * * *

The mechanical *trill* rung out incessantly, growing louder and louder, ceasing only when Hydo raised his hand to the sensor pad beside the pod, allowing entry to his friends. He tightened his black robe and braced himself for the onslaught of questions and accusations he knew would be arriving along with Hanson and Urdo. As his friends appeared in the descending glass chute, he saw the anger in Urdo's face and the confusion in Hanson's.

They both leapt forward, nearly knocking one another over to reach him first.

"Where have you been?"

"Gredoria thought you'd been attacked on your travels!"

"He's going to *kill* you."

Hydo raised his hands slowly, nodding along to his friends' concerns. "Enough. I'm fine, as you can see for yourselves."

Hanson shook his head, his golden plait falling over his shoulder, his blue eyes wide. "You've been here this whole time and not thought to contact us? To return home?"

He appeared hurt and it wounded Hydo to see it. Hanson was his closest friend, perhaps even closer than Urdo, though all three had been raised as brothers. Hydo inclined his head slowly, offering his friend an apologetic look. "I've had important matters to attend to."

"Is *she* one of those matters?" Urdo snapped, looking over Hydo's shoulder.

Hydo whipped around to see Octayn standing in the doorway, a white linen from the bed wrapped around her body, her blonde hair cascading down her body.

"I told you to wait for me in the bedroom."

"And I told you that no one orders me to do anything. Now, what is the meaning of this?" She drew her hand out before her, gesturing to Urdo and Hanson. Hydo could see the look in his friends' faces—exasperation. They didn't understand who Octayn was—*what* she was.

"I told you, if I didn't return to the Blade, Gredoria would send them for me."

Urdo pivoted on his heel to stare at him. "Who is *this*, Hydo?"

"This is—"

"You may call me Octayn."

Hydo wrung his hands together. This wasn't going as he had envisioned. He believed that Hanson and Urdo would understand if they had it explained to them the right way, if they could hear it from him. Octayn was a fiery woman. She did not possess the disposition Hunters were accustomed to. He wouldn't fault her for that. He loved her for it. But it wouldn't be an easy transition for his brothers.

"Octayn? That doesn't sound like a Daharian name," Hanson piped up, looking from her to Hydo.

Hydo hadn't thought of it, but he supposed Hanson was right. He noted the intense stare Urdo fixed on her, his anger unabated by any introductions. Octayn held his stare with ease, confident in her position, in her power. Hydo couldn't help but feel his attraction for her intensify—she was a woman who couldn't be intimidated. But he didn't sense that his brothers had come to do any intimidating.

"We should sit, we can explain," he began, knowing his friends needed an explanation.

"We don't need to explain anything," Octayn spoke, her voice clear and authoritative.

Urdo practically rolled his eyes. "*We*? Please, girl, leave us to speak with our friend for we have—"

Before he finished his sentence, a wall of fire erupted on the white stone floor, climbing seven feet high, flicking between Octayn and the Hunters. Hanson and Urdo immediately scrambled back, stunned. Hydo took a deep breath, watching with confliction. She had produced a shield of fire, without any noticeable effort or exertion. She was incredible. She knew so much more of their Fire-Wielding than he did, and he yearned to learn from her. But he also saw the fear in his brothers. He saw the hurt that he had created—it wasn't just surprise at learning that he had found another like him, but confusion as to why he wouldn't rush to share the news with them.

"Octayn."

At the sound of her name, she extinguished the flames, turning her green gaze to him, her expression softened.

I'll tell them nothing you've told me, he pushed the thought to her, careful to conceal his mind from his friends. She nodded slowly. She looked over Hanson once more before turning her fiery gaze on Urdo. "Speak to me so informally again, I'll burn you where you stand."

Hydo took a deep breath, knowing Urdo had meant nothing by the epithet, but knowing Octayn was accustomed to much more than most.

"My love, just give me a moment to speak with them."

She nodded slowly, tightening the sheet around her body as she turned and walked back down the hall.

Hanson turned to him, his blue eyes filled with confusion. "Love? You *love* her?"

"Can we sit? Please?"

Hanson sat, but Urdo refused. Hydo made them drinks. Urdo downed his but Hanson wouldn't touch the glass. Urdo paced, continuously turning his gaze to the doorway, as though he suspected Octayn to return at any moment. Which, Hydo knew, she might do. In the short time that he had known Octayn he had learned many things—chief among them being that no one told her what to do. They asked. Everything was a question, and her answer was absolute.

Hydo regarded his friends with remorse. "I'm sorry I worried you both."

Urdo glared. "Worried? We thought members of the Bakora might have ambushed you on your travels. We thought you were dead. We were more than worried."

Hanson stood, as if in solidarity, beside Urdo. "Gredoria instructed us to go straight to Haycith—we told him we would check here first. You were supposed to return a week ago."

"I know. Just let me explain."

Hanson sat once again, but Urdo remained standing, as though to sit would be to surrender some of his anger. Hydo told them what he could. Octayn had appeared at Haycith on his last night, she was a Fire-Wielder, he had spent the past week with her and he was in love with her. They stared at him, silent and incredulous.

Hanson was the first to speak. "I'll be the first to admit that the woman is a vision. And I see how important it is to you that you've found another Fire-Wielder. But *love*, Hydo? Be serious, you just met the woman."

Hydo held his friend's disbelieving stare. "It is love. She is my *everything*."

"You barely know her!" Urdo exclaimed, waving his hand out in frustration.

"I do though. I do know her. I cannot explain it, but Octayn and I know one another. We know one another's thoughts, bodies, and abilities. It is as though we are one."

His friends remained silent. They doubted his words but they both knew him to be a highly self-aware man. Hydo didn't live an illusory life, he didn't proclaim love for anyone, he didn't shirk his responsibilities for anything. He had a history of reliability that could act as a testament for his current claims. "She's like me. I'm not alone anymore."

Hanson tilted his head at him. "You've never been alone."

"Brother, I can't explain it. You do not know the Fire, how hard it is to have powers so great you doubt your own ability to control them. Octayn was raised by Fire-Wielders. She has such incredible control. Control that she can teach me."

They all remained silent. Hydo had had a Fire-Wielding parent who was not around to teach him the necessary skills. His Hunter brothers knew how the woman had died, and how she had taken Hydo's father with her. They would say nothing on the matter.

Urdo finally sat. "We didn't come here to convince you of who you do and do not love. We came to bring you home. Gredoria needs you."

"I don't want to leave her here, though I know I must return."

Hanson leaned forward in his seat. "We will explain to Gredoria that you found another Fire-Wielder and he won't be angry. He will understand."

"No. We will not be telling Gredoria about Octayn."

"Why not?"

"He just doesn't need to know."

Urdo stood quickly. "What are you saying? We should keep information from Gredoria—from our Lord Protector?"

"I know how it seems, brother, but it is for the best right now. Gredoria wouldn't understand."

"*I* don't understand, Hydo. We are Hunters. *Hunters*. We do not put anyone before our brethren let alone before our Lord Protector."

Hydo didn't know how he could explain it to his brothers. He knew how they felt, and he knew how he seemed to be acting to them—as though he were under a spell. But it was no spell. He loved her. He *knew* her. He wouldn't betray her for the world.

"I will figure out what to say to Gredoria, but I ask that for now you say nothing to anyone."

Hanson rose. "And what will you tell him, Hydo? How will you lie to him?"

"I will omit. I was held up. He needn't know details."

"I don't like this," Hanson said. "You're asking us to lie."

"I am asking you for your loyalty," he corrected.

Urdo spun, angry. "You have it. You've always had it! If you wish to keep your secrets, so be it. I will keep your secrets too. For one day, Hydo, you will be the Lord Protector, and we all know it. What will you do when one of your Hunters acts with such treachery? How will you respond when you have the power Gredoria has now?"

Hydo let his shoulders drop, his breath exhaling softly. "In truth ...I'd kill a Hunter who dissented as I have."

"Then you would not blame Gredoria if he killed you for these trespasses?" Hanson demanded, turning his gaze from Urdo to Hydo.

"I cannot live without her. And if you ask me to, I would hope Gredoria put me out of my misery."

* * * *

He held her tightly in his arms, his lips grazing her forehead. "I must return with them."

"But why?"

"If I cannot tell Gredoria about you I need to explain my absence away as a simple travel delay."

She pulled back from him. "Your friends. How do we know they will not tell?"

He knew Hanson and Urdo waited for him on the rooftop. They had promised silence and he, in turn, had sworn to return to the Blade with them. "They're my brothers. They would never betray me."

She seemed nervous, and when she was nervous, she was angry. "There are things you still do not know. Things Gredoria Vane could find out if he knew my name."

He took a deep breath, calming his own natural tendency to respond with anger. "What don't I know, Octayn?"

"I will tell you everything when you return."

"Octayn," he pressed.

"Your friend was right, earlier."

Hydo stared down at her, confused. "Right about what?"

"My name. It isn't Daharian."

She moved away from him, leaning against the wall. Small streaks of fire ran up her hands and arms and he thought she was perhaps unaware of it. "Think about it, Hydo. I have no Daharian sigil burned into my neck and I have no Daharian name because..."

He had, of course, noticed that she bore no sigil. All Daharians had the burn of their kind on the base of their neck. A form of organization implemented by Prince of Daharia after the Great War. But he had cared too much about her Fire to worry about her sigil. Admittedly, he had not thought once about her name, for he knew little of such things. It was a beautiful name. He looked her over, noting the challenge in her stare, willing him to figure out that which she was hinting to him.

He took a step towards her and he suddenly knew. The truth hit him, a vicious jolt to the system. He stared at her, as if looking for other signs to his newfound truth, wondering how he couldn't have figured it out sooner. He knew he should care, he should *truly* care about this information. And yet, he did not. Her people were the sworn enemy of Daharians—they were the reason Hunters existed. The Blade of Light had been last used against her kind. The practice of branding sigil existed to differentiate from her people. He hadn't been able to figure it out because he had never met one of her kind—he only knew of them as the enemy.

He grabbed her hands and watched as her small flames transferred to his skin. "You are not Daharian."

Chapter 5

Present Day

"Tell me then, Kohl." She had dropped the bag from Teck to the ground, and crouched beside it. They had run far, and if she needed to wait to hear Kohl's thoughts, then she would at least catch her breath while doing so. Falco knelt beside her, but Kohl remained standing. He appeared nervous and that concerned her.

When Kohl remained silent, Falco snapped. "We haven't got time for this!"

"Well, I don't know how to explain it. It's Hydo. He speaks about your mother, Jessop."

Jessop studied Kohl's worried expression, the concern that kept his lips parted, his eyes wide as he waited to gauge her reaction. She couldn't understand the importance of such a declaration from Kohl.

"He knew her. He killed her. I imagine her name would come up."

It had been over a decade since the murder of her parents, but the tone of her voice when she spoke of it was as sharp as ever.

Kohl shook his head, kneeling opposite her. "He speaks about her in the present, as though he *still* knows her. He said 'Octayn will need to know this.' He said it just like that."

Jessop felt her chest tightening and she realized it was her body reminding her to breathe. She sucked air in sharply. She didn't understand. She stared into his hazel eyes, angry that he would delay their quest for this. "My mother is dead. I saw him kill her with my own two eyes."

Falco stood beside her, his hand running down her arm. "As did I, brother. You walk a fine line with these stories."

Jessop stared at Kohl, studying the confused expression on his face. He brushed his blond hair back, revealing a large bruise swelling on his cheekbone and a cut near his ear. He paid the wound no notice as his fingers grazed it. Kohl was many things; weak was not one of them.

"They're not stories and I meant no harm by them. I just thought you should know what I heard."

Jessop stood, brushing sand off of her. "Enough. We don't have time for this. Hydo is a sick man; a sick man who instructed Hanson to take *my* son. There are people fighting for us, as we speak. We won't waste any more time on this."

She swung Teck's pack over her shoulder and began to walk off, her boots light on the dusty sand, when Kohl yelled after her. "But Jessop— what if your mother lives?"

She rounded on her heel, flicking up a storm of sand, closing the space between her and Kohl in an instant. "She's dead. I sat amongst her ashes. She burned to death in that fire." Her words were sharp and angry, and she glared into his dark eyes with challenge. She blinked, and she could see her mother before her, on the ground, their home burning down all around them. Her father, blood covering his body, Hydo fleeing, and Falco trying to save her. She could see the flames and smell the smoke ...

"But Jessop, one of your parents was a Fire-Wielder. It's how it works. You wouldn't be one otherwise." She was amazed that Kohl hadn't instantly backed off, as he would have once done. He remained still, his gaze still locked upon her.

Jessop knew how it worked. Fire-Wielding was inherited, if one parent had the Fire, the children may have the ability; if both had it, then the children would certainly have it.

"What does it matter if one of them was a Fire-Wielder?"

He stared at her, as if waiting for her to realize what he was saying. "A Fire-Wielder can't be killed in a fire. Hydo told me as much. Your kind doesn't burn like we do."

Jessop said nothing. She felt anger at Kohl for telling her these things, especially in this time and place. If one of her parents had had the ability, which they would have had to, why had she never known? She couldn't imagine why they would keep the ability a secret, even within the confines of their family home. And as far as not burning went, she had kept a natural distance from fire all her life, as any would after losing their parents the way she had. She had never thought to see how her flesh fared in an open flame—but she couldn't deny that on the occasions where a burn might have occurred, she had coped better than most.

Falco readjusted his position, moving slightly in front of Jessop, as if shielding her from the news Kohl had shared. "Jessop's father was dead before I ever entered the house, and it was no flame that claimed his life. He could have been the Fire-Wielder. The flames would burn a Fire-Wielder once deceased."

Jessop felt both thankful and horrified. They never spoke of these things. They spoke of Hydo, of vengeance, of strategy—never of her parents burning. He was right, though, her father could have been the Fire-Wielder. Jessop and Falco had been open with their son about his and their gifts since his first breath; it felt odd to her that her parents hadn't acted the same towards her. Perhaps they were waiting to learn if she had inherited the abilities too.

She would never know though. Octayn and Hoda had died years ago. She and Falco knew it. Hydo definitely knew it. Whichever mad way he spoke of her mother now, whatever coping mechanisms he had devised to live with his trespasses, was not her concern. All that mattered was Jeco. She looked to Falco. "We must go now. For Jeco."

"But Jessop..."

She ignored Kohl's protestations and Falco's conflicted gaze, taking off across the dune. She could hear them quickly walking behind her. She couldn't stand speaking about such things. She couldn't be distracted when her son needed her. But Kohl had laid a seed in her mind that was undeniably growing. The fire Hydo had set would have never killed her. Had she known what she was then—had one of her parents told her— perhaps she could have done more to save them.

Jessop pushed her boots into the sand, climbing the edge of a dune wall. The idea that she might have saved her parents wasn't the most severe of her contemplations. The most dangerous of thoughts, itching at the corners of her mind, flicking like a whip against her heart, daring her to believe it, daring her to imagine for just a second, was that her mother could have somehow lived. Her rational mind knew it wasn't true. Hydo speaking of her likely meant nothing. He spoke of her. He had a fractured mind and a wounded heart—Jessop had done much to progress his insanity in the time since she had arrived at the Blade. If he spoke of Octayn as though she lived, perhaps it was because she had trapped him in a memory where she *did* live for so long.

Jessop wiped her brow with the back of her arm, dabbing away the sweat and sand. The heat of the desert was not helping. She couldn't think clearly.

She needed her son back in her arms. Her mind ached. Her body ached. She knew tears would form if they could—but it was too hot for tears. No matter the desert, the fire burned inside her eternally, drying her tears. Since becoming aware of the flames, she felt them always. They itched under her skin, constantly wanting to break free, constantly hungry to consume. She felt her breathing grow heavy—as though a vicious weight sat mightily upon her chest. She ran a hand over her heart, pushing her boots harder into the sand, willing herself forward.

Mama!

Jeco. It was Jeco calling for her. Or was it? She spun around. She saw Falco and Kohl—they watched her keenly. Concern filled their eyes—their faces. Did they speak?

Mama!

She needed to get to him faster. If only she could breathe a bit easier. She dropped Teck's bag. She could remove her leather vest. Her hands were trembling, her fingertips numb, twitching under her weakened sense of control. She needed—

Falco locked her in his embrace with immense force. She grabbed onto him. She needn't have opened her mind to him for she was quite incapable of closing it off to anyone in the moment. She felt him instantly, like a rush of cool water. He moved through her mind, easing her thoughts, laying them down to rest, silencing the voices. He held her and it was the only time she felt the flames dissipate—as though they knew they could not touch Falco Bane. He held on to her and healed her tormented mind. He healed her as he always had.

He kissed her temple. "As I always will."

* * * *

Jessop rolled to her side and found Falco watching her. They had walked for many, many miles, long into the night. When the dunes became too dangerous for Kohl to travel over, his eyes not as familiar to darkness as hers or Falco's, they had begrudgingly agreed to make camp. Teck had supplied her with a bag that contained two small tents, several canisters of dried, salted meats, and two leathers filled with drinking water. He had ensured they could survive at least several nights in the desert if they were smart about it.

Jessop stretched out, knowing she needed to get back on their path soon. They had rested enough for her. Even as her mind seemed to descend into madness, as her body ached and protested further movement, she knew she *needed* Jeco. The rest could wait.

Falco held his hand out, a pincer grip on a shining jewel. She focused, and realized what it was that he held for her.

"You brought my ring?"

It was not the dark, shimmering band she wore most days, but the large shining black stone, surrounded by weaving ropes of white crystal. She took the beautiful piece from him.

"When I commissioned the piece, I explained something to the jeweler. He was an older fellow with long silver hair, someone Corin had introduced me to. I had him come to the Pit, and there we sat for a long time."

Jessop sat up, turning the ring over in her hand as she listened to Falco.

"I told the man who made it to imagine one who had lived in darkness all their life, feared by all, fearing even themselves at times. I told him to imagine a darkness that consumes you, that you get lost in, one where you feel as if you are entirely alone. I told him to imagine this dark place, and to wonder what it would be like for a man to have lived this way for all his life, before finding a single source of light."

He turned a teary gaze to her. "I was the darkness and you were the light. I spent half our lives together waiting for you to realize you should leave me. I spent it feeling certain that you did not love me as I loved you, for I was inherently unworthy of such love. A warlord. A killer. I felt myself beginning to lose my mind ...You were there, every day, refusing to leave, refusing to abandon me, no matter the cost. And I knew the only thing left to do was to let you love me. To let your light in. And when I did, I felt true contentment for the first time in my life."

Jessop pushed the ring back on her finger and leaned against him. "Falco, in my life, it was *I* who was the darkness, and you the light. When we had Jeco ...I felt fulfillment. I had everything then. And we ruined it. *I* ruined it. We need him back, Falco. I can't live without my son."

They held one another tightly, yearning to correct the course their lives had taken. The Hunters were brave and selfish, always focused on the Blade, and never on others. She and Falco had lived that way—and they had lost their son for it. She wished they had done many things differently. As she held Falco, she saw her hands, locked around his back, ignite.

Her heart began to race, knowing the flames controlled her too greatly. She immediately lifted them away from him, and as she did, he let out an audible cry. He suffered as greatly as she did. As she realized she was not alone in her grief, in her madness, the flames extinguished.

* * * *

Jessop pulled her boots on and fixed her blades once again. Falco knew her mind and refused to let her leave alone. He would go with her to the caves. Once ready, they brought their small tent down with ease. In the dark, Jessop could see Kohl, sitting off on the lip of a sand dune, staring out into the night sky. She let Falco finish rolling up the tent and she walked to Kohl.

She stood behind him in silence, but she knew he sensed her. The air was cool, the night a welcome reprieve from the scorching day. She looked out over the many dunes. She could hear life within the desert. She remembered learning stillness with her father Beyond the Grey. They would sleep beneath the stars, breathing as one with the wind, their eyes on the stars above, and they would listen for the movements of the desert creatures. She could hear them now. She could feel her father at her side—

"I will not stay behind." Kohl's voice wrenched her back to the moment.

"You cannot keep up."

"If I fall back, leave me."

She nodded down to him. Jessop could not deny his strength or tenacity, though neither were qualities that had led to her feeling any love for him. Falco was as strong as he was tenacious, braver and more skilled with a weapon than any in their lands. But he wasn't trusting, he never had been. It was Kohl's trust that had won over her reluctant, devious heart. It was destroying that trust that filled her with a guilt she could not escape, a resentment she could not suppress.

"I'm sorry I have such anger for you. One day we are embracing, and the next I would consider killing you if I had to."

He looked her over cautiously. "I feel the same. Though I think we both know I could not bring myself to kill you."

She thought of Aranthol and all Kohl had done to punish her. She could still feel the blade in her stomach, placed by his hand.

"But I also love my brother, Jessop. Despite the years and all we have said and done and been told. I had forgotten what it was like to be amazed by him daily. His power is without compare ...being near Falco is intoxicating."

Jessop knew of what Kohl spoke. It was the quality that made Falco a charismatic leader. He was powerful, confident and bold in everything he did. He was singular, and they all knew it. But his skill with a sword had nothing to do with why she married him. She could have married many men who could have defended her; Kohl could have been one of them. She married the man who taught her how to defend herself, at all costs.

"Kohl—"

"It's fine, Jessop. I see what you two have and it is not what we had. It's not something we could have ever had."

"No. It's not."

Slowly, he got to his feet. He faced her and placed a hand firmly on her shoulder. "Let's go get your son."

As Kohl walked past her when a pain seized his body, forcing him to his knees. He threw his hands to his head, hissing loudly, his eyes squeezed shut. "Falco!"

He appeared from the shadows and knelt before his brother, supporting his shoulders. "What is it, Kohl?"

Slowly, Kohl lowered his hand, though his face remained contorted. "Urdo—It's Urdo. He is trying to push a thought to me."

Jessop felt her heart quicken—news from Urdo meant that he was alive. He had survived the Soren and would be looking to join her side soon. Kohl rested his shoulders, his face relaxing as he allowed Urdo to enter his mind and speak with him.

She knew that Urdo would not have been able to so much as prod hers or Falco's minds, let alone enter them, and it made her instantly thankful that Kohl had insisted on following.

Falco squeezed Kohl's shoulders. "Speak to me, brother? Do they come to us—did the vessel return for Azgul?"

Slowly, Kohl blinked. He was crying. Jessop thought of Urdo, of Dezane, of their warriors, of the Hunters they had left behind. She knew many things could happen in battle, no matter how expert the warriors.

She sucked in air sharply, preparing to hear the worst. "What did he tell you?"

He glanced up to her, blinking away the tears. "Many died ...Mar'e is near death. If they do not get to Falco soon, she will die."

Jessop exhaled deeply. She tried to imagine Mar'e, injured in battle. Jessop had nearly killed the woman herself. Falco had already healed her once before from a mortal wound. Jessop felt ...at odds.

"We need to stay where we are so they can reach us sooner and Falco can heal her before it's too late."

Jessop rested her hand on Falco's shoulder. If Mar'e had been wounded in battle in their presence, she knew she would not intervene if Falco healed her. She knew Kohl did not deserve to suffer the further agony of losing a woman who so clearly cared for him. But she *hadn't* been wounded in their presence. She looked from her husband, to Kohl, and sighed. "We aren't waiting here for anyone."

Chapter 6

Azgul

Twenty-five years ago

Hydo tapped his foot against the white stone floor, keenly aware of the sweat trailing down the back of his neck, and of how hard he was working just to control his breath. She had kept such a great secret from him, and when his eyes were on the floor he felt anger, but the moment they looked upon her face ...His love for her was consuming.

"How can this be true? To enter Daharia would mean facing Soren, Ophidia, desert creatures which have no name—you would have needed an army for safety."

"I was helped in gaining access to a portal from Bakoran into Daharia. From there, I manned a Soar-Craft through *Haren'dul Daku*—"

"You crossed *Haren'dul Daku*—the Golden Death Valley—on your own?"

"My abilities—and coin—go a long way with the Soren and Ophidia and unnamed beasts of the Shimmering Death sands. Indeed, the no-man's land between Daharia and Bakoran is a dangerous place, and I did not pass unscarred, but pass through I did."

"Hunters have been bringing in Void-Voyagers for decades, for this reason exactly—to prevent the opening of portal walls between our territories. How did you find one?"

"When was the last time you were in *Haren'dul Daku*? Who was the last Void-Voyager you brought in?"

Hydo was silenced at her question. He had never been to the no-man's land at the edge of Daharian territory. He knew his comrades hadn't either.

The portal walls had been built by desert mages, on Hunter authority, to prevent easy access to Daharia. There were a handful of those who knew how to use the portal wall to travel to Bakoran—Void-Voyagers. Hydo didn't think he'd even seen a Void-Voyager since childhood. Anyone who was caught planning to open a portal, anyone who so much as spoke of leaving Daharia, was brought in for interrogation. And it had been years since he had so much as heard a whisper of Bakoran. He had believed Void-Voyagers were a nuisance long since corrected. Apparently, there were still those who wished to open the portals.

She ran her fingers over his; the sensation of her smooth skin brushing over his calloused hands calmed him. He had wondered more than once since meeting Octayn if this was an ability of hers—to simply calm another with her touch.

"I came here, to Azgul, first, though I kept a low profile. Like you, I searched for another of my kind, who was not of my kin and also a Daharian. I traveled Beyond the Grey and through the Oren desert mages' territory. I traveled far before I found my way back to the Red City. It was here that I heard several of your Hunter brethren in a tavern, speaking about the Hunter who was also a Fire-Wielder, searching for other Fire-Wielders. They spoke your name and it did not take me long to find Haycith."

He stared at her long, beautiful fingers, and the way they expertly caressed his tense hands. "I can't believe this. And yet it makes perfect sense. You're from Bakoran."

"Before I met you, I found many in these lands with extraordinary abilities. I had thought twice that I might have found a good match—two men of different tribes who each possessed the power to contain my fire. Clearly, neither situation worked out. But while they had great powers, they were not Fire-Wielders. There are no true Daharian Fire-Wielders, Hydo. It is a gift of the Bakora people."

He let her hand fall from him. He knew what she insinuated. It would be a lie to claim he had never thought it himself, but he would never admit it, never voice it. "I am a true Daharian. I am a Hunter of Daharia. The Hunters were designed to keep your kind out of our territory—I *am* a Daharian."

She dug her nails into his hands, reminding him to remain calm. "Do not deny your true nature out of love for your Hunter status. You possess a bloodline that traces you back to Bakoran—to *our* kind."

"This is treason. Bakora are not permitted to enter Daharia. If I am of Bakora bloodlines, I am an enemy to my Lord Protector."

Octayn scoffed loudly. "Trust me, your Lord Protector Gredoria Vane already knows that all Fire-Wielders originate from Bakoran. He knew it when he picked you to be a Hunter."

"Why would he do such a thing?"

She cocked her head at him. "Isn't it obvious? He chose you and trained you and kept you in the dark in order to have an elite Hunter who possesses the powers of his greatest enemy."

Hydo thought of Gredoria. The man was more than his Lord Protector—he was his mentor. He was the closest thing he'd had to family since the accident. He thought of his mother—of her abilities. Had she known what Octayn claimed? That Fire-Wielding was a gift of the Bakora bloodline alone?

The Bakora were Daharians' natural enemy. A lifetime ago it had been the battle between the Bakora and the Daharians that won the territory the Hunters now patrolled. The Prince of Daharia had forged a weapon to combat the Fire of the enemy. Of course, Hydo had thought of the fact that Bakora had fire abilities. But he had thought if they had it, others did too; he hadn't assumed what Octayn now told him. If Gredoria had known all these years, how could he have not told him?

"I have spent my entire life studying Gredoria Vane, Hydo. I am not just any Bakora. I am Octayn Oredan, daughter of Mei and the late Ore Oredan, niece of Ozea Oredan."

He stared into her shining eyes, wondering if he had even heard her correctly. She spoke the admission so simply, and yet the meaning behind her words gave explanation to her natural authoritative tone and regal airs.

"No. You're not an Oredan."

She sighed. "I know. It's difficult to—"

"This is *not* possible. The Fire-Wielding, and the secrecy, the breaking into my home, and wanting everything you want ...But *this*? You're claiming to be an Oredan?"

She straightened her stance as a wall of fire erupted from her sides, flying out and climbing the walls. "I *claim* nothing—I am Octayn Oredan, niece of an Emperor, second in line to the throne of Bakoran after the untimely passing of my father."

He stepped towards her, unafraid, his own fire igniting around his frame. "Your family is the sworn enemy of the Blade and of my Lord and Protector."

"Look at your flames—you are Bakora and that makes *me* your sovereign, not Gredoria Vane."

He knew she was right. If all she said was true—and he knew, somehow, that it was—she was his rightful leader. He wondered if it somehow explained his natural submission to her, if through their blood and heritage, he sensed her authority.

As they fell silent, their respective flames died out. He held her gaze as he processed all he had come to learn. "He is a father to me, Octayn."

She reached for his hand. "Would you rather have a father who could give you a Blade, or a wife who could give you a galaxy?"

He knew he loved them both. But however short their time together had been, he knew he could not live without Octayn.

"You see Gredoria's intentions so clearly for they mirror your own. He wants a Hunter with the Fire. You want a Bakora with the destiny and skill of a Hunter."

She took a step closer to him and raised her hand to rest on his cheek. "As Empress, I will rule Bakoran one day, and who better to live at my side than he who is destined to also rule Daharia?"

He cupped her hand with his, feeling his heart tear. He loved her, but he knew what that love meant. He had spent his entire life preparing to fight an enemy he had never known. An enemy who they all believed would never return to their territory. He shared blood with the enemy ...he felt like a fool. Gredoria had known for all these years. He had been using him. And Octayn had sought him out the instant she'd heard there was a gifted Hunter with the Fire. He couldn't help but suspect that she was more like his mentor than he ever wished to believe.

He rubbed his cheek against his shoulder to wipe away the tears. "Do you want me at your side because you love me, or because you love *this*?" He asked, igniting a small flame across his hand.

"You must realize that the flame is not like your mind reading—it is not some well-practiced ability. The flame *is* you—it is an extension of your very being. You are the Fire. The Fire is you. And I am in love with your Fire."

For Hunters, Sentio and skill with the blade were the most important of abilities—but they were *just* that, abilities. Skills you could hone. They were not who you were. The Fire was something different, it was not something that he could always control, it appeared often in anger, especially in his youth, and it had grown as he had. He did not know as much about the flames as Octayn did, or as much about Sentio as Gredoria did, but he did know one thing. He loved her more than his brothers.

* * * *

Hydo had spent weeks traveling between his home in the city and the Blade. He did not seek permission to leave the Blade and had avoided speaking to Gredoria whenever he could. He intentionally filled his mind with thoughts of his parents, so that if his mentor sought to discover the true meaning behind his recent broody absences, he would believe that his mentee struggled over hardships from long before.

"You think of your parents now, more than ever, perhaps because of your failed mission to find other Fire-Wielders," Gredoria had said.

He had told Hydo to sit and speak with him, but Hydo had resisted. "It is helpful to me to be in spaces that were once theirs, amongst things they handled, possessions they loved."

"Of course," he had said, his beard catching the light as he raised his hand to Hydo's shoulder. "Just remember, you *have* a family still."

Hydo had nodded to him, forcing a faint smile to acknowledge the sentiment. He could not deny that speaking with him, lying to him, despite knowing he had been lied to by him, was not easy. He loved him still.

Octayn turned in his arms, drawing Hydo back to the moment. "You should be as forthcoming with him as possible. Do not distance yourself and risk your rightful spot in the Blade."

They had remained in bed late that morning. He rested on her abdomen as she ran her fingers through his dark hair. He simply couldn't bring himself to return to training that day. "If I cannot have him find out about you then how exactly can I be forthcoming?"

"If he grows worried about you, he *will* find out about me. Your friends already present a great risk to us."

He thought of Urdo and Hanson. He had spent no significant period of time with them since returning to Azgul with Octayn. He knew he needed to remedy that, but being away from her was a pain he could barely endure long enough to train and make the necessary appearances in the Blade. "They would never betray me." Even as he spoke the words, he questioned their truthfulness. He was betraying them, by keeping Octayn's true identity a secret, by forcing them to lie for him, by neglecting to tell them of his and her plans.

"Once we are wed, you will have the entire Bakoran army at your disposal and none will betray us," she reminded him.

Hydo knew that even though what she said was true, their futures would not go entirely as Octayn envisioned. They would have to wait a long time to ensure the opportune moment of reuniting Daharia and Bakoran under one leadership. That would mean living apart, ruling apart, and keeping their marriage a secret for many years. He wondered how they would make such a relationship work once children were involved.

He turned over to face her. "What will we do when you are pregnant?" "I could be pregnant now. It has no bearing on our immediate plans."

"Your family would not be angered to know you'd had a child before marriage?"

She cocked her head at him and sat up straighter, forcing him to sit up as well. "Hydo, things for the Bakora are not as they are for Daharians. Having children, extending our lineage, it means everything to us."

"I understand that. I just think given the chance, if we were wed before you had any children, it would seem more appropriate, I suppose."

"Those are Daharian ideals. There is still much about me that you do not know."

He felt his jaw clenching uncontrollably. She angered him like no other, and yet, he could not help but love her. "Then tell me."

She stood from the bed and wrapped a robe around herself. "I already have children, Hydo."

He stared at her blankly. His initial reaction was surprise, but he didn't know why, considering that every day seemed like a new opportunity for her to tell him something astounding.

"With who? Where are they?"

She sat at the edge of the bed. "You must understand ...they are Bakora royalty born in Daharia. Until such a time that I can test their abilities and cross them over *Haren'dul Daku* to gain access to a portal, I must take extreme measures to ensure their safety."

"You won't tell me where they are?"

"Where they are does not matter half as much as *who* they are. The children were had with gifted men I once knew and cared for. But, of course, they were no Fire-Wielders. It could be several years before I learn if the children inherited my fire."

Hydo felt light-headed. She had two children. He didn't care that she had already bore children. He cared that she had been with any other long enough to have children.

"I have higher hopes for the boy. He just showed such great potential before I had to leave. His father had many abilities—that tribe is very gifted."

Hydo leaned forward as he caught her words. "The father *had* many abilities?"

Octayn looked him over slowly, as if trying to gauge his reaction. "It's complicated. While all children are special, mine in particular are of a unique, royal importance. I couldn't let a father interfere with their destinies, not once I knew he wouldn't be the one to rule Bakoran with me."

His heart quickened at her words, resisting the truth she was offering him. "You killed the fathers."

"I did what was best for my children."

"Octayn…"

He leaned forward, rubbing his head, feeling as though he might wretch. He knew that he was not a royal or a parent and that he, too, had killed before. But she was admitting to murder, and she had committed such a heinous crime against a Daharian. To become the Hunter he was, his mentor had beaten him within an inch of his life. He had trained every day for years. He had trained keep Bakora out of these lands.

He had seen how dangerous she was but had somehow had never viewed her as a threat. In choosing to love her, he was putting all those around him at risk. Treason in theory and in practice were, all of the sudden, very different. "There is much I can live with, including your true identity, your children, and your plans. But if we are to be together, you must swear to not kill any more Daharians."

She touched his hand warmly. "I understand that even though you are of my people, Daharians are also your kind. I know that hurting them hurts you."

He could feel his anger dissipating and was certain it was her touch.

"I will be the Lord Protector—any children of *ours* will be the rightful leaders of both Daharia and Bakoran. But as I will one day swear to protect the Bakora, you too will have to protect Daharians."

She held his gaze intently before nodding. "I see no reason to have to kill any more of them."

He knew she chose her words carefully. She was raised to rule and her diplomatic nature and imperious ways had become more and more visible each day. She wouldn't make promises she believed she wouldn't keep. But he knew better than to push the matter further.

"I just can't believe you have two children."

She smiled. "Yes. As I said, the boy showed great promise early on."

Hydo found himself smiling. A boy. A fatherless boy. He suddenly felt himself filling a very different role, one he knew he could fill well. "And the second child?"

Octayn's smile softened and her eyes fell to the bed. "The second child was very recent, such a short time before we met. It's difficult for me to speak about."

"We will return your children to Bakoran. They will be with you."

She blinked away a tear. "I know how I must seem. No one could understand abandoning their children ...but I do it for their safety."

"I know."

"The boy, he is so gregarious, strong and bold ...I know who he is and I can sense his future. But the second child..."

Hydo waited patiently. She dabbed her eyes with their bed sheet. "This beautiful girl, who made no noise at birth. She was not unwell, but she did not cry. She simply looked at me, in silence, with bright green eyes."

Chapter 7

Hara'agul

Present Day

Kohl remained kneeling, his tears streaking his cheeks in the darkness. Falco mirrored his position. Jessop stood between the two. She stared down at Kohl, then looked to Falco, who looked, in silence, at his brother. "We will not wait here for them, Kohl."

Kohl kept his gaze fixed on Falco. "What do you mean? Jessop, Mar'e is dying and Falco could save her if they reach us in time."

Jessop shook her head. "I'm sorry. Falco and I carry on for Jeco."

Suddenly, Falco was pulling Kohl into a tight embrace. They held one another tightly, and for the first time, Jessop felt like the one on the outside. The two men who loved her most also loved one another. After years of rivalry, years of hatred and mutual plotting, their brotherhood ran deeper than any rift she created.

She turned from them. "We must go now."

Slowly, the men rose. Kohl wiped his face with the back of his hand. "Could you please consider waiting?"

Falco stepped away from Kohl, joining Jessop. "I won't wait, brother."

"But—"

"My son is missing because of her, Kohl. She was too weak for this war!"

Jessop's angry yell echoed about them before disappearing on the sands. She had so recently tried to kill Mar'e it felt odd to be discussing the fate of her life once again. She blamed Mar'e for Jeco's abduction, and though she knew that blame was somewhat misplaced, had Mar'e never been in the Blade, the abduction might have never occurred.

He shook his head at her. "Have you no heart?"

"Don't ask questions you already know the answer to."

* * * *

They walked through the dessert in the darkness, the light from the stars barely touching the soft sand underfoot. Falco walked close beside Kohl to help guide his path. She crossed her arms and leaned back as she began to slide slowly down the steep wall of a dune, her boots skimming over the fine sand. She had loved Mar'e once ...Or at least she had thought she had.

Perhaps it had always been hatred—a child's longing for acceptance and friendship was a blinding force. Perhaps what had once seemed like love had really been something quite different. Maybe all of the years of shunning and rejection had ensured that Jessop would one day be the one to try to kill Mar'e Makenen—or at least be the one responsible for her death. In childhood, Mar'e had always been blinded by her own self-regard. Jessop should have known these were qualities she would have carried into adulthood, qualities she would have brought into the Blade.

"She deserves our help."

"Not now, Kohl," Jessop barked, her hands curling into fists. She could not stand to hear him ruminate over the state of their lives, their wrongdoings and losses, any further. It was tedious to think about, let alone voice.

"Why not now, why can't we at least—"

"We *know*, Kohl. You lost everything, I ruined your life, nothing is fair. She's going to die—and even though *I* am the one who knew her best, it's you crying through the night."

Jessop had rounded in the darkness, her feet expert on the sand, her eyes keen in the shadows. She did not struggle as he did and she stood inches away from him. Falco, just as adept, had his hand on her arm, warning her against doing anything she would later regret.

She saw the reproach in Kohl's eyes as he took an angry step towards her. He moved with such force that Falco landed his hand heavy on Kohl's chest, forcing him back from Jessop. Thought Falco held him back, Kohl had a finger in her face, pointing at her with anger.

"Yes—*you* knew her best but you did not care for her most. And not everything is about *you*, Jessop. We all suffer! We have all been wounded. We three here have harmed one another greatly—but are *we* allowed to suffer aloud? Are we permitted to say anything that might anger you? You do *not* control me. Everything I do for you, I do out of love, not allegiance.

You should act like my friend—not my Lord Protector, because in case you forgot—*that's* Falco."

Jessop remained still, stunned, and silent. Perhaps she had been acting like Falco wasn't the Lord Protector. She was accustomed to his leadership, and to her being the natural exception to his rule. As he claimed a new frontier, the one they had most coveted, she should have shown more support. But Jeco ...She could not pander to custom when her son was missing. She could not mourn the potential loss of Mar'e, nor any other, when Jeco was in danger.

"I allow you to do things because I am the most powerful."

Jessop hadn't intended to say the words aloud and felt a heat rising in her neck as she heard them escape her mouth. She wasn't that person, or at least she did not want to be. She was powerful, perhaps the most powerful, but she was not a tyrant. She had controlled Kohl for so long, through strength and manipulation, she now realized she had never really stopped.

"I'm sorry. I don't mean to, not anymore, but I still do. I act like I can control you because if I wanted to, I could."

She felt shame. She felt more than shame—she had acted towards him as Hanson or Hydo once would have. "I don't know what to say."

He inched closer to her as Falco slowly lowered his hand. "You don't allow me to do anything. When I do as you ask, it's out of love, not fear."

His words wrapped around her and her skin shivered. She saw the small flames licking over her fingertips, illuminating the three of them in the darkness.

She forced her gaze up, first to Falco, then to Kohl. "Since we battled in Aranthol, things have been complicated."

"They've been complicated much longer than that."

"Yes, they have." She could feel Falco's tense stare but she couldn't focus on him. She couldn't carry on this way, acting as she did towards Kohl. "I know I'm not your Lord Protector. You're a skilled Hunter and I'd always choose to have you fight at my side rather than against me."

"I'd never raise a blade to you again, Jessop. I can't live with what I did to you."

"It was I who first betrayed you—"

"*Jessop!*"

She noticed the sound of her skin being punctured before she actually felt anything. Her flames flickered as she looked down and saw the metal shaft of an arrow protruding from her chest. She fell forward, Falco quick to scoop her up. She heard Kohl's sword sing, as it was unsheathed. Falco shimmied down the sloping wall of the dune, holding her tight against him.

She heard the whistling of another arrow and the *ting* of metal as Kohl struck it out of the sky—she was amazed at how long she had overlooked his abilities.

She felt wet; the blood was soaking through her clothes. "Falco."

He lowered her gently to the ground, keeping her close to him as he knelt down. "You're fine, my love."

She closed her eyes. She could hear sand kicking up. Another clash of metal and an arrow slid to a stop in the sand beside her. "They're coming."

"Kohl's got it covered."

Falco had an obvious confidence in Kohl that she had never had. "Are you sure?"

At her words, a wild scream encircled them. Kohl had killed one of the attackers.

Falco nodded, his hand wrapping around the arrow. "Of course I'm sure."

She knew he needed to remove the arrow if he was going to heal her. She felt swelling throughout her body and her mouth tasted acidic. He needed to be quick. "Do it now."

She tried to ignore the feet in the sand, the running, the sound of Kohl swinging his Hunter's blade. She could sense him and she knew that he felt no fear. Despite the darkness, despite the pressure of having to fight alone and defend them all, he felt nothing. He was confident. She had fought so hard to keep him safe. She had torn his memories and made pacts with Trax, she had worried so greatly about Kohl leaving Azgul to fight ...It had been misplaced. She hadn't known him well enough.

"He's a *Hunter*, Jessop. He's trained all his life for this," Falco reminded her.

His words reminded her of a conversation she had once had with Kohl. He had looked at her with such seriousness. "Jessop," he had said, "You act like I'm some childhood friend who spent the past twenty years as a tailor or rug maker. I was raised in the Blade. I have been fighting all my life ...I'm not fragile."

As she thought on the memory of Kohl, Falco slipped into her mind, numbing her as best he could. There was an immense pressure in her chest, right beneath her collarbone. She felt her flesh begin to rejoin, the sinewy muscles, torn by the arrow, grasping to one another, the flesh weaving into a new scar.

"You need to forgive him, Jessop."

She hissed as the scar came together tightly. "For Aranthol or for trying to kill me?"

"For loving you still."

She heard the clashing of swords, the scuffling of boots, the sound of flesh slicing as Kohl defended them. She winced under Falco's touch.

"Do *you* forgive him?"

"I sentenced him to death days ago, and I've threatened it for years. And yet, despite every opportunity, I do not kill him and he does not fear me. We are brothers."

She felt as though she were seeing Falco differently after so many years. He had spoken of the brotherhood with vitriol, he had cursed them for turning their backs on him, for making him into their enemy when he was destined to be their leader. He had told her again and again how they lived by a hierarchy, how the Blade came first, nothing was ever more important than your brother or your Lord Protector.

"All these years, it hasn't been hate, but love, hasn't it? The hurt endured because you loved him."

He moved her into a resting position against the dune wall and kissed her softly before standing and unsheathing his onyx blade. "Perhaps my hurt endured because I loved him then and I love him still. And perhaps your hurt endures for the same reasons."

He said nothing more, staring into her eyes, as if waiting for her to speak first. When she said nothing, he disappeared from the sandy enclave.

Jessop pushed herself up further, sitting upright. She knew from Falco's words, and from Kohl's, that things would never change for the three of them. They would never be able to live together in the Blade. They loved her. And it would have been easier if she loved neither, but that wasn't the case. She loved Falco, and yet, Kohl could not let her go, as she could not seem to let him go.

She didn't understand what had become of her life. They had spent so many years planning their revenge against Hydo that their lives had been about nothing but their agenda. Then they'd had Jeco, and their planning was reinvigorated, for their son was another reason Hydo had to be removed from the Blade. And having achieved everything they set out to, they had lost what mattered most. Jeco was gone.

She needed to get to her son. She got to her feet, shaking off the injury, embracing the new scar and sense of determination she felt. She made her way around the dune wall, her ankles rolling in the soft sand. She took a deep breath, regaining her footing. Kohl and Falco fought their attackers, their fighting styles so distinct from one another. Falco never took one heavy breath, never huffed or gasped. He fought with alarming ease. Kohl had begun to fight with more flair than he ever had in the Hollow, but his form was still rooted in tradition.

The attackers were desert brigands, but of what tribe or heritage, she did not know. She tried to focus on one, but they moved quickly. From underneath a black tunic she saw skin that appeared to glisten, as though perhaps not skin at all, but scales. Their eyes glowed, but not as those of the Kuroi did, with a soft lighting, but as though they were creatures of the night. And they fought with exceptionally long blades, though strapped to their backs were quivers filled with the metal arrows they had used to initiate their attack. She watched as one charged Falco and was stunned by the screeching cry the assailant let out—a wild war call that sounded more beast than man. Jessop threw her hands out before her, and with all her focus, she ignited a fire around the attacker. Falco then cut him down with ease.

She counted six more, following their quick running forms around in the dark. She unsheathed her sword, and her shoulder seared with pain. She heard the arrow, and shot her sword through the air just in time to stop it. She was weak—more injured than she had originally thought, more injured that she had been in quite some time.

"Falco," his name barely passed over her lips, but he heard her. He flicked his gaze to her, his sword clashing with another's. He moved their fight nearer her, and as he struck down his opponent, he leapt to her side.

"We've got this," he answered, and she lowered her blade, resting her injured body. Kohl and Falco circled her continuously, keeping the attackers at bay, and one by one they brought them down. Jessop knelt, her blade in her hand just in case, resting. She needed sleep, though she had been so certain of the contrary when they had made camp. She needed water. She needed her son.

As Falco struck down the last one, she took a deep breath, urging herself to rise up and carry on. They did not have time for rest—they did not have time for recovery. She watched as Kohl leaned over one of the fallen brigands. They were men, but they were also something more. With the scales and eyes of desert creatures, it was as though they had further adapted to their terrain than Jessop and Falco had to the perpetual night of their own. As Kohl pivoted around to face her, Jessop saw the attacker move. With scaly fingers wrapped around his hilt, he lunged at Kohl's back.

Jessop threw her hand out and a spear of fire extended from her palm. Kohl leapt to the ground, rolling out of the path of the flames. The brigand burned before Falco threw a dagger, ending what would have been a much longer death.

Jessop fell forward, her hands burying in the fine sand as she tried to catch herself. She could hear her heart beating, the blood pulsating through her body. Her chest tensed, willing her to breathe deeply, but she couldn't. She couldn't focus.

Mama!

She knew it was in her mind. He wasn't there. They weren't at the caves yet.

Mama!

She cupped her hands over her ears, drowning out the sound of his beautiful, little voice, as she buckled forward. "Stop it. Stop it!"

She felt Falco's arms around her, she felt him inching into her mind. "We will get him back. I promise."

She nodded, focusing on Falco's presence in her mind, focusing on his breathing. She knew that she was losing her mind. All that mattered was getting their son back.

"I'm sorry," she whispered, although she did not know who she spoke to. And as her vision began to blur, she passed out.

Chapter 8

Azgul

Twenty-five years ago

Hydo navigated the familiar backstreets with ease. He had left the Blade that night with Hanson and Urdo, sneaking off to their favorite Azguli tavern. It had been time to repair some of the damage he and Octayn had created. She had agreed, encouraging him to reaffirm his relationship with Urdo and Hanson. He knew she had ulterior motives in her support—she worried for their secret and his path to becoming Lord Protector. Hydo understood that Octayn had no friends, she had no siblings, and the bond he shared with his brethren was not one she would ever be able to comprehend.

They walked through the streets, lighthearted and merry. Hanson swigged from his flagon before tripping on an errant stone on the path. "Not—where did that come from? Not all of us have secret girlfriends to go to every night."

Hydo clapped his friend on the back. "I'm blessed. With my brothers and my woman."

"And your abilities."

"And your destiny."

"The *greatest Hunter they've ever seen*, the infamous Hydo Jesuin!"

"Ha! That is how the Council always talk about you."

Hydo smiled as his friends laughed. Even if they found joy at his expense, it felt like familiar times, before his life had become so greatly complicated. That night, they had spoken of training and Gredoria. They had an upcoming mission Beyond the Grey to see a Kuroi leader's son that everyone spoke highly of. He couldn't explain it, but since learning that Octayn had been involved with a Kuroi man for so long, and had borne his children only to murder him, Hydo felt an anger whenever the tribe was mentioned. As though he needed to feel hatred towards them in order to not feel the shame of having let them down so greatly. He didn't understand it and he couldn't speak to anyone about it. He just knew he was not looking forward to the trip.

"At least we aren't expected to marry ...Relationships are hard." Urdo's voice pulled Hydo back to the moment and he realized the conversation had carried on without him.

Hanson scoffed. "Relationships? I can't even get a woman to speak to me!"

Urdo had never struggled to find company, but Hanson always had. He was too shy, too nervous, and the drink only forced him to over-correct—his humor suddenly confusing and abrasive, his questions too probing.

They rounded a corner and found the stairwell to an underground tavern that they had frequented many times before. "Alright, gentlemen, this is where I leave you."

"Stay!"

"Just for one more drink?"

Hydo laughed, embracing each brother quickly. "Speak tomorrow, brothers."

* * * *

Octayn rolled over in their bed, nudging him gruffly. "Hydo, what is that?"

He ran a hand over his face. He could hear the buzzing of his pod, alerting him to company. It took him a moment to fully wake up. He felt as though he had only just gotten to sleep, having left Urdo and Hanson at the tavern before returning home. He felt as though he knew what had happened. Many nights before this one, when all three had drunk too much, they would sleep at his city home instead of returning to the Blade.

He rolled out of bed reluctantly. "I'll deal with it."

He walked down the pristine hall, reaching the doorway for the pod. He raised a hand over the scanner pad and a screen lit up, showing a grainy picture of his brethren standing on his rooftop, as he suspected. He rested his hand against the pad, granting Hanson and Urdo entry. He ran a hand through his messy hair and prepared glasses of water for his brothers. They could sleep the drink off and leave early for the Blade.

As the doors opened, Hydo knew instantly that things were not as they usually were. Urdo's mouth was bleeding and Hanson's eyes were wide, bruises already forming. Whatever had happened had had a sobering effect on both of them, as they approached Hydo with obvious fear.

"What's happened?"

Urdo leaned against the wall and slid down it, resting on his haunches.

"Tell me."

Hanson's eyes darted about the room, alert and paranoid. "It was an accident."

"What was?"

Urdo stared at the white floor. "We're going to be kicked out of the Blade. Executed."

"*Executed*? What are you talking about?"

"Your brothers killed someone."

They all turned at Octayn's voice. She stood in the corridor, wearing her long white robe.

Hydo shook his head, "Do not say such things."

But Hanson and Urdo said nothing in their defense. Hydo looked them over but neither would meet his gaze. "Tell me this is not true."

"Urdo killed no one." Hanson kept his eyes on the ground.

Hydo stepped back involuntarily, the words stunning him. He rested his hand against a chair, steadying himself. Hanson meant he had killed someone. An Azguli? He was a Hunter—killing outside of sanctioned missions was a trespass punished by execution. But they had said it was an accident. They must have been attacked; they must have acted in self-defense. Many of the Aren zealots knew Urdo worked keenly to bring about the end of their group—perhaps *they* had done something.

Octayn glided into the room, her shoulders back tight, a look of impatience crossing her face. "Where is the body? Or is it bodies?"

Hydo could hardly believe her voice was so calm and smooth. He knew the Bakora were a different kind, with a culture that tolerated violence much more so than the Daharians' did, but still ...He could not help but think of how she had killed and how all of this was much more familiar to her than to the rest of them.

"On the roof."

At Urdo's words, Hydo lunged forward. "You brought a body to my home?"

Hanson stepped between the two of them. "We didn't know what else to do."

Hydo raised his hand, warning his friend to stay back. "Tell me exactly what happened." His deep voice shook as the nausea seized him.

"I was speaking to a woman, she was married, a man grabbed me, and that's when Urdo got involved. The fight just broke out."

Octayn sighed heavily. "Just take me to the body."

Hydo turned his gaze to her. "What? Why?"

"Why do you think they brought it *here*?"

"I..." but Hydo's voice trailed off as he looked over the guilty faces of his friends. They had brought the body here because they needed help getting rid of it. Because they had always turned to him for guidance, mocking him one minute for his destiny to be their next leader, and relying on him the next for help. They had implicated him in their trespass.

"You have both risked my rise to Lord Protector by bringing me into this."

They said nothing. They already knew as much. Urdo used the wall to get to his feet and stepped back into the pod. Octayn was quick on his heel, followed by Hanson. Hydo waited, hesitant, imagining the future he had worked so hard for disappearing before him. Octayn stared at him expectantly. "Let's go."

Slowly, he stepped through the doors and joined them.

They traveled up through the floors of his house in complete silence. When the doors finally opened, they were embraced by the warm Azguli winds. The crimson sky was dark, but not dark enough to conceal their presence on the rooftop should a Soar-Craft fly close overhead.

They moved towards Hanson's vessel. Hydo slowed his pace as they approached the old machine he had picked up on a bargain several years back. He came to a full stop several feet behind Octayn and the others, not wanting to get any closer than he had to. Hanson and Urdo climbed the side of the Soar-Craft and, with a forceful heave, lifted the body of a man over the doors. They lowered him to the ground. His head knocked the rooftop with a *thud*. Hydo's stomach turned. He had killed before. But it had been ordered, it had been as a Hunter, not as a man. He realized then that he had started to separate the two, as if Hunting were little more than an occupation, despite having been raised to believe it was his whole identity.

Octayn stood over the body. "This is it?"

Urdo nodded. "This is him."

The man looked only a few years older than Hanson or Urdo. He had a strong jaw and bloodied fists. It helped Hydo to know that he had at least been capable of putting up a bit of a fight. He intentionally kept his gaze on the fists, ignoring the man's trunk, where he knew Hanson would have inflicted the fatal wound.

Octayn looked over the man with her dispassionate stare. He knew he needed to help, he needed to deal with this burden so that she didn't have to. He took a small step forward.

"We—we should move it somewhere it won't be seen."

Octayn ignored him as she ignited her hand, shooting flames, like arrows, at the body. Hanson and Urdo jumped back as the man's clothing caught fire. Octayn forced the flames to grow at a supernatural rate, hissing and whipping about, resisting the wind with anger as they burned faster and faster. Soon there was nothing but the smell of burning bone. Urdo turned away, raising his arm to protect his face from the heat. Hanson covered his mouth with the back of his hand. Octayn, unblinking, kept her focus, destroying all evidence of their crime.

Hydo felt lightheaded. What his brothers had done and what Octayn now did for them, what she had done in the past—he condoned it and it called into question the kind of Lord Protector he had always envisioned himself becoming. He fell to the ground, the smoke from the body trailing high from his home, a beacon of disgrace. Hanson turned to him, but remained still. His brothers had betrayed him with their carelessness. They had endangered his life and his future.

Octayn finally finished, leaving nothing but a pile of ash on the ground. Such power was mighty—mightier than Hydo's, certainly—but it was also terrifying. He stared at the ashes, knowing that he had come to both love and fear her. He supposed he didn't fear her, he feared how much he loved her, knowing he would do anything for her, however treacherous.

She turned to him with her cold green eyes and crossed the rooftop quickly, her robe trailing behind her, a vision in white against the crimson sky. She reached her hand out to him, a trail of blue fire running over her fingers. She looked so powerful as he sat weeping over this terrible accident.

She kept her hand out, palm up, waiting for him to take hold. "It won't always feel this way."

He thought, perhaps, that it *should* always feel this way—it wasn't meant to be easy because it wasn't right. He thought of standing on his own, refusing her hand, and with it, her way of life, and walking away from them—his love and his brothers. He imagined never seeing her again. He looked into her beautiful face and could instantly hear her laugh, could feel her lips on his, could picture her first thing in the morning when she woke up. He imagined never holding her again.

He looked past her and saw his brothers. They had come to him in their greatest hour of need. Octayn had provided for them, taking the lead in a time when he could not lead. He knew that power and strength were two very different things—he *had* strength, he was naturally gifted, but power required loyalty and a long, forceful reach. Power required control. Control of the Blade, control over the Hunters ...over Octayn? She could do as she wished as long as it was for their shared prosperity.

He took her hand. If he walked away he would lose them all, and with them, his future. If he stayed, he could learn to lead, and to rule, as she did. He rose to his feet. Octayn nodded to him approvingly. "They owe you their allegiance now."

Her words burned him, despite how closely they mirrored his thoughts. "I believe they would have given it to me before this. I had faith in them."

She kissed him deeply, her lips firm against him, forcefully pulling him against her with hunger. Just as abruptly, she stepped away from him, breaking their kiss without warning. "Who needs faith when you have certainty?"

* * * *

"Speak with me, Hydo. Tell me what troubles you." Hydo looked down at Gredoria's outstretched hand and knew that his mentor was not asking Hydo to join him—he was demanding it.

Hydo took a seat opposite him. He had thought for some time that Gredoria was ailing, his voice had become breathy and slow, his movements somehow more delicate and less certain. It would have been disrespectful to ask after the man's health, when the Blade knew that he was Gredoria's successor.

They sat in Gredoria's vast chambers, silently staring at one another. He had sent for Hydo early that morning and as luck would have it, Hydo had just snuck into his own chambers minutes before the messenger arrived. He had been uneasy in his own home since the incident. The body had changed everything for them. Octayn had shown her leadership in the face of death and trespass and Hydo had made a decision for his life. He had chosen her. He had chosen her plan, to become a ruler as she was, to learn to lead as she could.

His friends fared less well. Hanson had tried several times to tell him the story but had been incapable. Urdo had finally told him what he could and it was mostly what Hydo had already imagined. Hanson had been drinking, as they all had. They had been rowdy, but not dangerous. A woman had spoken with him, he had bought her a drink, several men had appeared, and when one claimed she was spoken for, a fight broke out. That was all Urdo could tell and it was all Hydo could tolerate knowing.

He sat opposite Gredoria, trying to look at ease, completely incapable of recalling how he used to sit, speak, or even think *before*. He remembered always feeling calm in his mentor's presence. But everything had changed. Gredoria sat very upright, his shoulders tight back, like Octayn. His hands rested on his knees. While he stared at Hydo, he did not pry at his mentee's mind. After a long silence, he sighed heavily.

"Hydo, let's not pretend things are as they once were. We both know you are set on a path to take my place here. Up until very recently, nothing seemed more important to you. I won't force your thoughts from you, but if you can no longer disclose them to me, you make it very difficult for me to trust you with the Blade of Light."

Hydo shifted in his seat. He felt uncomfortable with his mentor's candor. Gredoria always spoke in soft, lofty terms. It was more than simple discomfort though; he felt angry. Gredoria had been lying to him for all these years, and now he suggested Hydo couldn't be trusted. He forced himself to look into the eyes of his mentor, his Lord and Protector. He leaned forward, his dark hair falling about his face.

"Did you know all Fire-Wielders are of Bakora lineage?"

Gredoria sat back in his seat and breathed heavily. "This is what's bothered you? You figured it out. Well, of course I knew."

"Wh—*what*?"

Up until that very moment, Hydo had thought there was a small chance Octayn had been wrong. Perhaps Gredoria hadn't known and hadn't intentionally deceived Hydo all his life. Hydo felt his heart racing as he stared at Gredoria. He could picture every conversation they'd had, he could feel the edge of his mentor's sword in the Hollow, he could close his eyes and instantly be writhing in pain, refusing to give-in, refusing to quit, surviving the rites required to be a Hunter.

"I've always known. It's my job to know. Keeping it quiet was simply part of the deal."

Hydo stood and then quickly sat back down. His mother's face flashed before him. "What deal?"

"Bakora are not permitted to live in Daharia. Your parents were Bakora, though, and they had angered the Bakoran Emperor Oredan. I granted them clemency, and in turn, they let me raise you as a Hunter. Not just *any* Hunter, Hydo. *My* Hunter. Having taught you our ways, knowing you had the gift of Fire, we knew you'd be an unstoppable Lord Protector."

Hydo felt his stomach turning. His throat burned. He didn't understand. His parents had given him up so they could escape Emperor Oredan and live in Daharia? Had they wished to keep him? If they had been able to raise him, would that fateful accident that claimed their lives somehow have been avoided?

"You need to remember your true path, moving forward, not living in the past."

Hydo quickly shut off access to his mind. "How could you have kept this from me? After my parents died there were so many times you could have told me. I wouldn't have left you."

"You were on a path to glory and success. What good would telling you have done?"

"To avoid me finding out from someone else!" Hydo was on his feet. He had never raised his voice at Gredoria.

Gredoria narrowed his eyes at him. "How did you find out? Daharians know next to nothing about Bakora—thanks to us and our ability to keep them out."

Hydo glared back at his mentor. Octayn had been right—she had been right about everything. He had never been more thankful that she had found him. She had tried to tell him what kind of man Gredoria was and he hadn't listened. He could feel the flames running down his arms, his heart was racing, tears welling in the corner of his eyes as he stared at his mentor.

The fire extend down his hands, licking his fingertips. "You betrayed me."

Gredoria did not fear the flames. He had helped Hydo learn to calm them through his adolescent years. It still amazed Hydo that in this moment, his mentor did not fear him at all. Gredoria was righteous.

"I did what was best for you. I pushed you as I did, and kept from you what I kept, to guarantee your path to greatness. I chose you as my successor, Hydo."

He had lied to him for so many years. He had lied to everyone, knowingly breaking their own laws to allow Bakora into Azgul, to ensure a child of Bakora lineage would become the next Lord and Protector of Daharia.

"You have to understand, the Bakora are a ruthless type. Your parents' death was no accident. Who better to defend the Blade from Bakoran than a Hunter with the Bakora Fire?"

His flames extinguished as he honed in on Gredoria's voice. "What did you just say?"

"I said who better than—"

"No! About my parents' death."

Gredoria looked at him with wide eyes, his hands resting at his side. "I wanted to keep all of this from you. Truly. I never wished for you to know."

"Tell me now or so help me—"

Gredoria took several deep breaths before speaking again. "Bakoran is run by the Emperor Ozea Oredan. He is a ruthless, merciless, man…"

Hydo kept his mind sealed as tightly as he could, knowing Gredoria spoke of Octayn's kin. He could not pretend that he was surprised at Gredoria's words—it would be a lie to describe Octayn as anything less than ruthless, and he had been raised knowing the Bakora were the enemy for a reason.

"Your parents angered him. To this day, I don't know how, but they ran. They made it to Haycith. This was so many years ago …It was still early into my tenure; I wanted to assert myself firmly when it came to defending our territory. When I learned of their presence, I went to confront them. I was stunned to find they had such a young child with them. More than that—they nearly killed me. I'd never seen such abilities—I had never met a Bakora. I had only ever heard of the Fire. We all knew that while their powers were great, I had an army of Hunters who would come for them if need be.

"I knew instantly that there was a better opportunity to be found. I made a deal with them that ensured I would train you. I tried as best as I could to hide them in Haycith, and for many years they were safe, but Ozea Oredan got to them eventually. Their death was no accident—they were murdered for their betrayal."

Hydo suddenly couldn't feel his legs. He hadn't known that both his parents had been Fire-Wielders and he had no recollection of the events, obviously, for he had been too young. He fell, knocking a table in his attempt to catch himself. Octayn's uncle had killed his family. Gredoria had lied to him for his entire life. He was full-blooded Bakora. "The Council …do they know?"

Gredoria knelt before him. "They know you are Bakora, but they do not know about your family or what happened with Ozea Oredan."

"You've lied… You're a *liar*."

Hydo had felt all his life that he would kill for Gredoria Vane—and he *had*. He had been certain that he would also die for his Lord and Protector, if it had ever been necessary. His mind ached. His stomach felt tight with knots. He closed his eyes and saw the dead man Hanson had killed.

"What did Hanson Knell do?"

Hydo blinked and saw Gredoria's angered face. He had been in Hydo's mind and he knew. Hydo scrambled to his feet as Gredoria stood.

"Nothing. He did nothing."

"I saw your mind, Hydo. Hanson Knell killed a Daharian?"

"No. Of course not."

Hydo grabbed Gredoria's arms. It had been a mistake. The death was an accident. Letting Gredoria into his mind had been an accident too. Hanson had trusted him.

He jerked free with an angry tug. "Release me at once! Where is Hanson now?"

"You cannot punish him—his treachery is no worse than your own!"

Gredoria balked at the claim. "I have *never* killed an innocent Daharian, Hydo Jesuin."

"It was an accident."

"An accident punishable by death," Gredoria hissed, turning away from him and making his way for the door.

"What if it had been me? What if I had killed a Daharian—would you execute your lifelong project, your greatest student?"

Gredoria stared at him with cold eyes. "You're of the Bakora people. I've spent every day that I raised you preparing to kill you if I needed to."

Hydo felt a pain in his chest. He had believed Gredoria loved him. His mentor pushed past him, making his way for the door. He was going to find Hanson and sentence him to death. He would find out about what they did with the body. He would find out about Octayn.

Without thinking, Hydo threw his hands out, aiming at the back of Gredoria's mind, and within seconds he was inside his mentor's mind. He didn't know what to do; he couldn't think clearly, his own mind aching from Gredoria's admissions. He looked for the memory of the past moment they had shared. Gredoria tried to expel him with a violent force. Hydo had no choice but to harm him into submission while he searched for the memory. He tore at the thoughts he passed through. He saw faces and images, places and people he'd never met—he ripped each thought into shreds. And as he searched, a different thought crossed his mind. Gredoria would have memories of Hydo's parents.

He searched, wrenching through the fortified walls of thought and time and memory. He ripped apart dreams and fears, he overturned memories that hadn't been touched in decades. He moved through the colorful waves of light, slashing and cutting and burning, knowing he was nearing his mother's face.

And then, like a vision, he saw her. She was younger than he had ever been able to recall. Her black hair ran to her hips and she was smiling, calling his name and beaming with joy. He wanted to grab on to her. He wanted to be with his parents one final time ...The fire appeared out of nowhere. It burned the memory to ash. Hydo could hear screaming—was it him? His mother's face was gone. Everything was going blank.

His head hit the ground with a violent smack. He rolled to the side, grabbing at his head. He took deep breaths as the ceiling came into focus. "What have I done?"

He hadn't been thinking clearly. He had been so consumed by the memories he had lost sight of ...of everything. He blinked slowly, pushing himself up, and saw Gredoria kneeling on the ground. He leapt from his position, locking his arms around his mentor.

"Gredoria, speak to me. Are you alright?"

Gredoria looked up at him and smiled. Hydo felt a wave of relief rush over him. His mentor was strong—the strongest. He had done him no harm. Gredoria slowly got to his feet, continuing to smile at Hydo. Hydo smiled back. "Oh, I've never been so thankful—"

"Who are you, boy?"

Hydo knew it was just an accident, a small injury caused by going through his mind too quickly. "Hydo, sir. Your pupil."

"My what? What a funny word. Why would I have a pupil?"

Hydo felt the pain returning to him. The guilt was instantaneous.

He could barely breathe as he kept a hand on Gredoria. "What is your name?"

Gredoria opened his mouth, prepared to answer, but said nothing. His eyes narrowed, his lips remaining parted, as if the answer rested on the tip of his tongue. "How odd ...I can't seem to recall. Isn't that funny?"

Chapter 9

Present Day

Jessop woke to the pale light of early morning creeping through the tent. She was in Falco's arms. She could tell by his deep breaths that he was still sleeping. She sat up slowly, cautious not to wake him. As she rose, her shoulder stung, and instantly she recalled the attack from the previous night. She pulled at her tunic and saw the raised scar, red and angry, on her skin. She covered the fresh injury back up. Whenever Falco had healed her before, he had *completely* healed her—no residual pain left lingering. She knew their quest for Jeco was wearing greatly on them both.

She ran her fingers slowly over the side of his face, her thumb brushing over his long scar before combing his dark hair back. She knew that as she felt the madness claiming her mind, she had to keep faith. They would retrieve their son, and they would return to their lives—restored in every sense of the word. They needed to carry on, but he could sleep a few moments longer. She pulled apart the tent flap and crawled out onto the sand. To her surprise, Kohl was already up. He had built a low-burning fire, and he had a large blanket wrapped around him. He had reworked his tunic to cover his face and protect his eyes from the sand. He looked over her slowly, as if assessing her for injuries.

"You're alright."

She stood and stretched. "How long have you been out here?"

"All night."

She looked down at him quickly. It was no longer surprising, really, the lengths he would go. "You should have slept."

"I believe we are officially in the beginning of true *Haren'dul Daku* territory—no man's land. Couldn't risk Soren sneaking up on us again, and Falco had to be with you while you recovered."

She nodded but did not voice her thanks. She knew that there were more important things to be said. "About last night..."

"We don't have to talk about it."

"I'm sorry we couldn't wait for her."

"She's strong. She'll hold on until they find us."

Jessop nodded. She knew Mar'e's fight and the way she was driven by her emotion. It was a form of strength. She hoped Mar'e would survive.

"It is difficult to know that had we three been there, she probably wouldn't be hurt. Many more would have survived."

Kohl's eyes were on the small flames. "I know. I've spent my entire life in the Blade believing Hunters lived to protect. But *whom* were we protecting against? First, we were told it's the Bakora. Then, it became about keeping Falco at bay. Who were we protecting from him though? Daharians ...or Hydo?"

Jessop stared at him. Kohl was different. She knew that they had destroyed parts of one another. And they could not apologize or forgive one another enough to make up for any of it. She had believed this whole time that she had set off a series of events that had shattered his way of life. But she couldn't deny that, as they traveled closer to the lands where the Bakora and Daharians once fought, the land Hydo Jesuin had fled to, it seemed many events had been set in motion long before her arrival in the Blade.

"You were not wrong to protect Daharians from Falco—or myself, if you had known of me then. But we would have never become as dangerous as we were, or as we *are*, if Hydo hadn't done all he had done. He's responsible for all of this."

Kohl shook the blanket off and pulled his tunic off, uncovering his scarred body. She saw the maimed Jeco scar that he had originally cut into himself to gain entry to Aranthol, the one that she had destroyed. She saw all his wounds, all of the scars Hanson had inflicted. He began to fold the blanket up when he paused, staring at her.

"Is he though? Or were we just too foolish to ever look with our own eyes, to ever discern the truth on our own without relying on him? Did he destroy Aranthol, or was that me? Did he nearly kill me, or was that you? He might have set fire to your home once, but I plunged a sword through you."

Jessop bristled at his words and how reminiscent they were of Urdo's, raising a hand to the scar he had left on her. "He destroyed my family."

He stared at her still. "If it weren't for what he had done, you and Falco wouldn't be together."

"You think I should be thankful?"

"Of course not. But if he hadn't done what he did, for whatever reasons he did it, you would have never fallen in love with Falco, you would have never had your son; you would have never come to the Blade ...I would have never fallen in love with you."

"A preferable ending for you then."

"Hardly. I'll live with this pain all my life, and it will be worth it for having lived for the briefest of time under the belief that you loved me."

"There are days where I hate you. And there are days where I love you, Kohl. Just not as—"

"Not as you love Falco. I know."

She knelt before the small fire. "You'll love another, Kohl. In time."

"Not as I love you. Not as you love him."

"Mar'e will survive this. You cannot deny the feelings you two might have for one another."

"She deserves better than a broken man."

"Any would be lucky to have you, brother." Falco spoke. They turned to see him exiting the tent. He looked over Jessop slowly, as Kohl had. "How is your wound?"

"Healing."

"Let's go then."

* * * *

It didn't take long for the heat to set in. Jessop removed her leather vest, stuffing it into her pack. Falco and Kohl walked without their tunics or vests, using the lighter material to cover their heads and necks. They had one flagon of water left for sharing, and they each had sipped at it with great caution only once or twice in the several hours they had spent crossing the dunes. She hated the bright light reflecting in the sands, so much hotter than any territory Beyond the Grey.

"I heard you both this morning," Falco suddenly broke the long silence.

Jessop looked him over, the sweat trickling down his muscular, scarred form, his skin burning under the heat of the desert, his voice dry and hoarse. She did not worry if he had heard them—she hid nothing from him.

Kohl glanced at Falco, carrying on steadily through the sands. "You know how I feel about Jessop."

"Not that. I was thinking about Hydo and how all of this started. How we all got ...*here*, I suppose."

Jessop and Kohl looked to one another before returning their full attention to Falco. He leaned into the dune wall as he scaled it, Jessop and Kohl at his side. As they crept over the sand lip, he stopped climbing. He ran his hands over the back of his neck and stared out over the vast desert. "My parents were terrified of me."

Jessop whipped her head to the side. In the years they had been together, he had never spoken of his family.

Falco continued to stare, looking out into the horizon. "There—that dark patch in the distance, that must be the caves."

Jessop followed his gaze and saw as he did, a dark ridge in the horizon line. She felt her heart begin to race. "Jeco." She did not wait for either of them, sliding down the face of the dune wall with ease, forcing on through the heat and scorching sands. Kohl and Falco were quick to reach her side.

Despite their hurried pace, Falco continued with his story. "Like Hydo, I'm from Haycith. My parents knew something was different about me early on ...I could move objects with ease. I once struck my mother with a large vase. It was an accident, but after that, she was always so afraid of me."

Jessop couldn't believe Falco was divulging this history. She was torn between his voice and her view of the caves. She took his hand, by way of offering her support and encouraging him forward.

"I was so young. Whenever I was overly tired or losing my temper, objects would go flying. My parents knew of a family—the parents had died in a terrible accident, but they'd had a Hunter son. They thought the Blade could handle me. It was that or death, really—they thought I'd kill them on accident, or kill myself."

Jessop squeezed his hand tightly, imagining Falco as a young boy; he had probably been identical to his own son. She knew he would have been so confused—much more afraid than his parents. Jeco's ability was a point of pride for her and Falco. She couldn't imagine ever sending him away for his gifts.

"My mother was really too young when she had me. And I don't remember any father."

Jessop and Falco both turned to look at Kohl as they trudged through the sand. He kept his eyes trained forward. "She was so young ...beautiful, with blonde hair and warm skin. She would wash my feet in a small bucket when I came in from the fields. We had no coin and barely any food ...I think we were living in a shed on someone else's land."

"She knew things were different about me, I suppose, when I told her I could hear her sadness. She was afraid and sad every day, and I could hear her thoughts. I began to voice them to her, unaware of what I was doing ...She wasn't afraid of me, but she knew I could have a better life elsewhere."

Jessop remembered once being in Kohl's mind and seeing such a woman. She had been so young Jessop hadn't ever considered she was Kohl's mother. She looked to Kohl but said nothing, and the three of them carried on in silence. Jessop wondered if Kohl would ever return to the woman—Jessop had found her location, after all. She had forced the information from Hanson before Falco took the Blade.

Jessop stared ahead when she finally spoke, unable to look at him. "Would you go to her now that I could tell you where to find her?"

She knew why she struggled with the question. In the passing days, though she no longer had nightmares about Kohl, she once again feared losing him forever. She wondered if it would always be that way for them— if they would spend their lives torn between wishing the other dead and wishing they could love each other differently.

Kohl said nothing, but in her periphery she could see him thinking hard on the question. Finally, he shook his head. "I couldn't bring her into all of *this*. She's safer not knowing me."

Falco scoffed, pulling Kohl and Jessop's stares. He kicked up a mound of sand. "We are as dangerous as they come—*everyone* is safer not knowing us. All of Daharia fears me. And for good reason too."

He spoke the words with an odd tone, as though they were both a point of pride and a mark of shame. They instantly reminded Jessop of how Falco once was as a boy—arrogant and lonely.

"They will not fear you when you lead them. They will respect you. As we do."

"She's right, Falco. The same act that seems treacherous when executed by your enemy is seen as brave when committed by your leader. Daharians feared you because of Hydo, and Aranthol, and the belief that you would one day harm them ...Knowing you will use your power to keep them safe will win them over."

Falco laughed, pulling his hand free from Jessop as he leapt down the sloping curve of a dune. "Keep them safe ...I couldn't even keep my own son safe."

Jessop felt the words burn her as keenly as a branding iron. She had let him believe he was to blame for Jeco—knowing full well that he would have already been blaming himself. Just as she blamed herself and as Mar'e and Kohl had blamed themselves.

She leaned back as she slid down the slope, quick to land at his side and grab him in her strong hold.

"You mustn't think like that."

She reached up and touched his face, forcing him to look at her. "It's not your fault. Do not take blame from Hydo and Hanson—this is *their* doing."

"It's as you have been saying—you blame Hydo for setting events into motion that ruined your life ...Well, I set the events into motion that led to Jeco being taken. By reclaiming the Blade I put him at risk."

"You *had* to take the Blade back because of what Hydo did—what *he* started!"

"No, I didn't! He may have wronged us years ago, but we could have moved on. We are all responsible for our own actions, Jessop."

She knew he was right, as Urdo and Kohl were right. She had remained incapable of accepting their notion of responsibility because then she would have to admit she was more monster than martyr. In every act of violence she had committed, she'd had the convenience of blaming Hydo—never having to admit that a part of her relished in her abilities. Abilities that had only continued to grow. She was a Fire-Wielder—Hydo hadn't made her dangerous, she was *born* dangerous. He had done nothing but provide her a target for which to aim.

She could not face the person she had become. She had pretended life in Aranthol was a great pain she had suffered because of Hydo, when in reality she had loved their Shadow City. She had claimed manipulating Kohl had been an arduous task, when the truth was much harder to admit. She had loved the way he'd loved her—instantly and without apology.

"You're not a monster, Jessop. If you were, you wouldn't feel so terrible for your inability to love him back. You wouldn't regret hurting him so." Falco spoke clearly, knowing there was no longer a point in shielding Kohl from such things.

"When you know so much, how could you possibly make the mistake of blaming yourself for our son?"

"Because, Jessop, what if we aren't the heroes here? What if we aren't the oppressed mighty few, rising up to reclaim what's rightfully ours? What if everything truly would have been better if we had stayed in Aranthol?"

Jessop knew his words gave voice to thoughts she had long since wondered. Too much of what they had done had felt wrong to claim it was for a greater right. "I know—"

"No. Just, no." Kohl finally spoke, appearing at their side, his hands on either of their shoulders.

"You two are hardly heroes—you're violent, selfish, and you think of no one outside of your own family."

Jessop glared, but if Kohl could sense her anger, he didn't show any sign of caring.

"But you're not *wrong*. Hydo doesn't deserve the Blade. Long before anything was set into motion, we all knew the Blade would be handed over to Falco. That is what was right. And that is what we will ensure happens. And after Falco, it seems very likely that Jeco will rule. Which requires us getting him back. Enough of this contemplation—we have a boy to rescue."

Jessop knew instantly that Kohl had the same quality Falco possessed, the one that she did not. He had the great ability to lead. His words moved her and she felt more confident in their mission than at any stage prior. She suppressed a smile. Falco turned and embraced his brother, clapping him firmly on the back. Jessop couldn't help but watch them with amazement, and a critical eye. She wondered if their bond would always be like her own with Kohl, constantly shifting between love and hatred.

She heard the spear before she saw it—the distinct whistling of a fine weapon cutting through air. She threw her hand out quickly, only seeing the weapon once she had frozen it mid-air. She flung it to the ground as its owner appeared on the dunes.

"Falco," she spoke, and in unison, he and Kohl unsheathed their blades.

There were three women, two still carrying spears. They wore no garments, but their bodies were covered in a thick, black paste. It was thick over their smooth, hairless heads and around their jaws and cheeks, protecting their skin from the heat of the desert, Jessop imagined.

Kohl spiraled his sword about his sides. "Dezane wasn't lying when he said this was a treacherous place."

Falco laughed. "What I don't understand is why they all try to kill us? Why not just keep walking?"

Jessop shook her head, ignoring both of them as they made light of the situation. She couldn't, not when they were so close to the caves.

The three women made no sounds. They walked in unison, almost as if gliding over the sand. Jessop knew they were supernatural beings by the way they moved and their unblinking stares, but she did not know in what way. As they continued their approach, one threw another spear. Falco deflected it with ease before using Sentio to wrench the last remaining spear from the hand of the third woman, tossing it across the dunes.

When the women came to an abrupt halt, Jessop thought that perhaps, without weapons, they would reconsider their attack. The three of them stared at Jessop, Falco, and Kohl, still unblinking, emitting no noises whatsoever. Jessop was willing to let them leave in peace, in order to get to the caves faster. But she quickly realized the women had no such intentions.

Each of their bodies began to tremble. The women held their hands out, their paste-covered skin shaking violently, still maintaining perfect silence, still staring. Jessop could hardly believe what she was witnessing, but it seemed as though all of their hands were melting under the black-paste, losing the shape of their fingers and thumbs and wrists.

Jessop glanced to Kohl and Falco, who remained equally transfixed and horrified. "Anyone know what they are?"

Their hands were beginning to take new shape. Their arms grew longer, flatter, forming sharp edges and a fine point—their hands had become long black swords.

"I've never..." Jessop began, but her voice trailed off, uncertain what to say.

The three began to extend their arms out, testing their weapon limbs. Once sure of themselves, they smiled as they began their descent on Jessop, Falco, and Kohl. Jessop took a step forward, leaving Kohl and Falco behind her. She threw both hands out before her, focused with all her might, and let the fires that had been bursting to break free, fly from the palms of her hands. It was a relief and she could feel her muscles relaxing and her skin cooling as she allowed the flames their escape.

The fire encircled the women, but to Jessop's amazement, they remained silent. She knew after holding the blaze for a long moment that the flames should have been fatal. Slowly, she lowered her hands, expecting to find the bodies, charred in the sand. Instead, the three women remained standing, completely unharmed.

"Neat trick," Falco mused, walking past Jessop, his sword at the ready.

Jessop couldn't believe it. They were immune to her powers. She unsheathed her Hunter's blade and took quick strides towards the women. They may have been fire proof, but there was nothing her sword couldn't cut down. Jessop swung her blade, engaging the woman who had thrown the first spear, as Falco and Kohl covered the other two.

Her sword met the woman's blade-arm with surprising ring. "What are you?"

"*What are you?*" The woman spoke back, and to Jessop's surprise and horror, she spoke in Jessop's exact voice.

"Well, that's terrifying," Jessop balked, forcing the woman back against a dune wall. Jessop's fighting ability was superior—but the woman was incredibly strong. Jessop ducked her sword-like arms and avoided falling into her grasp or getting kicked by one of her long, paste-covered legs.

"Well, that's terrifying," the woman mimicked, still staring at Jessop with unblinking eyes.

"Enough already!" Jessop threw her free hand out, willing the woman to fall to her knees with Sentio. But nothing happened. Jessop's hand was outstretched, as useless as her flames had been. She stared at her fingers, knowing this was the first time since Falco had taught her Sentio that it hadn't worked.

"Sentio doesn't work on them!"

Just as Jessop yelled to the others, the woman kicked her violently in the side of the head. She flew to the ground, rolling in the sand. Her head throbbed in pain. The fire didn't work, Sentio didn't work, they had turned their arms into blades—Jessop couldn't fathom what the women were.

She rolled to her back and with a quick flip, she was once again on her feet. As she turned to face the woman, she was stunned to see her own reflection before her. She blinked and refocused, knowing it had been a firm kick to the head. But, still, standing before her, was a perfect version of herself.

The woman had changed shape once more, turning into an identical copy of Jessop. Jessop stared at the version of herself—amazed at how identical the replica was. The only difference, if she could think of one, was that her copy didn't blink—and though she had hands that matched Jessop's, she did not carry a weapon.

Jessop sheathed her sword. "If you think I won't kill you just because you look like me, you're in for a treat."

Jessop hadn't fought without a blade in the longest time, and a part of her longed to win a fight with her bare hands. She twisted her body and executed a perfect roundhouse kick against the woman. She ducked under angry swings and struck with neat precision, hitting the woman in the face and throat. It *was* confusing—seeing her own face bleed, but it did not deter her. As she ducked low, she heard the whistling of another spear. She fell to the ground, letting the weapon travel over her.

With a sickening pierce, the spear struck Jessop's attacker in the chest. Jessop rose quickly, turning to see Falco wink at her—he had used Sentio to throw the weapon.

Jessop turned back and found that the woman was beginning to shift back into her original form, blood pooling from her mouth and chest—she was dying. She leaned over the woman and wrenched the spear free from her, bringing about a much faster death. She turned and found that her attacker was not the only one to have changed shape—Falco and Kohl both fought identical versions of themselves. Jessop watched Falco's fight. He moved with a grace she found mesmerizing. She would always know Falco, even blinded, she could hear his step or recognize his breath. Without hesitating, she threw the spear with all her might, and struck his attacker.

As Kohl brought his own attacker down, Jessop walked to Falco's side, taking his hand in hers. Kohl spun on them as he sheathed his sword. "What is wrong with you two—you could have killed one another!"

Falco turned to him. "There was no such risk."

"But they were identical to us."

"We can sense one another," Jessop explained.

Kohl shook his head, as if he should no longer be amazed by the connection they had. "Of course you can."

Chapter 10

Present Day

Jessop rushed ahead, fearing neither Hydo nor Hanson, nor any other monster that could be hiding within the caves. She thought only of her son. Falco was at her side, but Kohl was more cautious, taking a wider berth of the caves, ensuring they did not run into a trap. They were a small range of caves that backed into the dry hill where the sands trailed up sparsely before blending into the persevering desert shrubs.

"*Jeco!*"

"Jeco! We're here! *Son!*"

Jessop and Falco ran into the mouth of the cave. There was no light and though that did not hinder her or Falco greatly, Jessop ignited her hand to help in their search. "Jeco!"

Her heart was beating with such a violent force it caused a sweat to break out on her brow. She was anxious—more than anxious. Her son had been missing for days—*days*. It had been the worst time of her life.

"Hanson! Where are you?"

Jessop ran down through the deep cave, her heart never slowing. She felt the panic growing with every second that Jeco remained missing.

"Where is my son?" Her voice echoed all around them as a spout of fire erupted from her hand, trailing over the cave walls in a winding pattern before escaping out into the desert. She followed the fire's path and found Kohl standing in the cave entryway.

"There's a natural spring behind the caves, footsteps in the dampened soil—small ones. He would have been here as recently as this morning, perhaps last night."

Jessop turned to Falco and saw the pain in his face, the disappointment—the fear. She turned, glaring back at Kohl. "Your mentor will die for this."

"Given the chance, for *this*, I would kill him myself."

She threw herself against Falco, her arms locking tightly around him as the tears burst forward. She was not an emotional woman—she was a warrior. She did not suffer the actions of others. She *took* action. But this pain was too great. It was more than torture, more than suffering. This, Jessop truly believed, was what dying felt like. And as she held Falco, she knew her husband felt it too.

"He's not here, Falco. Our boy isn't here."

She fell to her knees and he fell with her. She cried, as she never had before—the waves of pain rushing through her, escaping her in agonizing sobs. Her body heaved as her strong muscles rippled, her stomach violently turning. Falco held her as tightly as he could, crying and fighting for breath.

They held one another in their grief and she wanted nothing more than to fix everything, for Jeco to have been with them, safe…

"*Argh!*"

Kohl fell to his knees, grabbing his head, pulling both Jessop and Falco from their own pain. She knew instantly it was Urdo, forcing his way into Kohl's well-fortified mind as he had before, to tell him of Mar'e's condition. Kohl rubbed his head tightly, hissing for a moment before relaxing.

Finally, he opened his eyes. "Urdo told me we to stay here—they're close. And they're bringing reinforcements."

* * * *

Jessop started a small fire for them, using kindling that Kohl had gathered from the hillside. Falco refilled their flagon with fresh water, and they shared the last of the dried meat. She knew Teck had kept them going this far with his foresight. She bit into a leathery strip of meat and sipped water, though it did nothing but add to her nausea. She needed her son back.

Falco squeezed her arm, answering her unvoiced thoughts. "We will get him. He was here—he *is* alive."

She handed him the flagon and turned her gaze to the small fire she had made. "I know we will. What I don't understand is why would they take him to Bakoran?"

Kohl shifted in the sand opposite her. It had grown dark in the desert but her fire kept a warm light on all of them. "It has something to do with the woman—Octayn."

Jessop moved back, readjusting to be further away from the fire. "Not this again."

"Jessop—"

"I remember my mother—I remember her life, and her death, and I remember her smile and her glowing green eyes, and—"

"Her what?"

"Her glowing green eyes."

He furrowed his brow, the movement twisting the star-shaped scar carved into his cheek by Falco so many years before.

"What?" she pressed.

"The face of the woman I saw in Hydo's mind—she was a beautiful woman, but she didn't have glowing eyes."

Jessop thought on his words. "You have no Kuroi blood—you cannot see that my eyes also glow. Neither can Falco."

Falco leaned forward. "That is true, but I can see how *you* see another Kuroi when I see your memory of them, for it's my witnessing a memory, not my witnessing *them*."

"How so?"

"I can see your memories of Korend'a or Trax or Dezane—and I see the way their eyes glow. I can see Trax's memory of you, and the way your eyes glow to him. But I could also see Kohl's memory of you, and your eyes do not glow in those images."

Kohl moved closer, his eyes fixed on her. "Which means I would have seen Octayn's eyes glowing if it were your mother?"

Falco shook his head. "No, actually you wouldn't have. Hydo has no Kuroi blood—he would have never seen the way Kuroi eyes glow so he would have no memory of Jessop's mother's eyes that way."

Jessop looked between the two of them. "Then there's a simple solution to this—let me see the memory you saw."

Kohl leaned back from the fire, silent, dropping his gaze from her. "What is it?"

Falco looked her over with his gray eyes. "He does not want you in his mind again, I think."

She felt offended instantly, and then remembered she had no right to feel so, not after all she had done to him. She had tweaked and removed memories, tortured him, torn through his thoughts and used her abilities against him to propel her own agenda. She had no place in his mind.

"Oh." It was all she could manage.

His tight expression softened at her voice. "No. It's fine."

She looked up at Kohl's words. He was nodding, as though convincing himself that it *was* fine.

"Kohl, I know my mother died. I don't need to see the face of the woman you're thinking of. I have no place in your mind any longer."

"It is I who must know, now. If I cannot trust you to enter my mind then what am I even doing here? Just do it."

"Kohl—"

"I said do it."

Jessop stood and quickly made her way to Kohl's side. She didn't want to hurt him any more than she already had. Slowly, painfully aware of his fear and Falco's eyes on her, she raised her hand to his face. She remembered holding him in the Hollow—certain Falco was going to execute him. She remembered everything between them and she forced it all down into the deepest parts of her mind where it could live forever, in hiding. She took a deep breath, closed her eyes, and once again entered Kohl O'Hanlon's mind.

* * * *

Jessop turned in Falco's arms, shifting her back to his chest, facing the fire. On the other side of the glowing embers she could see Kohl's back rising and falling with slow breaths. She didn't think he was really sleeping, but she couldn't be sure. Falco slept, but it was with unease and restlessness. She felt him twitching and tensing, whispering under his breath. They had not spoken much after she had found the memory.

It hadn't been her mother. Of course it hadn't. The woman was undeniably beautiful and there had definitely been a surprising resemblance between her and Jessop's mother—the long blonde hair and green eyes. But sure enough, the Octayn of Hydo's memory was not Jessop's Octayn. "What are the odds of Hydo knowing a blonde, green eyed woman named Octayn who *isn't* your mother?" Kohl had asked, staring at her with confusion.

She had no answer for him, for she had no explanation for any of these things. She didn't know whom Hydo had known. She didn't really know anything about Hydo, she realized. Which was odd, considering the time Falco had spent schooling her on his former mentor, preparing her to help take him down. She knew about his abilities, his training tactics, and the strength of his mind. She knew exactly how long it had taken her to trap him inside a memory. But she had never once used that time during his deep sleep to peruse his mind, to find out more about the man. She had never seen reason to. As she stared at Kohl's slowly rising shoulders, thinking about the things he had brought up, she wished she had taken advantage when she had the chance.

"Why didn't you just kill him when you had the chance?"

Kohl's voice didn't surprise her, but his line of questioning did. Unlike Falco, he did not have unfettered access to her thoughts, he hadn't truly known what she had been thinking when he'd asked the question. But somehow, nonetheless, he had known. He rolled over on the firm ground and stared at her from across the crimson embers.

She readjusted her position on Falco's arm. "I suppose we wanted more ...We wanted him to be shamed in front of all of you, to admit his trespasses against us, to admit what he did to my family and to Falco. If I had just killed him, he would have died a hero to Daharians everywhere."

"I wish you had just killed him."

"So do I."

They stared at one another in silence, the fire between them slowly dying out. "In hindsight, knowing how I reacted when you brought him to the terrace, if you had done something sooner, I probably would have killed you."

"You would have tried and you would have failed."

"I know."

She held his gaze, knowing they had not spoken in the middle of the night like this for quite some time. "I know nothing about him, really. Which is odd, given my focused plans to kill him."

Kohl moved, so he was no longer resting on his shoulder. "What's there to know? He was the youngest Lord Protector there ever was, best friend to Hanson and Urdo, he had led well all those years since Falco had disappeared."

"Best friends with Urdo? Hanson I can see, but Urdo?"

"Yes, but you could have actually watched them grow apart in my lifetime. We never knew what caused the rift."

She would ask Urdo about it. She needed to know more. She had never thought that the face of the woman from Hydo's memory would have been that of her mother, but she would have been lying if she claimed the entire thing hadn't piqued her interest somewhat.

"Gredoria Vane was the Lord and Protector before him—he's still alive isn't he?"

Kohl shook his head once more. "Died a year ago or so. I met him once, actually. As mad as they come."

Jessop had never asked Falco about the history of the Hunters, so she knew very little about what had happened before Hydo Jesuin. "What do you mean?"

"Quite literally that. He lost his mind. They found him rambling in his quarters one day, all alone, repeating *Hadonia, Hadonia* ...over and over."

"What's Hadonia?"

Kohl smiled. "*Who*, you mean. Hadonia was his wife."

Jessop thought about it. Imagining losing so much of yourself with a fractured mind. "He didn't know his own name, but hers he never forgot."

She could feel Kohl's intense stare. She wanted to look away from him, but she couldn't.

His eyes were filled with love and sadness. "I know what that must feel like."

* * * *

In her dream, Jessop saw five men, laughing and speaking amongst one another, with children playing all about them. One of the children was Jeco. She stood adjacent to the group, but they did not seem to see or hear her. She watched as Jeco played swords with another boy, one with flaxen hair and bright green eyes. The boy was perhaps a year older than Jeco and he played well with her son. Jeco was laughing.

The children were dressed all in white—ivory tunics and breeches, even the female child, whose long golden hair was tied back. These were children who trained. Jeco was dressed as they were, but his gray eyes and dark hair set him apart. Jeco was not the only one to stand out—one of the men had dark features. His skin was golden, as Jessop's, he too had dark hair, and as he turned to reach for a drink off the table, she saw that his eyes glowed. Jessop knew instantly he was part Kuroi. And though he did not have the same shared qualities of the others, there were different features that they had in common. All of them had strong jaws, muscular and lean bodies, scars—even the youngest, who appeared several years Jessop's junior, had a long scar down his jaw. Warriors dressed in white.

"*Cara'ka, Jeco*," the golden-haired girl spoke, taking Jeco softly by the hand and leading him to the table near the adults. Jessop did not know the language the female child spoke in, but she watched keenly as the girl pulled fruit from a large serving bowl and expertly carved it into small, edible pieces with a sharp blade. She pushed it towards Jessop's son and then poured him water into a golden chalice. It was only then that Jessop noticed the finery—the serving platters and goblets were gold and encrusted with glittering gemstones. The table and chairs were covered in ivory linens that bore no wrinkles or stains. The garments the men and the children wore were of the finest making. Jessop had been accustomed to such luxury in Aranthol—but she had yet to ever see it elsewhere in Daharia.

"Misa, *casos*," one of the fair-haired men spoke. Again, Jessop could not understand the language, but by the tone and the look in the man's eye, she knew he was the girl's father.

Jessop walked closer, rounding the table until she could kneel beside her son. He seemed so content. His hair was clean and combed, he had lost no weight, and he smiled with each bite of food. She slowly reached her hand out, needing to brush his hair back, to whisper his name and tell him she loved him, when suddenly a movement in the corner of her eye halted her.

Hydo. He wore his black Hunter's clothing and his dark eyes were focused on her. He could see her as clearly as she him. She stood, leaping in front of Jeco. "What is going on? Where is this place?"

He raised his hands slowly, as if offering peace. "You're in a dream, Jessop. I simply arranged a visit. To show you what life was like for us, what it could be for your family."

Jessop wanted to kill him, to strike him down where he stood, but she knew what he said to be true. This was nothing more than a dream. "I will kill you for taking my son, Hydo. Do you hear me? I'll kill you for taking him from his family."

"I would never take him from his family."

He slowly extended his hands out and Jessop sensed the shift in the dream. The eyes of all the men and children were now on her. They could see her. They could hear her. They no longer laughed in conversation; they did not sip their drinks or eat their meals. They stared in silence, directly at her. She turned quickly to see Jeco, staring up at her, his gray eyes growing wide. "Mama."

"*Jeco!*"

Jessop woke, her scream echoing through the cave.

Falco grabbed her instantly, pulling her into his embrace. "It was a dream. Just a dream."

She was shaking in his embrace. Sweat covered her body. She could see Kohl sitting upright, his hand on his Hunter's blade, alarmed by her scream. The fire had died out completely. "It was more than a dream. It was Hydo ...He was in my head."

Chapter 11

Haren'dul Daku

Present Day

The morning light barely cracked through the cave. Jessop had started another fire. They had discussed her dream at length and had come to few conclusions. She sat, the lengths of her index fingers pressed firmly against her mouth, as she remained crouched down against the smooth wall of the cave. Falco stood opposite her, arms crossed, leaning against the stone. Kohl was reclined by the fire, his hands firmly gripping the sides of his head.

"An apparition—he used Sentio to appear in your dream," Kohl recapped.

"Jessop's mind is far too strong," Falco said. "My love, how are you certain it wasn't simply a *very* realistic dream?"

"I just know."

He nodded but she wasn't certain he believed her. And she didn't blame him. Her mind was as strong as he said—strong enough to live out her double life in the Blade, stronger than Falco's, stronger than any Hunter she knew. Except for Hydo, it seemed. Though she had been the one to put him in such a deep sleep none could recover him.

"The mind is weaker in its subconscious state. Yours is very well fortified in your waking hours, but as you sleep, your defenses lower," Falco spoke, finishing her thoughts.

She had not opened her mind to him, nor anyone, that morning. Not since the dream. He simply knew, as Kohl had known her thoughts without entering her mind that previous night. They simply knew her.

She didn't know what face she had made, but Kohl rolled up to a sitting position. "Jessop, even with lowered defenses your mind is a fortress—as impenetrable as a seasoned Hunter's in waking hours."

"Not to Hydo."

They sat in silence for a long moment before Falco pushed off the wall. "What about the others in the dream—you said they became aware of you?"

"Yes, five men, a handful of children. One who had so many similar features to me, but also to the others, he was part Kuroi ...At first, it was as though I were invisible to them, then at Hydo's will, they could all see me."

"And you think they were real too?"

"I think it was all real."

"Good."

She glared at him, unsure of how any part of their situation could be characterized as *good.*

"You said Jeco was well and being taken care of, he was with other children, happy and content—if that is true, then it is a good thing."

She realized the truth in his words. If it were real, Jeco had also been real, and he had been happy. She thought on him and how he had seemed and then remembered Hydo's words ...

"Hydo said something to me—I nearly forgot. I threatened him over taking Jeco from us, and he said '*I would never take him from his family*'."

Kohl stood. "This must have something to do with the Octayn coincidence."

"Kohl—"

"I'm being serious. Jessop, I can *feel* this—something isn't right. Something about this woman and Hydo, something about your family, it all feels wrong."

She said nothing. She didn't like his words, but that didn't make them untrue.

* * * *

She had decided they could wait till sundown. If Urdo hadn't arrived by then, they would continue on in their search. She couldn't waste any more time sitting in the caves, contemplating the strength of her own mind or the state of her life—worrying constantly about her son.

She paced the width of the cave, watching Kohl and Falco spar in the corner of her eye. Their camaraderie was still odd to her—so recently each had been determined to kill the other. Theirs was a relationship she would never understand. A small part of Jessop felt disturbed by the realization that Falco had always been *more* Hunter than he had let on. He had missed his brothers, loved them more than hated them, longed to lead them more than punish them.

But Falco was not what mattered most, getting their son back was. Jessop watched as Falco twisted Kohl's arm back in a quick, paralyzing motion. Kohl hissed, but rolled out of the hold with expert motion, only to fall quickly back into another trap. He was no match for Falco. As she had long known, he never had been. Her eyes trailed over the wild mess of scars that covered both of their large frames. She wondered if the rite of passage they had undergone was partly responsible for their quickly restored friendship. They were forever bonded by their shared past. The thought was not impossible for her to imagine. Jessop had scars that bonded her to the both of them too.

* * * *

Jessop found Kohl sitting at the mouth of the cave, sipping from the flagon of water. His eyes were red and his cheeks splotchy. She knelt beside him. "I lost my temper with you again ...I'm sorry."

He sipped the water once more before sealing it. "You and I can't spend our lives apologizing to one another."

She took the flagon from him and opened it for a small sip. She held the cool water in her mouth for a long minute, letting it swirl about her tongue before swallowing. "Have you been thinking about Mar'e?"

He nodded, his gaze stuck on the darkening horizon of the desert. "She'll make it and Falco will heal her."

"Maybe. But then what? We are walking towards a war and we all know it. It's you and Falco, leading a new generation of Hunters—a new army—against Hydo and Hanson and all those who fled the Blade with them."

"We don't know what we prepare to face. But we were made for battle, Kohl. And it is not just Falco and I who map this new course."

"I keep thinking that if Mar'e survives it all, maybe I could be with her. Maybe being with her will help me stop wishing I was with you."

"Kohl—"

"You betrayed me. And I know that most of it wasn't real ...but I close my eyes and I can still remember holding you, sleeping at your side, feeling as though you were mine. What's wrong with me? I tried to kill you and yet still..."

"We have done unforgivable things to one another. But you deserve better than to live with this torment."

"Don't we all."

She thought of all she had done and all she had harmed. Even those closest to her were in danger of her rage. She had lived her life with an agenda—to avenge her parents. She hadn't been a very admirable person along the way.

"No. I don't think we all do. I don't think I do."

He turned to her, a perplexed look painted across his face.

She handed him the flagon back. "This life is all I know, Kohl. How to kill, how to fight, that's it."

She stood and so did he. He fixed his hazel eyes on her. "We are the same. Hunters are raised with a blind mission. Protect the Blade. The difference is that we have our brothers."

"It's quite the difference."

Slowly, he reached out and rested a firm hand on her shoulder. "You are one of *us,* too, now."

"Is that what we are to each other? Siblings?"

"No, of course not. I'll always love you. And I'll always hate you. But you have my loyalty—as does Falco."

"I think you're a good man, Kohl."

"When you say such things, remember I burned your city to the ground."

"Kohl—"

"Maybe there is no good or bad ...Maybe everyone is both."

"I don't believe that. There is pure good in this world—and your mistakes don't change what I know is in your heart. I *know* you are good, Kohl."

"And what of Mar'e? Is she good?"

Jessop could picture the woman perfectly; beautiful and challenging, but *good.* "Yes. I think she is."

"Hopefully, I'll get to find out."

"I hope so too."

"I'll do things differently with her, than I did with you, if she still wants me. Maybe that will make the difference."

"What do you mean?"

"I don't want to love another so quickly, so hard, again. If the pain isn't excruciating enough, the embarrassment lives on."

Jessop grabbed his hand tightly. "Don't. Don't do anything different. You loved me instantly and without apology, and it changed everything for me."

"It didn't change enough."

"Kohl—"

"I love him, too, Jessop. I really do. The hate was a lie created by Hydo. I'm glad Falco has you."

Before she could say anything further, he pulled his hand free from her, leaving her in the dark.

* * * *

Jessop rolled Teck's pack up tightly. Night had fallen and they would leave the caves to continue their search. Jessop had been uneasy since her conversation with Kohl. There had been so much retrospection in their time together crossing the desert. None of it brought her closer to Jeco. She couldn't understand how the three of them—the most skilled in battle—had become so seemingly delicate overnight.

"Nothing will be the same till he's back," Falco answered her unvoiced thoughts. His voice was barely a whisper but she heard him perfectly from the shadow of the cave where he sat, watching her.

She sighed heavily, rubbing her temples. She couldn't tell if he had been in her mind or if he simply could see her distress—had she left her mind open to him or had he found a way in, as Hydo had done? "Falco, I need to be able to keep Hydo out."

He moved with silence and grace, through the cave, to her side. "You will. You have always been able to. He takes advantage of your vulnerability."

"I don't know how to bolster my defenses in my sleep."

"Then what if we act preemptively?"

"How so?"

"Get in his mind before he can get in yours."

She turned in his arms. "Late tonight. When he is sure to be sleeping."

"Late tonight it is."

* * * *

"Do you think Urdo ran into trouble?" Kohl asked as they made their way out from the caves. She was angry that they had waited as long as they did and still the others had not arrived, but at Kohl's words she grew worried. They had encountered attack after attack since crossing into *Haren'dul Daku*—there was no saying what Urdo had possibly faced.

"No, they're safe in their Soar-Craft. I doubt all the desert brigands have Bakunawa cannons." Falco answered with confidence, but Jessop could tell he wasn't truly certain. She wondered if Kohl could also tell, or if Falco's subtleties were still only visible to her.

She refocused her thoughts. She could not continue to focus on Falco and Kohl, on herself, or on Urdo. She instead focused on Hydo and how she intended to enter his mind late that evening. She had entered the minds of those in her proximity countless times, even if the person were out of sight or on the other side of a wall. But to enter the mind of one of the most powerful Hunters of all time as he hid in an undisclosed location was something she did not know how to go about without—

"*Ouch!*" Jessop rolled down the sandy dune, knowing something had tripped her up.

Falco was at her side in an instant, helping her up. "What was that?"

Kohl looked down at her with a light amusement in his eyes. "Are you alright?"

"It's not funny, Kohl."

"Jess—"

Falco shook his head. "Jessop doesn't just fall, Kohl. Not ever."

It took him a moment to understand what they were saying. With keen vision in the darkness, an incredibly light step, and wildly accurate senses, Jessop *didn't* just fall on accident. She never tripped, never slipped on a slick floor, never so much as rolled an ankle while walking idly. Something had caused her to fall.

She stared at the sand beneath her feet but saw nothing. There was a light breeze that shifted the fine grains. There was a faint whistle in the air. But there was nothing to be seen. Just as she was about to admit that the trials of their recent affairs must have thrown her off her usual pristine balance, she felt a shift in the sand beneath her feet. It was the oddest sensation—as though a large mound had appeared under her heels and disappeared just as quickly.

She instantly unsheathed her Hunter's blade. "Something is in the ground."

Falco swung his own blade about him in a deadly spiral. Jessop shot her gaze to Kohl, his hand on his hilt, his eyes scanning the ground. "Unsheathe your blade."

He pulled at the hilt, nodding to her, when the dune beside him spouted up like a water fountain, a wild explosion of sand and dirt and shining metal. Jessop saw Kohl fall to the side just as she covered her eyes against the debris. She tried to maintain her footing, but the ground shook violently. She fell into Falco, toppling them both to the ground, her sword falling from her grip. They rolled down the quaking lip of the dune, sand flying in their eyes, filling their mouths, a mechanical scream filling the air.

They sprawled across the desert floor, coming to a slow stop where the dune leveled out. Falco still had his blade, amazing Jessop that he hadn't accidentally cut her as they fell. She turned her gaze from him, back up the dune wall to where Kohl was, to find a sight unlike any other she had ever seen before. The creature that had burst through the ground was a giant serpent—though not one made of flesh and blood. The entire body of the beast was made of fused bones, and not the bones of any reptilian animals, but the bones of men. Leg bones and skulls, tiny metacarpals, and hips, all meshed together, hundreds upon hundreds of them, intricately bound together, forming the towering body of the serpent. The head was the only part of the giant snake not to be made of human bone, instead being fashioned by shining metals, forming a menacingly sharp jaw. Its eyes were completely clear, like glass. Jessop could do nothing but stare as the snake used its long tail to hold Kohl twenty feet above the ground.

With a deep breath, she threw her hand out and called for her blade. As it came flying into her grasp, she made for the beast.

Falco grabbed her shoulder, pulling her back. "Jessop, don't!"

She froze. She watched as Falco sheathed his sword. He raised his hands out, palms forward, and took a slow step towards the creature. "It's one of the Ophidia, beasts that clean up the ravages of man."

Jessop didn't know why he was telling her this. "And?"

He smiled at her calmly. "Their entire kind is loyal to me."

He held his hands out and continued to approach the beast with slow caution. Jessop had no idea what Falco was saying. She had heard of the Ophidia but she had never seen one and never imagined that the description was of something so colossal.

The creature stilled and regarded Falco with what looked like a sense of recognition. It lowered its great body down, the crunching of bones and squeaking of metal deafening to Jessop. Her heart raced as the massive creature approached him, cocking its silver head from side to side. Slowly, it relaxed its tail, letting Kohl fall to the ground. It slithered over the sand, the bones of the dead creaking and cracking, the sand grinding between them.

Falco kept his hands out. The Ophidia was but a foot away from him now, and he stood only several paces ahead of Jessop. She was prepared to kill it, to set it ablaze with her mind if it made one foul strike against him. She flicked her gaze to Kohl, who had a look of shock and horror plastered so visibly across his face it was almost amusing. But then the Ophidia blinked, silvery metal eyelids moving up over its glassy eyes, and retracting back down. And instead of the eyes being clear orbs, they were filled with images of Falco. He was younger, but not a child. Jessop watched with amazement as the images of her husband smiling and meeting with the Ophidia kind played before her in the eyes of the giant snake.

Slowly, the images went away. Falco outstretched his arms and the snake slithered forward, nestling its massive head against Falco. He ran his strong hands over the metal head of the creature, soothing it. "Return home, young one."

They broke their embrace slowly and the Ophidia turned from Falco, slithering up the dune wall, paying no attention to Jessop or Kohl before shooting its powerful body across the sand, disappearing down the dune and into the night.

Falco turned back to her, calm as ever. She stared at him waiting for further explanation. She didn't even know when Falco could have formed an allegiance with such wild creatures without her having known.

He smiled. "Being Lord of the Shadow City does come with perks."

Chapter 12

Haren'dul Daku

Twenty-five years ago

"Careful where you step—Ophidia are rampant here," Octayn warned. Hydo turned to regard her by the spring behind the caves. She had shown him the spot, suggesting it as a resting stop for the night before they continued their travels to Bakoran. He couldn't believe he was in *Haren'dul Daku*— no man's land. They traveled by Soar-Craft and while they had remained mostly unseen, they had come across a band of Soren once. Though they had been no match for himself and Octayn, he had felt unnerved by the way they stared at him—as though they knew he was a Hunter. He had ensured there were no survivors, no one to run off and whisper that Hydo Jesuin was crossing the desert towards Daharia's greatest enemy.

He moved closer to her. "I've heard stories of the giant beasts."

She dabbed her mouth with the back of her hand, slowly rising from the spring. "Real and quite fire-proof."

He pulled her into his embrace. "Remarkable."

She kissed him, but Hydo felt her hand quick to her stomach. He immediately loosened his hold on her and rested his hand over hers. "That they are."

He leaned his forehead against hers. "I wasn't talking about the beasts."

* * * *

He rested, his hands behind his head, his eyes studying the cave walls, Octayn sleeping beside him. In truth, he could not reconcile the state of his life. He knew that he could not live without her—but he still did not fully comprehend what living *with* her would entail. The Bakora did not share Daharian beliefs. Octayn had a certain comfort with killing that he, as a Hunter, could never understand, empathize with ...or tolerate. And yet, he knew what he had done to be with her in this place. He could barely close his eyes without picturing Gredoria's face.

He turned to look upon her perfect form. They had mapped out their plan and they knew it would take many years to see through. Many years that they would have to spend apart.

He didn't want to think about that, thinking instead of Urdo and Hanson. The relationship with his brothers had changed. They all had seen what had happened to Gredoria, but Hydo would not admit his role in it. Even if it hadn't been for Hanson, he could not speak of his actions. They knew, even if they didn't discuss it—they knew what he had done.

Hanson had changed almost overnight. There was no longer any joy in his voice, his step was no longer light, his mood no longer carefree. Rather, he was despondent. Urdo drank. He drank through the day and through the night. Had Gredoria still been their Lord and Protector, Urdo would have been punished, if not forced into help. But Gredoria did little more than sit with his wife in silence, smiling at her idly. Hydo was thankful that Gredoria's mind was intact enough to remember Hadonia, but too ruined for any of the Council to discover if his sudden descent into instability was the result of foul play. And overnight, Hydo was the new Lord Protector. The formal ceremony hadn't yet occurred, but it was as good as done.

There were members of the Assembly Council who disapproved—they either didn't trust the circumstances of Gredoria's ailment or they thought Hydo was too young to rule. But it had been made clear on too many occasions that Hydo would be the next Lord Protector after Gredoria, by Gredoria himself. They could not deny him his position, as none of them could deny his ability to claim the Blade if he chose to do so by force. He shook his head, pushing the thoughts away. He could hardly recognize his own mind.

Several months ago, Gredoria had been a father to him, Urdo and Hanson his brothers. He would have never kept such secrets, never become implicated in such trespasses, and never contemplated his ability to take the Blade by force. He watched Octayn sleeping peacefully. She was the most beautiful creature he had ever seen—and possibly the most powerful. It wasn't just her Fire, though that was a force to be reckoned with, it was *her*. She had a hold on him that he could not deny. It had been there from the first. What he had once instantly believed to be the thrall of her beauty, he had soon come to believe was their shared nature—they were both Fire-Wielders. And that meant more than he had ever known. She was changing who he was, and while it was different, it wasn't necessarily worse. He was becoming more powerful under her influence.

The loyalty was not one-sided. They had spoken at length about what Gredoria had admitted to him. His Bakora parents had been murdered by Octayn's uncle, the Bakora Emperor. She hadn't seemed surprised by the information and had quite simply told him, "If you want him to die for it, I understand. Just give it time."

Hydo had learned that conversations could change people and that information could lead to death. He had learned of Gredoria's true nature, and now Gredoria didn't recognize his own reflection. He had learned of the Emperor Oredan's role in the death of his parents, and just like that, him and Octayn had tweaked their plan to involve the death of a royal.

* * * *

They traveled in their Soar-Craft, keeping low to the dunes. Octayn slept frequently, her hands on her small stomach, her blonde hair a wild mess about her face. His dark eyes skimmed the desert horizon. He could not believe he approached a portal wall that could lead him to Bakoran. In truth, if he were forced to speak candidly, he'd had many reservations, long after the planning was complete, but once she had told him, he knew he was fully committed.

He was still a young man and a great part of him longed to resume his life with his brothers—training, drinking, blissfully unaware of the truth of his bloodline, his history, or the actions of those around him. But if he returned to such a life, it would be one Octayn was not a part of, and that instantly reassured him of his decision. He had known for many years that he would rule Daharia, that once Gredoria stepped down, he would assume the mantle of Lord Protector. And if he thought on it with an uncritical mind, those things *had* happened. They simply hadn't happened in the manner he had once anticipated.

While he had always believed he would be a great leader, he had not envisioned a future where he would be known for much other than his abilities. Octayn had changed that. With her, he would assume the kind of prominence that would long outlive him. There had been countless Lord Protectors, countless legions of Hunters, but none among them had been able to reconcile Daharia and Bakoran. When all it would take was a child born of both realms' leaders, with the powers of both Fire and Sentio, who could *rightly* be in a position to declare themselves sovereign. He kept the Soar-Craft true as he slowly reached over and rested his hand on Octayn's swollen abdomen.

* * * *

The portal wall was like nothing he had ever seen before, and he had been travelling Daharia for all his life. His entire world, the deserts of *Haren'dul Daku*, the very skies he flew in, came to a sudden, blurry halt. The clear surface shimmered and swelled, as though alive, and, like looking through wavy glass, it obscured everything on the other side. Even if the other side looked like complete and total darkness, it was blurred. Hydo stared and stared. Each day he spent with Octayn he learned more about his life, his world, his destined path—the secrets Gredoria had striven to keep from him.

The Void-Voyager was dressed in ridiculous garb. He had fine boots and an expensive coat, but his tunic and breeches were tattered. Hydo imagined the finer things had been obtained through unlawful means. He wore a leather cap that was near too small for his head, and one eye was mechanical. "Are you crossing over or not?"

Octayn took Hydo's hand tightly in hers. "Yes, we are."

"Dandy, this way," he ordered, making his way towards what appeared to be his makeshift office. Hydo had to duck to fit under the thatch hut, but found that the inside was quite modern. The floor might have been sand, but the table at which the Voyager worked was made of shining metal, his documents were neatly ordered in glass trays, and soft light emitted from well-made, ornate fixtures.

He pushed two documents into Hydo's hands. "These are your standard indemnity forms. Sign them, pay the toll, and we'll be on our way."

"We're married—we only need the one form," Octayn lied, grabbing one paper from Hydo and pushing it back at the Voyager.

The man said nothing, simply holding out a quill for them. Octayn snatched it out of his hand and signed the forms. She wrote down a family name that Hydo had never heard before; he briefly wondered if she had made the name up then and there, but he doubted it. She then pulled a small velvet purse from her pocket and dropped it on the table. The distinct sound of coins clinked loudly. Again, Hydo didn't ask.

The Voyager pulled the bag open just enough to peek at his payment. After a quick minute, he nodded to them. "Bakoran it is then."

"Let's get a move on then," Octayn answered sharply. The Voyager flicked his gaze between her and Hydo, but said nothing.

He shuffled them out of the office. "Alright, alright."

Hydo squinted as they stepped back out into the heat. "How exactly do we do this?"

"Don't you worry your head about how we Voyagers do what we do," the man laughed, rubbing his hands together. "Just hold your breath and hold onto each other."

Hydo watched the Voyager continue to rub his hands together. He began to move them faster and faster, creating a friction that seemed to almost spark. He seemed to be mumbling to himself, but Hydo couldn't make out any words.

Octayn held his hand tightly. "Take a deep breath, Hydo."

Suddenly, the Voyager threw his hands out, his palms facing the wall, and a giant vortex of blue and gold light appeared. The center was a black hole. The sound was deafening, as though the world were being sucked into the center of the swirling darkness.

Hydo looked down to Octayn.

She squeezed his hand tighter. "Deep breath!"

He listened to her, breathing in as much air as he could as he pulled her into his arms. He held her tightly and continued to suck in air, drawing it deeper and deeper into his body. Then, with a nod from Octayn, they leapt into the portal wall.

* * * *

It had felt like dying. No amount of oxygen could have been enough. There had been no light. There had been no sound. It felt as though a thousand tiny pieces of glass had been cutting into him. The sensory deprivation and slow suffocation had been enough to convince him he *was* dying. And then, without warning, they landed firmly on the ground. Once again, air filled their lungs, and they could see and hear and move without agony.

"That was..." He began, getting to his feet, but his voice trailed off.

"I know."

Hydo wanted to say more—to ask more—but his eyes had fallen to an entirely new and alarming sight.

The border of Bakora was a wall of azure fire, so thick and high one could barely make out the standing guards on the other side. Hydo let his gaze travel far, but no matter how many miles his keen eyesight could take in, he still saw the fire. The border's blaze seemed never ending.

Octayn noted his stares. "It cannot harm us."

He looked down to her. Her blonde hair whipped about her, her long white gown kicking about her feet in the sand, her bright green eyes always on him, always unblinking. To Hydo, she was like a Goddess of Fire, terrifying and beautiful.

"It harms none?" he asked.

She smiled at his naiveté. "I didn't say that. Fire-Wielders are rightfully Bakora—they are welcome to pass through the blue flame without suffering its burn."

He stared at her for a long moment, refusing to be near the flame. He had been exposed to fires many times and he had learned that he did not burn as others did—but this was not Daharia and that wall was no natural flame.

She pulled him forward slowly. "Don't you trust me?"

He knew the answer should have come to him instantly. He was in love with her. In truth, he was *more* than in love. He would never voice it, but Octayn had become all-consuming to him—she ruled his every thought, she determined his every action. He did not fear her superior Fire-Wielding, for he knew that if she were an enemy, he could strike her down—he feared something much greater than that. He feared that if she were an enemy, despite ability, he *wouldn't* be able to strike her down. He was compelled by her every word and movement, admittedly enticed by her dark plans—she controlled him wholly.

Not just a man, but a Hunter, and not just *any* Hunter, but the newest, youngest Lord Protector of Daharia—he did not simply fear that he would do whatever she wanted him to, he feared *what* she wanted. His gaze traveled over her beautiful face to find her spare hand holding her abdomen. She had two children in Daharia whom he would now be responsible for, whom he would have to find and return to her unharmed and proven as Fire-Wielders. Those children would be *like* children to him, he knew as much. But the child she carried was *truly* his.

"Of course I trust you."

She smiled up at him, but quickly let it melt away. "Be sure to stay behind me so the guards don't kill you."

Without hesitation she pulled her hand free from his and marched towards the blue wall of fire. He could see it in her walk, the same regal authority that had once puzzled him when they had first met was so obvious after all this time. She had been trained to walk with power and grace, to speak with influence and education. She was a monarch. And he would follow her anywhere.

He quickly leapt after her, remaining right behind her as she stepped into the blue flames. Of course she had been right, the flames did not harm him. Once fully immersed in their wall, the sound of wind whipping through the fire was near deafening, and he paused for just a moment to see the wall of fire that surrounded him. It was powerful, frightening, and beautiful, just like Octayn.

He stepped forward, touching his foot down in Bakoran—the enemy's territory. *His* territory. Instantly, his eyes fell to the guards. There were perhaps twenty in the immediate vicinity, marching down the border wall. They wore white linens under gold chest plates, on their heads sat gold helmets shaped to form a giant flame, and their weapons were golden spears and swords.

"*Cazai caren, esa Octayn Oredan!*"

Octayn's words were an authoritative call, ringing out over them all. She raised her two arms high up in the air and, with a heavy clap, brought them down to her sides, the motion causing something Hydo had never seen before. It was as though she had pulled all of the air from the space around them, as if she had created static electricity all about them. He could feel his skin tingling. Suddenly, completely white flames erupted all around her. The fire flickered down her arms, over her chest, and through her hair—a brilliant, pearl-white.

As the flames extended out around her they whipped the air with a loud, thunderous *crack*. And just like that, the guards fell to their knees.

Octayn extinguished the white flame and the air lost its charge. He moved to her side, amazed that once again there was more he had not seen, more he had not known. "What was that?"

She smiled to him. "It's an Oredan thing."

* * * *

The guards had organized an escort to the Oredan palace. They rode in gilded carriages, pulled by young guards. Hydo felt uncomfortable with the practice, as he felt uncomfortable with the way Octayn reclined back, sipping her beverage and picking at the fruits the guards had brought.

She bit into a piece of fruit, her green eyes watching him keenly. "You'll grow accustomed to it. It's the Bakora way."

"Hunters live in service. You live to be served."

"Perhaps that's why we are such a good fit then."

He found it difficult to focus. He was *in* Bakoran, he was being seen by Bakora society, and he was traveling to meet Ozea Oredan, who was not only the sworn enemy to Daharia but the man responsible for killing his parents. While Hydo knew the current Emperor would not survive much longer, according to Hydo and Octayn's plan, nothing currently stopped him from contacting the Blade and informing the Council that Hydo Jesuin had impregnated Octayn Oredan and had crossed into their territory. Nothing but the hope that as an uncle, he would believe Octayn's story.

They had not traveled far but already the landscape had begun to change from desert to lush, forested terrain. As they moved closer and closer to the city, the guards raised a curtained wall around their chariot, ensuring they could not look out and none could look in on Octayn. While Hydo felt trapped and uncomfortable, Octayn seemed to relish the privacy. She laid out across the cushions of the chariot, keeping one hand on her abdomen, and the other firmly on Hydo.

Chapter 13

Haren'dul Daku

Present Day

They had traveled as far as their legs could possibly take them that night, thankful that they had crossed the terrain without further disruption or attack. They made their small shelter in the fold between the desert and the adjacent hillside, their canvas tent shielding them from the desert winds. The three of them sat cross-legged, forming a small triangle.

"Just close your eyes and seek him out," Falco advised.

"Focus on his image, his movements, his face as you last saw it," Kohl added.

Jessop rested her hands on her knees, her eyes shut, her mind focused on Hydo. The hour was late and she intended to enter his dreams as he had entered hers. She took slow deep breaths and thought of Urdo and how he had taught her to search with Sentio.

"Imagine where he sleeps."

"Think of how he—"

"*Stop!* Both of you, I can't focus."

They remained silent and she continued to concentrate on her breathing. Her palms were moist and she rubbed them over her knees. They had traveled so far through the desert. Her hair was coarse and matted, her skin raw from the sand and wind, her feet blistered. Her mouth tasted of dust and dried meats. Her shoulder ached from injury. The men were just as worn. Falco's hair stood on wild end, his skin red from the heat, his gray eyes exhausted. Kohl's clothes were tattered, his lips so chapped they bled, the skin over his knuckles cracking from dehydration. She felt their pain—and the pressure for them to make real progress.

Jeco needed them. And they needed to find him. She knew of no others who could carry on through such conditions and she knew nothing would stop her now, as nothing would stop Falco or Kohl. They were trained to see through their missions and retrieving Jeco was the most important task any of them had ever had to undertake. But they were falling sick to the treacherous wasteland. She needed to find out where Hydo was.

She knew this was not the exact same process that she had done with Urdo. She was trying to enter a mind from a distance. It required a degree of abstract focus that she knew well, but typically her targets were within sight. She took a deep breath and kept her eyes shut. She could hear her own breath, the breath of Falco, and that of Kohl. She blocked it out. She focused on her heartbeat. She focused on the darkness within herself. She found herself drawn into the shadows of her inner being. She saw flashes of her life—of the men she sat across from, of her son, of her parents. She walked away from them all. She knew, somehow, that she needed to immerse herself in the shadowy void of her own mind.

She breathed deeper and deeper, each breath propelling her towards the shadows. She saw nothing and no one. She heard no desert wind, no breathing, and no heartbeats. She felt surprisingly calm. Fear was an emotion that had eluded her for many years. Without her son, she had been reminded of its treacherous hold. But in this shadow place, hidden deep inside herself, she felt nothing at all. It was isolation, and silence, and in some ways it seemed tantamount to peace, to true, inner calm.

She pushed through the shadows, and some part of her knew that she was in complete control. She felt invincible in this place, not for being all-powerful, but for being immune to harm. She felt safe. She felt as though she hovered above all others, watching them live their lives, watching them sleep and eat, make love and kill. She felt as though all she needed to do to peek into their existences was open the right door, a door hidden in the darkness.

She focused on Hydo. She focused on his dark eyes, on their dark history. She pictured his face and his gait. She imagined him speaking with Jeco, and just like that, Jessop knew she had found the door. She reached out in the darkness, and found her hand pushing on a door...

The room was completely white and gold. There were white sheets that hung from the ceiling, so long they pooled in a fold of lush fabric on the floor. Jessop found that the ceiling with its gilded molding had an intricate mural painted in gold. It took her a moment to realize the painting was of a fire. She looked down and found that the white stone floor had the exact same golden fire drawn into it. She turned about. The room was decorated in fine materials and ornate furniture. Tables held gold platters of fresh fruits and meat and chalices filled to the brim with cool drink.

She had no recollection of this place and yet it seemed somehow familiar to her. She thought of the men she had seen when Hydo entered her dream—of the white linens and gold utensils.

"Welcome, Jessop."

She spun around to find Hydo standing several feet behind her. He was dressed all in white and his hair was pulled back tightly. Standing next to him was one of the men Jessop recalled from her own dream, the one with the glowing eyes. Jessop imagined he was about the same age as her, and she noticed the hilt of a dagger peeking out above a strap on his shoulder and what appeared to be a silver coil—perhaps a whip—tucked on his hip. As she had suspected before, he definitely had the build and presence of a warrior.

She turned her gaze away from the young man. "Where is my son, Hydo?"

"I assure you he is safe. He is being well cared for."

Jessop let her hand wrap around the hilt of her Blade. "Can you die in your dreams? Or will I have to wait till I find you in person?"

At her words the younger man took a step forward. Jessop pulled her blade but Hydo raised his hands, urging them both to calm. The younger man stepped back. Jessop kept her eyes fixed on Hydo—they both knew his young friend was no match for her.

"Jessop, how you have your mother's aggressive flair ...In truth that is the only similarity I see; it amazes me they made you a Hunter."

"Speak of my mother again and you'll get a lesson in why they made me a Hunter."

Once again, the younger man made a move forward, but Hydo was quick to stop him, placing his hand on the man's shoulder. "No, Calis."

"*Vei con harana mei*, Calis." *You cannot fight me*, she warned the young man. He stared at her with his glowing eyes, a blank expression on his face.

"He does not speak Kuroi," Hydo explained.

Jessop was certain he was part Kuroi—his eyes were an obvious tell. She couldn't imagine how a man of Kuroi descent didn't know the language. "You can't speak your own tongue?"

He narrowed his gaze at her. "You're half Bakora and you can't speak *your* own tongue."

Jessop didn't know of what he spoke. But his words did not matter to her. "You know nothing of what I am."

"I know more about you than you know yourself."

"That's enough," Hydo spoke, raising his hands as if to ease the tension. "You both have much to learn from one another but—"

Jessop pulled her blade free. "I'm not interested. Where is my son, Hydo?"

Calis moved faster than she had anticipated. With an angry *crack* his silver whip had laced around her sword-wielding arm. The sharp metal tip slapped her with an agonizing sting. Just as she was about to wrench the man forward with his own weapon, the whip ignited, a dark blue flame erupting around its silver coil.

For a second, Jessop almost laughed, knowing she was more resistant to flames than most, but then she felt it. The fire actually burned her. She hissed in agony, falling to her knees.

"Jessop, you need to let us explain everything to you. You *can* be reunited with your son, but first we must speak in person," Hydo explained, taking a step towards her.

She resisted for long enough, finally screaming out in pain as the fire burned her flesh. With all her might she wrenched her arm and Calis flew forward. The pain was excruciating. She needed to escape the dream.

She loosened her arm free, but the moment he regained his footing, he lashed at her again. She remembered the mage and the damage he had done to her back with his whip. She pushed the thought out of her head, focusing on Calis. The whip cracked the air beside her face with a vicious bite. She had barely rolled out of the way in time. She threw her blade into her other hand—dominant or not, she was a better swordswoman than most. She leapt up and carved the air with her weapon, aiming for the young man. He flipped back with spry mobility, barely escaping her attack. As he readied his stance, he pulled his dagger loose, tightly wrapping his fingers around the hilt.

"Both of you—*stop!*" Hydo yelled, but Jessop knew she wouldn't be able to leave with Calis attacking her.

He struck at her with swiftness and precision, his feet moving perfectly, his arm in flawless form—he had been trained very well. But not as well as her. She sidestepped his strike with ease, carved his blade back, and executed a crescent kick against his face. He fell to the ground, his blade over his body like a shield, his loose whip tucked between his fingers. She pulled her weapon back, ready to strike him, when strong hands grabbed her shoulders and wrenched her back.

She flew off her feet and toppled backwards into a table. The golden plates and chalices clattered about her as she grabbed the heavy tabletop to regain her balance. She was amazed by Hydo's strength. She knew he did not have his Hunter's blade, but as he squared off with her, he called Calis's dagger to his hand. Sentio worked in their dreamland.

"Good to know," she mused, and with an easy push from her mind, Hydo went flying back. She held her burned arm tight against her chest, her blade in her left hand. She might not have been fit for the fight, but she welcomed it. She pushed herself off the table as Hydo recovered, but before she could strike at him, Calis leapt at her. With a slight swipe of her fingers, she used Sentio to also send him flying across the room.

"Tell me where my son is!" she demanded, closing the space between her and Hydo with ease.

Hydo spun the blade about him in a manner near identical to Falco. "She asked me not to fight you!"

Jessop didn't know whom he spoke of and it didn't matter to her. She swung at him, and despite his claims, he was quick to parry and attack. She was injured and in pain, but she had longed for the moment where she could fight Hydo. "Don't make me explain to her that I had to kill you," he growled at her.

She struck his blade with hers, forcing him back. "You couldn't kill me as a child. What makes you think you could kill me now?"

"You know nothing about what happened that day," he answered with his own strike. She blocked and attacked once more.

"Just give me my son back!"

As she leapt in the air, prepared to strike him with a hook kick, he used his Sentio. He flung her to the ground with a vigorous force. She felt the rib break but refused to scream out. She rolled back, threw her legs up, and leapt to her feet.

"I trained the best there ever was, girl, and it's not you." He cut the air with his blade. She blocked, but she struggled to counter-attack with her broken rib and burned arm.

He swung down on her again. Their blades sung as they met. She used all her might to hold his weapon off. She saw Calis behind him, watching with visible concern. He would not intervene now, not while it appeared Hydo dominated their fight.

"I knew when his skill overtook mine—that was never the issue. The issue was *you*."

Jessop didn't follow his angry diatribe. She forced his blade back and struck at him. He blocked and returned the attack.

"Where is my great student now? When his love is so close to death, where is Falco? Nowhere to be seen!" Hydo yelled, spinning in a fluid motion and bringing his blade down on her with might.

Before Hydo's strike could connect, strong hands caught his forearms, rescuing Jessop. "Don't be so sure of that."

Falco stunned them all. But as his scarred hands sent Hydo flying across the room, Jessop knew it was really him—he had come for her. His dark hair still wild, his scarred face staring down at her, concern filled his eyes. As Calis took a step forward, Falco swung his arm and sent the man flying back into the white-covered walls with a violent force. He struck the wall and Jessop could hear the *crack* of his head against the hard surface. His body fell limp to the floor—he was unconscious.

Falco corrected his stance and pulled his blade free, spinning it about himself in the same manner as Hydo. He took a quick step towards Hydo, who threw his hand out in an attempt to use Sentio on Falco. Falco waved his hand and instantly cut through the man's supernatural abilities with his own. "Where's my son?"

Their blades clashed with a violent *ting*. Jessop watched with amazement as Hydo fended off Falco's attacks with some of the fastest defensive moves she had ever seen. Their form *was* astoundingly similar. They both moved constantly, spinning in circles, twirling their blades about themselves with ease. Though Falco found it visibly easier.

She had truly underestimated Hydo's skill with a blade. But it was true what he and all of the others had said—Falco had long since surpassed his corrupted mentor. Falco swung his blade about and with a sharp inward curve, he sliced Hydo's side open. Hydo stumbled back, quick to grab at the wound. His blood pooled through his white tunic.

He held his side, flicking his gaze between Falco and Jessop. "Neither of you understand. You *have* to understand."

"Understand what?" Falco demanded.

Jessop felt the ground beneath her feet begin to shake. "Falco," she whispered. The entire room was shaking. She looked to Hydo, who seemed unsurprised. She knew that he was somehow responsible for the quaking; he was kicking them out of the dream world. The linen fell from the ceiling. The chalices tumbled to the ground. The room was growing darker and darker.

Jessop blinked and she saw Kohl's face above her own. Suddenly, Falco's face appeared above her. "Is she okay, Kohl?"

She was confused for a moment until she tried to move. She could barely breathe and her arm felt as though it were on fire. She hissed as she looked down and saw that the linen of her tunic was singed black and her arm, where the whip had wound about her, was *truly* burned. Her skin was red and angry, the flesh crisped and boiled. Falco had his hands on her, his eyes shut as he focused on healing her.

Kohl poured the last of their water over the burns and she cried out as the cool liquid washed over the charred skin. She felt the rib heal first, which allowed her to take deep breaths as Falco worked on her burns. She stared at the wounds, realizing that she could have died in Hydo's dream. That he could enter her dreams and kill her there, if he so chose.

Chapter 14

Haren'dul Daku

Present Day

Her arm would never be the same. In function, she was perfectly healed, but Falco could only do so much about the scars, and it seemed that each day they passed in *Haren'dul Daku*, his healing abilities weakened. Jessop knew it was Jeco's absence impacting his focus and ability. The angry red whip line circled her arm three times and ended in a sharp point just at her shoulder.

She tore her gaze away from the wound and focused on her tunic. With a rough rip, she tore the charred sleeve off. She quickly evened it out by removing the other sleeve. They were not willing to waste any more time resting, no matter their weakened bodies and dwindled supplies. They needed to push on. She could hear footsteps, though they were not those of Falco or Kohl, for she knew their steps. It was the sound of several men, approaching quietly. She didn't have the energy to fight any more desert attackers. She was wounded, confused by all that had happened, and beyond tired. Some part of her knew she needed Falco and Kohl to handle whoever approached them—but a larger part of her knew she would never admit that aloud.

She listened keenly to the steps as she slipped out of their small tent, knowing whoever approached would be right behind her. She closed her eyes, focused all of her strength on her Sentio, and leapt out, a wild scream escaping her as she sent the group flying in all directions. It was only as one rolled across the sand, cursing profanities, did she realize whom she had attacked.

"*Urdo*? Urdo!"

He had found her. In the barren wasteland of mayhem and death, he had found her. She jogged to his side and wrapped her wounded arm around him, helping him to his feet.

"I'm sorry—I—we've been attacked so many times ...I thought you were another desert brigand."

"It's fine, it's fine." He brushed off his clothes, spitting out a mouthful of sand. He finally turned his gaze to her, his eyes softening at her mangled, wild appearance, and the burns. He offered her a small smile. "I'm fine," he whispered.

He grabbed her with his rough hands and pulled her into a tight embrace. What once would have made her violently uncomfortable, she now welcomed, resting her head against his massive chest, hugging him back, knowing they were thinking the same thing—how thankful they each were that both had survived this long.

* * * *

Urdo had brought supplies, provisions greater than they had originally packed, weapons and fresh garments, and food and beverages, but there was more—he had brought warriors. Jessop embraced Korend'a tightly.

"Trax is well; he wishes he were here but he keeps the Blade secure and Azgul is calm under his temporary leadership," Korend'a explained.

"I couldn't think of any better to rule in Falco's absence." As Jessop spoke, her eyes fell to Falco, who approached her with Dezane in tow.

She wrapped her arms around the elder. "*Dorei, Mesahna.*" In truth, Jessop wished he hadn't come. He should have remained in the Blade with his son, but she knew Dezane was a true, experienced warrior, with untold powers. He would have never sent his armies into battle without himself present to lead them. She simply wished for his safety in a time where safety could not be guaranteed, in a place so dangerous it made her think light of their former home in the Shadow City.

"As good as it is to see you all, there is someone in need of Falco's help."

Jessop looked from Falco to Dezane and knew of whom the elder spoke. "Mar'e. Where is she?"

"The Hunter Kohl is moving her from the Soar-Craft to a tent as we speak."

"Take me to her," Falco spoke. Jessop nodded to him, thankful for his natural leadership in such situations, though they both knew the red whip lines she now bore were wounds he had only been able to temporarily heal.

Without his son, without his usual calm, his abilities were weakened. She hoped, for Mar'e's sake, that he would be able to help her.

Jessop looked around at the camp their troops had built to surround the Soar-Craft. Hundreds upon hundreds of warriors, both Kuroi and those of Falco's army, had disembarked and now worked in unison, lifting and transporting beams and canvas and casks. There were the tents for sleeping and the tents for provisions, and a much larger tent to act as a mess, where they could all eat together. There were barrels of water and crates of supplies and she saw several men laying stones for fire pits. Jessop knew just by looking at the preparations that what Kohl had said was true—they readied themselves for war.

"Jessop." Falco's voice drew her attention back. He had walked several paces with Dezane, headed for a row of tents. "Are you coming?"

* * * *

Mar'e shivered violently, her eyes clamped shut, her hands trembling around a blanket though she was covered in sweat. Jessop stood at the end of the cot, silent, admittedly more shaken by the sight of the Kuroi woman fighting for her life than she anticipated being. Kohl grabbed one of Mar'e's hands, whispering reassurances to her.

Falco touched her forehead as if assessing her. "She is still in the fighting stage. That's good."

Jessop looked to Dezane. "Can she hear us?"

The elder shook his head, keeping his glowing gaze on Mar'e. Jessop could sense how hopeful he was.

Falco gestured for Kohl to move aside. "Show us the wound, Dezane."

The elder stepped between the Hunters and Mar'e. His hand froze above the blanket. "I did what I could." Slowly, he pulled the blanket down.

Mar'e's abdomen was wrapped in blood-stained bandages. She had been sliced from shoulder to navel and Jessop could see that the bandages were holding her together. It was a miracle that she still breathed. Jessop immediately grabbed the woman's leg, as if to show support somehow. "Why did she not return to Azgul?"

Dezane stroked her dark braids back. "This did not happen in that first battle. We made camp when the vessel returned the dead to the Red City. The Soren came back in the night. Mar'e had been standing watch outside my tent."

Jessop understood. Mar'e had saved Dezane. She looked to Falco.

"I'll do what I can."

Falco laid his hands on her, his eyes closed. Jessop watched him as he focused on the injured Mar'e, his brow furrowing as he allowed his mind to explore her wound. Jessop knew when he had started, for it didn't take long for Mar'e to start screaming. With eyes tightly shut, she lashed out in pain, screaming for it to stop.

Kohl held her still, promising her she was going to be fine, Dezane spoke to her in Kuroi, advising her to fight through the pain, and Falco worked as quickly as he could, ignoring her violent resistance. Jessop knew the risk was great, but she had to ease her pain as Falco forced her flesh and bone to reconnect. She entered Mar'e's mind without warning the others, and found it to be alight with red, angry, fear. She didn't understand what was happening, she couldn't open her eyes to see Falco helping her—she thought she was dying.

Jessop worked quickly, washing over Mar'e's mind with cooling thoughts, calming her friend, attempting to numb her to the pain of her wound and Falco's healing. She pushed back in Mar'e's memories, flicking through years of images and sounds that Jessop had never seen, but seemed instantly familiar given their shared tribe and homeland. She pushed through the thoughts, going further and further, knowing that she could do for Mar'e what she had inflicted on Hydo Jesuin—place her in a memory for safekeeping.

She found the dam where she and Mar'e had played as children, swimming and drinking from the water, drying in the warm heat. She focused, and after a long minute, the screams died out. Jessop was at the dam. She knelt beside the pool and ran her hands through the water. She watched the ripple travel over the clear surface, expanding and splashing softly against the rim on the other side, where Jessop saw Mar'e standing.

"What is this?"

Jessop stood, running her hands over her tunic. "I've placed you in a memory, so you wouldn't suffer any longer."

Mar'e nodded, as if instantly understanding what magic Jessop had done. "I'm dying."

Jessop slowly walked around the perimeter of the dam. "Falco is trying to save you."

"Is he going to?"

"I really couldn't say."

"Days ago you tried to kill me and now your husband seeks to save my life."

"Kohl has begged him to."

"Is Kohl okay?"

Jessop stopped. She studied Mar'e's beautiful face, with her glowing eyes and full lips and long hair. "You really care for him."

"You're surprised by that. You must think so little of me."

"It's not that ...You just don't really know him."

"How long did you know him before loving him?"

"I don't—"

"Jessop."

They stared at one another, stubborn in their silence, and their independent senses of certainty. Finally, Mar'e spoke. "I would never harm him. If that's what you fear about my interest in the Hunter. If I survive, that is."

"Thank you."

In truth, Jessop couldn't articulate what the issue was. She didn't know if it was because of the feelings she harbored for Mar'e or the ones she still held for Kohl, that stopped her from encouraging their bond.

"Thank you for bringing me here. The last time we were here together we were so young."

Jessop nodded. "No need for you to be in pain while he works."

"Why did you choose the dam?"

Jessop shrugged. "As peaceful a place as any."

Mar'e walked along the perimeter of the water. "We never fought when we were here. I was cruel to you in childhood for your mixed lineage. But when we were here, I was never unkind to you."

Jessop thought on her words and realized they were true. When they swam as children, despite being of a desert people, they were at peace.

"Do you think we were ever really friends?"

"We were friends. We just weren't friendly."

They both laughed softly at the thought. It had been a lifetime for them both. Jessop knew that the Mar'e before her, the Mar'e whom Falco fought to save, was not the same girl who had taunted Jessop in childhood. Mar'e knew that Jessop was not the same—harder, angrier, and more impatient. But also more mature. Jessop, for the first time, had begun to take responsibility for her life and her actions. Kohl had helped her to do that.

"When we were children, you said that there was something different about my mother and me. You said you had heard your parents speak of it."

Mar'e sat beside the water; resting on the cool, damp sand. "And you want to know if I have learned anything more since?"

Jessop said nothing, her silence an answer.

"There have been many stories over the years. Some of which Dezane confirmed, like you marrying Falco and learning Sentio, and some which none could speak on with any real authority. Your mother was part Kuroi, but none knew of her ties to the tribe. Your father was a true man of the desert, but one with no history, no family of his own, and no sigil. And year after year, the Hunter, Hydo Jesuin, would come and argue with them, and then leave, always angry, always ready to return."

Jessop cocked her head. She had no memory of Hydo ever speaking with her parents before their death. Before she could say anything, Mar'e spoke again.

"Dezane told me that much. You have no ties to the tribe, yet you are of it. A Hunter, who ended up killing your family, made routine checks on you every year. First by himself, and then he brought the boy Falco with him."

"I can't—"

"There's more."

"How can there be more?"

"Dezane told me that many years ago, there had been rumors that a Bakora woman lived somewhere Beyond the Grey."

Jessop studied Mar'e's face, as if looking for further clues to the riddle she was telling.

"The only people with the gift of Fire are the Bakora people, Jessop. You are part of the tribe. But you are also part something else."

Jessop didn't know what to say. She immediately thought of what Calis had said to her in the dream world—that she was half Bakora. She had received so much information that her first instinct was to be mad—she and Mar'e had spoken for many hours in the Blade, before Jeco was taken, and at no point had she shared any of this with her. But she didn't have time for anger. She didn't have the energy for anger. She needed to use all the information she gained to rescue her son. She needed to direct every effort—

Jessop opened her eyes and found she was back in the tent, in *Haren'dul Daku*, with a hand on Mar'e, who was sitting up, alert. She had woken up, ultimately exiting the memory. Falco had saved her. Dezane embraced him. Kohl kissed Mar'e's forehead. And Jessop took a step back from all of them, silently exiting the tent.

* * * *

Jessop managed to walk off mostly unnoticed. She found a place to rest against the hillside and contemplate all Mar'e had told her in the memory. Fire was a gift of the Bakora people. Her parents had had no ties to any named Kuroi or anyone else, it seemed, for that matter. Hydo had visited her every year of her childhood, something she had no memory of. She found that the pain and exhaustion were forcing her to relinquish a sense of control. The armies had arrived and Falco could lead them better than any. She ran her hands over her hair and knew she had to carry on, with or without the Hunters, the Kuroi, or the soldiers. She leaned forward, prepared to get to her feet, when a bag was thrown to her, landing atop her boots. Daylight was breaking on the horizon and she could just make out the face—the young Hunter Urdo had chosen to accompany them.

Jessop grabbed the bag and stood. "You."

"They call me Hode Avay, but from a woman of your abilities, I'll settle for 'you'," he said with a smile, approaching her slowly. He fixed his pale blue eyes on her, running his hand through his short auburn hair. "There are clothes, provisions for bathing—your tent is being fixed now, you can wash in there, and you'll find a few other things."

She followed his gaze to the large tent in the distance. "Thank you, Hode Avay."

"Don't thank me, thank O'Hanlon."

Jessop pictured Kohl's face. He had been with Mar'e, rejoicing over her recovery, and yet, he had still thought of Jessop's well-being.

"Wait—I don't think he wanted me to tell you that. Pretend I said nothing?"

"Certainly."

* * * *

The tent was grand compared to their recent living quarters. There was a large bedroll and a great wooden tub with pails of steaming water surrounding it. She knelt beside the bedroll and opened the pack Kohl had put together for her. She would bathe and then she would leave. She could not let Jeco wait any longer.

Determined as ever to carry on, she still couldn't resist smiling when she found a comb tucked amongst the fresh garments. She used her fingers to brush out her wild locks as best as she could, loosening the matted tendrils before forcing the comb through. She hissed with each rough tug, but it didn't take too long for progress to be achieved.

Once she had finally worked through the mess, she stripped off her tattered garments. Her skin was so dry and reddened by the heat of the desert that it stung to drag the material over her body. She pulled her boots off for what felt like the first time in days—what *was* the first time in days. The leather of her shoes was well worn and true to her form; they had protected her feet well, but the skin was still hot and raw.

She poured two of the pails of hot water into the wooden tub before stepping in. The hot water was as welcoming as it was unforgiving—cleaning her skin and reminding her of her treacherous travels. She lowered herself slowly. As she reached for a third pail, she sensed him behind her, silent as ever.

Falco took the pail from her hands. Kneeling beside the tub, he poured the water over her back and shoulders. They remained silent as he bathed her. He cleaned her hair and ran his hands softly over her newly formed scars. He brushed the sand from her and rubbed her aching shoulders. When the water ran cold, he helped her from the tub.

He knew she had no intentions of staying.

"We must at least speak to Urdo first, and Dezane. We need to formulate a plan before we continue."

"We?"

"You think I would rest here when Jeco is still missing?"

She said nothing. She didn't think that of Falco. She knew he would do anything for Jeco. But Jessop felt a maternal bias that could not be explained. She had grown Jeco inside her body, she had carried him for many moons, she had birthed him, and she had been the first to hold him. She would die for her son.

"And so would I." Falco added, knowing her thoughts.

"I know you would."

"We will speak with the others. Then we will carry on."

* * * *

"Everything is as I feared it would one day be," Urdo whispered, his deep voice traveling around the small group. They had told him all that had come to pass since they were separated the day of the first Soren battle. Urdo and Dezane had both inspected the burn on her arm. She had described the whip Calis had attacked her with. She had told them of her fight with him and Hydo, and all Hydo had said.

Urdo studied the burns intently. "Dream traveling is *not* a Hunter skill—it is a Bakora one." Jessop had thought first to what Calis had said to her—that *she* was of Bakora blood and then she thought of what Mar'e had told her. She thought of telling the group but felt uncertain about how they might react.

"Fire-Wielders are all Bakora in one way or another; it is not a trait of Daharians," Dezane added.

"You knew my parents, Dezane."

"It doesn't have to be a parent—any Bakora blood could allow for the passing on of the skill."

"Mar'e, when Falco was healing with her, I spoke with her in a memory. She told me many things, including that Hydo had visited my parents every year of my childhood. Did she speak the truth, Dezane?"

She could feel Falco and Kohl shift in their seats, all eyes on her as she shared the new information.

Dezane held her gaze as he contemplated his answer. "Yes. Hydo met with your parents every year, before the year he killed them."

"Why?"

"I do not know."

"Dezane."

"I promise, *Oray-Ha*. They never told me."

"Was there a Bakora woman who lived Beyond the Grey once? Did Hydo know her?"

His gaze narrowed. Jessop knew he hadn't expected an interrogation, and she hadn't intended to give one.

Falco grabbed her hand. "A Bakora woman?"

Dezane ran a hand over his face, exhausted. "There were rumors but I never met any such woman. Bakora have never been welcome in Daharia, and had one been living Beyond the Grey, she would not have openly walked in my presence."

Jessop nodded. She knew her line of questioning had been hard for Dezane, and harder for the others to follow without context, but she had needed to ask what mattered most before she left.

"My gift of Fire ...the dream travel," Jessop spoke softly. They all knew what she inferred. They all knew what had been made so clear by recent events and Jessop's expanding abilities.

Falco shifted in his seat, moving closer to her. "But I am no Fire-Wielder and I have no Bakora blood, and I managed to follow Jessop into Hydo's dream world."

Urdo sipped from his flask thirstily before answering. "Tell us *exactly* what happened again."

Falco leaned forward, his strong forearms resting on his knees. "Jessop was gone. She was in Hydo's dream. Kohl and I were watching over her. She began to scream, like I had never heard her scream before, and it was then that the burns appeared. I touched her face, as if to enter her thoughts, and just like that, I was with her."

None spoke for several minutes, as if digesting the information he had shared.

Urdo stared at Falco, clearly eager to know more and perplexed by what he had already been told. "Hunters have tried to master the practice for years. We cannot do it."

"Neither can the desert tribes," Dezane added.

"It's like nothing I've ever heard of before," Urdo answered.

"Perhaps Falco *is* part Bakoran," Hode Avay suggested.

Kohl leapt to his feet. "He's *not* part Bakora. Can't you people see?" He looked over them, finally fixing his gaze to Jessop. "Wherever she goes, he will follow. When you love someone like that ...you could find them anywhere. Even in some dream world."

The silence that followed exaggerated the look of pain in Kohl's eyes. He loved her but he couldn't follow her anywhere, he couldn't find her anywhere. He would have never been able to save her. If she had chosen him, if she had loved Kohl, and ventured for her son with him at her side only—she would have died.

Kohl forced his hazel gaze away from her and turned, exiting the tent. She wanted to follow him. She knew Falco did as well. But they couldn't. Kohl's suffering could not take precedence—not when she had so little time to speak with Urdo and the others. She fixed her gaze to the old Hunter. "We cannot focus on Kohl. Not now. Not when we still don't know why Hanson and Hydo would take my son to these lands."

Urdo sighed heavily. "He's returned to her."

"He's returned to who?"

"I cannot believe it. After all these years." The old Hunter shook his head, taking a deep breath before reaching for his flask. They all waited as he gulped down the fiery liquid. When he had his fill, he shifted in his seat, as if trying to regain comfort.

"We were so young, as young as you lot are now ...Things happened that we couldn't have prevented or fixed. Hydo was searching for another Fire-Wielder. He didn't know he was Bakora, none of us did, and for that, he did not know for whom he searched. Or how dangerous the one he would ultimately find truly was. Her name was Octayn Oredan and she was the most beautiful and most terrifying woman we'd ever laid eyes on."

Jessop looked to Falco and instantly wished Kohl had stayed to hear the story—knowing that they were about to gain some explanation as to the woman he had heard Hydo speak of.

"Oredan? Like *the* Oredan family?" Hode Avay asked.

"*The* Oredan family. The leaders of Bakoran."

Jessop couldn't believe that Hydo had been involved with one of the enemy's own family members, and yet, she did not know why it surprised her. He was the enemy to her. She couldn't believe that there had been another Octayn and that the woman Kohl had heard Hydo speak of was relevant to their mission.

Urdo cleared his throat, drawing Jessop's attention back.

"He loved her instantly ...It was frightening to watch. He changed completely and immediately. His whole world shifted, and the importance of the Blade and his brothers fell far beneath the love he had for her. Something happened ...it gave her more power over him, over all of us really, and it ultimately, perhaps, led to Hydo becoming the Lord Protector—but he would never speak of it with me."

"What happened?" Falco interrupted.

"I cannot speak of it, Falco."

"You must."

"I've never told. None of us has."

Jessop could see the pain in Urdo's face. She did not want to see him struggle.

"Falco—"

"*Master Rendo*. Tell me."

Urdo looked away from Falco, to Jessop. He stared at her for a long time, as if worried most about how she would react to his news. "I am so ashamed."

Jessop pulled away from Falco and moved closer to the old Hunter. She took his hand in hers. "You can tell us, Urdo. Do not fear that I would ever see you different."

He took a deep breath as a silent tear streaked his cheek. "Hanson Knell killed a man. I was there. It was partly my fault. We took the body to Hydo and Octayn Oredan destroyed it."

Jessop squeezed Urdo's hand.

He squeezed her hand back.

"I don't understand how that could lead to Hydo becoming the Lord Protector?" Falco asked. Jessop knew Falco wouldn't have been angry at the news. They both cared for Urdo too much to let any past mistakes taint their view of him.

"I believe that Gredoria Vane found out about the murder and that Hydo shattered his mind before letting Hanson face execution."

When Falco said nothing further, Urdo continued.

"Shortly after that, Hydo left for a long while. He said he escorted Octayn back to Bakoran in secret and that we needn't worry any more, that he was devoted to his role as the Lord Protector. He returned, and for a long time, he was true to his word. He put all his energy into training Trax DeHawn. And then he found *you*," he finished, staring at Falco.

Jessop shook her head. "And now you think he has returned to Octayn Oredan in Bakoran—that he has taken Jeco there?"

She could picture the dream world vividly, where she had seen Jeco playing with the other children. It was a place of great luxury—not a wasteland desert.

"I'm starting to think he never severed ties with her at all. But still, what I do not know is why he would visit your family so many years in a row. What are the odds of him knowing another Octayn, and why try to kill her whole family?"

Chapter 15

Bakoran

Twenty-five years ago

Hydo shifted uneasily on his feet. The Oredan palace was grand, even to the eye of someone familiar with privilege and wealth. It was not laced with the modern fixings of the Blade. Instead, it remained fashioned in a historic, regal style: white pillars, gilded dressings about every room, long artful tapestries, platters of fresh foods upon every table, in every room, regardless of its engagement. He was accustomed to a childhood where servants had waited on him, but he knew them by name and history—in the Oredan home, those who served were silent. They kept to the shadows, and if you did cross one, they would stare firmly at your feet, refusing to speak a word. It was the coldness with which he was truly unfamiliar—the Oredan elitism that made him most uncomfortable, despite having perhaps felt elite all his life. It was simply different.

"You hate it." Octayn crossed her grand chamber to stand at his side. They looked out from her open balcony to see hundreds of miles of forest—so different from the deserts they had traveled across to be here.

"I didn't say that."

"Our children will be raised here. You must abandon these reservations ...You are Bakora."

"Do you think I've forgotten? Do you think for one second the fact that my own mentor lied to me for years about a murder your uncle—the *Emperor*—orchestrated?"

Seeing her expression immediately made him regret his words. If she were hurt, she never showed it. Her fire was fueled by anger. He could see the flames burning around their clasped hands. He took a deep breath and pulled her closer. "I'm sorry."

"We have a plan. Why must you make this harder than it already is?"

He kissed her forehead, forcing his own anger back. "Our plan worries me."

She turned from him and he instantly grabbed her wrists, stopping her. He loosened his hold but kept his fingers laced around her. "Where are you going?"

She looked down at his hands on hers before returning his stare. "To rest. My family can be tiresome. Dining with them tonight will be a long event."

"The way it is with your family is not how it will be with ours. I don't want our children to hate us."

"And what of *my* children?"

"The half-Daharians I didn't father?"

"Yes. Do you care if they hate you?"

He thought on it for a long moment. He was no longer the man he had once believed himself to be. He no longer looked at the same future he had seen set before him for so many years. He had never envisioned a partner and children. He had never pictured a true family. However unorthodox, that is what they would have—a *true* family.

"Yes, I would care. They are *our* children. And they will love us."

* * * *

Ozea Oredan's skin was completely gold. Hydo knew it wasn't really his skin, but gold painted onto it. He wore flowing white robes and every square inch of flesh that Hydo could see was covered in a thick gold paste. His eyes were green, like Octayn's, and they contrasted wildly with his gold eyelids.

Hydo controlled his breathing. He forced his anger down into the deepest parts of his mind. The Emperor had killed his parents and Hydo would have to spend an evening speaking with him as if he did not care—as if all were forgiven. He didn't know how he would be able to do it. But he felt Octayn's eyes on him. He sensed her and their child and he knew what he had to do. He took the Emperor's hand in his.

"Emperor Oredan, it is an honor."

"Hydo Jesuin, Lord Protector, welcome to Bakoran." His voice was high and tight, and he stared at Hydo with unblinking eyes. Suddenly, a bright flame erupted around their hands. Hydo refused to acknowledge the Fire, keeping his eyes on Octayn's uncle.

"Thank you for having me, and for keeping our meeting so *private*." They all knew that the surreptitious relationship would be widely disapproved of by both their territories.

"Of course, of course, thank you for bringing our Octayn back to us." She inclined her head slightly to him, not required to bow. "Uncle."

He turned his eyes back to Hydo, extinguishing the flames. "Let's sit, eat, and discuss the future of Bakora and Daharia."

* * * *

"That went better than I expected," Octayn spoke, wrapping her arms around Hydo as they entered her chambers.

"Because we remained civil?"

Octayn pushed herself up on her toes, her lips touching his ear as she whispered. "Because you're a terrifyingly good liar."

He could tell by the tone of her voice that she was pleased with the knowledge. He, on the other hand, felt sick. He had dined with the man responsible for killing his parents. He had betrayed Daharia.

"Ready for bed?"

He nodded. She was worth it. She was worth everything. "I must return to Daharia tomorrow, Octayn."

"I know."

"It kills me; the thought of being away from you. Of not being able to watch you every minute…" He sat on the end of the bed, running his hands over the fine linens.

"I can show you something. Something that only Bakora can do. It's a way we can be with each other every night."

He felt his heart fluttering at the prospect. "Anything. Show me and I'll do it."

She smiled. She pushed her hand into his chest, willing him to lie back on the bed. "We have the ability to see one another in our dreams. We can be together always."

"Is it hard?" He asked, immediately thinking the gift was similar to his own Sentio.

"For one of Bakoran—not at all. For any other, near impossible."

* * * *

The carriage waited, ready to return Hydo to the portal wall. As he resisted leaving, he felt certain that Octayn looked more beautiful than ever standing in her long, flowing robes, her golden tresses falling about her pregnant frame.

"I cannot bring myself to leave you."

"Think of the dream travel, as we practiced. We will be with each other every night."

"I'll do everything I can to be here for the birth."

"I know."

He pulled her into a tight embrace. "Everything we have discussed ...it's all happening."

"I love you more than I ever thought I would, more than I ever thought I was capable of." As she looked up to him, he saw she had tears in the corners of her green eyes. He had never seen her show sadness. It hurt him to see it.

"And I am just as in love with you ...My life is yours."

When he finally took a step towards the carriage, she grabbed his wrist. "Be sure to use the same names I used on the paperwork with the Voyagers," she advised.

He stepped into the carriage. "One Hoda Jero, returning to Daharia. Where did you come up with such a name?"

She smiled as she took a step towards the carriage, to whisper her answer. "The Jero couple are my daughter's guardians. The woman, Essa, goes by Octayn, so that my girl might know my name, if not anything else."

Hydo smiled at her. He knew he would have to find the Jero family someday soon to test whether Octayn's child had become a Fire-Wielder. Octayn had insisted that it was required before he could reunite her with her kin. All Bakora royalty needed to show they had the gift, a requirement to one day rule, she had told him.

Chapter 16

Jessop fixed her blades to her back and readjusted her sword on her hip. Her long dark hair was plaited and she wore a fresh black tunic, breeches, and her boots. She had repacked the satchel Teck had originally given her with a fresh bedroll and provisions. The heat of the desert was returning in full force, urging her to leave. She longed for more rest and food. But such wishes paled in comparison to her true wish—to have Jeco in her arms once more.

She couldn't force an army onward when they needed their own rest—a requirement for battle. They weren't even her armies to command. She couldn't help but recall her mission to save Aranthol. Against Kohl, she had failed. She knew she could not lead warriors again—not against Hydo Jesuin. She would go alone and she would return with Jeco. Any who crossed her would die on her blade—it was the simple rule that she had to continue to live by.

She ducked out of the tent and into the heat of the desert once more. To her amazement, Falco and Kohl stood before her, Dezane and Urdo behind them, then Korend'a, Teck, and Hode Avay ...and behind them, their entire combined armies ready for travel. Falco took a step towards her. "Where you go, I go."

Kohl stepped forward, his hand on his blade's hilt. "You are a Hunter of Daharia, Jessop; where you go, so go your brothers."

Dezane moved forward slowly, his glowing eyes fixed on her. "You're a daughter of the Kuroi, *Oray-Ha*, where you go, the Kuroi army goes."

Jessop felt the heat in her throat that would give way to tears, had she not been standing in front of warriors. She focused on the details of the men—their dress, their weapons, their armor. She focused so that she would not cry.

Urdo took a step forward, unsheathing his sword and kneeling. "My blade is yours."

Falco knew how their allegiance moved her and he was quick to take her in his embrace. She hid her face in his shoulder. He kissed the side of her head, whispering into her ear, "Let's get our son."

* * * *

The Soar-Craft flew in almost complete silence, save the faint *whirring* of the engines. Jessop was seated near the front, beside Falco, Urdo, and Korend'a. Kohl sat beside Hode Avay, who manned the vessel. She leaned back in her seat, her eyes fixed on her own arm, on the new scar. Forcing herself to focus helped alleviate her dislike for flying.

Like a snake, the scar was woven around her perfectly. She thought of Calis, the man who had burned her and of the whip he had used. She did not know how such a weapon could burn her, but if any were going to develop a tool that could burn another Fire-Wielder, it would be the Fire-Wielders themselves. Like the Blade of Light—a weapon designed to fight the Fire. It had surprised Jessop that, like herself, Calis was part Kuroi, and yet he seemed to know nothing of the tribe. She wondered if Hydo knew of her Fire, and if so, for how long?

"What if he always knew?" Falco asked, listening in on her thoughts. "I feel as though Kohl may be right in that all of this is somehow related. There's a reason Hydo killed your family with the Fire. If he had thought you were a Fire-Wielder, though, he knew you would have survived."

She did not know how to voice what she so feared. "He was stronger than I ever anticipated, better than I had once believed him to be."

He held her green gaze. "You knew who you were fighting."

"What if I can't kill him, Falco? He would have won our fight had you not intervened."

"I've got it, Jessop. I can do it."

"But—"

"I've got it."

Jessop knew Falco was considered the best for a reason. She had seen it in the dream world. He had fought Hydo with an ease that she simply hadn't been capable of. She had been wounded, and that had hampered her skill, but she had *gotten* wounded—when Falco hadn't.

She had wondered so many things in the days that they had traveled the desert and many more since her time in the Blade. Urdo had called her arrogant once, suggesting that had she ever opened her mind to the ways of the Hunter, she might have learned much more during her time with them. Jessop knew she was conceited; her skill with Sentio and the sword so greatly outweighed that of others. But there was much she had not known, much she still did not know, and there were those who were simply still greater in skill. Her Sentio was perhaps finally stronger than Falco's—but his skill with the sword, his ability to fight Hydo as he had ...She had been wrong to call herself the superior fighter.

She was turned in her seat to stretch her aching muscles, when her eyes fell on Dezane. Several rows back, he was seated with Teck Fay. The Oren and the Kuroi were natural enemies, both equally disapproving of one another's abilities and methods of sorcery. She nudged Falco, who turned and followed her gaze.

"They were speaking before we even boarded the ship ...It's been hours."

She couldn't make out any of their words, but Dezane leaned forward, his eyes fixed on the hidden face of Teck under the hood of his cloak.

"Do you know what they've been discussing?"

"Not at all, but I do know that that's a whole lot of desert magic right there."

* * * *

They made it to the portal wall of *Haren'dul Daku* without the interruption of another attack. Jessop was the first to disembark, her eyes scanning the wavy wall for any signs of a Void-Voyager. Falco had known many Voyagers, several of whom had retired from their illicit galaxy trafficking to live out their lives in Aranthol. She saw, some several hundred paces away, a small hut. It was a dilapidated wooden shack that appeared completely out of place beside the edge of a portal wall. But it was a start.

She ran to the small hovel, her boots light on the fine sand. She spun into the entrance and immediately dug her feet into the ground, forcing herself to an abrupt halt. Collapsed over the table was the body of a Voyager. His clothes were charred and his skin burned. Jessop backed out of the small space quickly, forcing the stench of burned flesh from her nostrils.

Falco had been right behind her. "One Voyager. Burned to death."

"We will find another. Korend'a will go; he knows those who lived in Aranthol, and which survived the fall of the city."

Jessop noted how he never directly said anything to blame Kohl for Aranthol. Had it been a different time, she might have said something. But it wasn't and she didn't, knowing that starting feuds over wrongs of the past would get them nowhere. This was Hydo's doing—he had known she was close and had sent Fire-Wielders to deal with any Voyagers on the portal wall.

As they gathered with the others, she found herself speaking with Urdo. "If he also knows battle is inevitable, he can't waste time killing every Voyager. We will fight in this territory or Bakoran, where he waits with the Oredan."

Urdo took a long sip from his flask. "He is buying himself time. But for what, I cannot imagine. Many Hunters left with him that day ...this battle will not simply be Bakora versus Daharian, it will be Hunter versus Hunter."

She feared many things, but she knew Jeco lived. It may have been in the presence of Bakora and deserter Hunters, but he lived. She would have felt it in her heart if it were otherwise.

Korend'a appeared at her side. "I will find you a Voyager."

"I cannot ask you to do that alone."

"Hode Avay travels with me and a handful of Kuroi. We will return safely."

She looked past Korend'a and saw Hode Avay speaking with Falco. She did not know what Falco said to him, but the younger Hunter nodded eagerly. She turned her gaze to Urdo.

"His skill is beyond his years. He will help find a Voyager."

As if he knew he was being discussed, the young Hunter approached, with Falco at his side. "The sooner we leave, the sooner we can return with a Voyager."

Korend'a quickly embraced Jessop in his strong arms. She clung to him tightly. These were not the same times they had once lived in. Danger was omnipresent, the threat of death more real than ever before. She had spent many years with Korend'a at her side. They had fought together, they had trained together, and he had been there for Jeco's entire life. She loved him as family.

She leaned her head against him. "Return to us, Korend'a."

He simply hugged her tighter.

* * * *

Several warriors buried the body of the Voyager, offering him blessings for his next life in their different and unique ways. Jessop watched from a distance. She knew the words the young Kuroi man spoke, though she could not hear him over the winds. She had known the blessings that were done by the tribe when people had been killed all her life.

She recognized some of the movements and the prayer that a young Hunter she had not yet met performed as he too blessed the Voyager. She had been present at a Hunter burial before—Daro Mesa's. Falco had killed him for her, as he had too greatly threatened their mission. She felt a sharp pain in her chest at the memory. Too many deaths had taken place at Falco's hands and hers, and many more were still to come. She tried to force the thoughts away, focusing on two of Falco's men who also performed rites for the Voyager. One involved chanting as sand was poured over the fresh grave. The other splashed strong liquor at the ground and gave what seemed to Jessop to be a toast to the man's life. The group's blessing was messy and incongruent, but it was beautiful.

It made her think of what would be done when she died. If this looming battle killed her, as this quest to reclaim Daharia had already nearly done, what rites would be performed for her soul? She thought on it long and hard and not for the first time. She had no answers and no instructions to give anyone. She thought that Falco would know what to do, better than anyone. It did not surprise her that in these thoughts, she imagined herself dying in battle and Falco surviving. He was the best.

"As Hunters, we never really know how long we have." Kohl's voice startled her as he appeared at her side. He sat down silently, leaning forward to watch the rest of the burial with her. "You'd think it would make us live more recklessly—an attempt to try everything before it's too late."

"Or to live more cautiously."

Neither said anything as the warriors finished the ceremony. It grew dark all around them. The heat had dissipated and their camp was once again nearly fully erected. "I couldn't kill Hydo, when I fought him. He bested me," she admitted.

"Falco will kill him."

Jessop shifted in her seat. She did not want to admit what she thought. She too believed that Falco possessed the skill to kill Hydo. But she feared for the Hunters as they prepared to fight their brothers and mentors. They had allegiances she simply didn't have. But as she thought on it, she knew she had developed bonds she did not wish to live without. Korend'a, Dezane, and Urdo. Urdo, who had become a mentor to her, had guided her through the Hunter life since learning her true nature. He had been the only one who could teach her when she'd believed she needed no further instruction.

"They say he's the best there ever was for a reason, Jessop. He can kill Hydo. And the rest of us ...We know which side of the war we are on."

She turned and looked into his warm amber eyes. "Hanson raised you."

"He took your son. He left me to die."

She continued to stare at him, wondering.

"I know he has to die, Jessop."

"How do you always do that?"

"What?"

"Know my thoughts."

He arched his brow at her, as if it were obvious.

"I know you're not in my mind, Kohl."

"I just know you. Call it a side effect of being completely in love with you still."

"Kohl..."

He shook his head, his golden hair falling about his scarred face. "It would be beneath all three of us if I ever pretended I wasn't."

She grabbed his hand. Her fingers curled around his and rested between them in the sand. "I would have never let him kill you."

They remained quiet. They both knew of whom she spoke.

Finally, he broke their silence. "Out of sympathy."

She shook her head. This time, she could not hold back the tears. Silently, they streaked her burned, dried cheeks. "Out of love."

She thought of all she had done to him; the pain and torment, the lies and manipulation. She thought of all he had done to her. He had nearly killed her. He had haunted her every thought for so long it had become near impossible to sleep or rest. She knew how she had hated Falco for having ever pushed her in Kohl's direction—not simply because she had betrayed her marriage to advance their cause, but because she *had* truly grown to care for Kohl in the process. Somewhere along the way, he had stopped being collateral. She had loved him and Falco had loved him, and Kohl loved them both in return. But the love, it was different. It was all different.

"I know you do not love me as you love him. And I can see it, you know?" he whispered. His voice was cracking softly over tears. "And I love him too. He's my brother, and my leader now. All that hate ...It was misplaced. You're right to love him more, Jessop. He is the better of us."

"I'm so sorry, Kohl. I know we keep promising to stop apologizing to one another. Maybe what we did to each other is simply beyond repair.

But Falco and I ...we were made to be with one another. We have lived as one for so many years. It's how we will always live."

He raised their hands and kissed her knuckles, his lips wet with tears as they pressed against her skin. "I know."

* * * *

Jessop rested her head on Falco's chest. It was late. Most of the camp slept, save a few. She found it near impossible to close her eyes in peace, for many reasons, not least of which was Hydo's ability to enter her dreams. She wondered where Korend'a and Hode Avay were. They had taken one of the Soar-Craft, unpacking all its supplies before leaving, and crossing the desert they had just made their way over. She valued their loyalty and their commitment. And as much as she wondered where they were and how long it would take to track down a Voyager, she also wondered about Kohl. He slept several tents over, alone. She knew he had spent several hours with Mar'e, who still rested. But he hadn't stayed with her.

Jessop knew how easily she could be in his mind. She knew how easily she could make him forget all of the pain she had caused him. He could forget he had ever been a Hunter, he could forget ever knowing her ...She could build a new life for him.

"It's not your place to control his life. Not anymore than you already do." Falco spoke. She, consumed by her thoughts, hadn't realized he was awake and in her mind.

"I didn't mean—"

"I know what you mean, Jessop," he interrupted, sitting up. She rolled to the side. They could see one another perfectly in the dark and she could see the look in his eyes.

"We both know he already loves you to the point of doing anything for you. Why must you try to control him further?"

"I'm *not* trying to control him further. I am trying to set him free."

"Then let him fall out of love with you on his own, in his own way. Stop messing with his head."

"You think that's what I'm doing?"

He reached for her. "No. I think you love him and you hate to see him suffer."

Before Jessop could say another word, a loud commotion broke out. She and Falco were quick on their feet, ducking out of their tent in search of the noise. A small fire burned thirty paces away, near the remaining

Soar-Craft. Surrounding the fire were a handful of Kuroi and a group of Falco's army—yelling and pushing one another.

Jessop and Falco ran over to the group, immediately forcing themselves into the middle of the fray. Jessop found the angriest of the Kuroi warriors and spoke with him, as Falco addressed his own men.

"Vara far'a harana?" What is the cause of this fight?

"Kasei ves far'a harana, far'a daku, far'a sus kesio," the young warrior answered her, his voice high and angry. *"Nas sus kesio, kesio ni Kuroi!"* Jessop bristled at his words. The soldier had complained that they traveled to fight, and possibly die, for just a boy.

She turned from the warrior and moved to her husband's side. The soldier had long red hair and dark eyes. His skin was covered with scars and black-inked designs. "Did you say you regretted risking your life for just a boy—for *my* boy?"

At her words, the group fell silent. The sound of the small fire flickering seemed, suddenly, thunderous. She took a small step closer to the man. "Did you?"

At her anger, the small fire grew into a raging inferno, a wall of flames rising up behind her, threatening them all. The man looked to Falco, instead of her. "I didn't mean it as it sounds. But this is going to be a war over one child..."

Jessop moved forward, prepared to kill the man. But she had not been fast enough. Falco twisted his hand in the air and just like that, the soldier fell dead in the sand, his neck snapped.

One of the fallen soldier's comrades leapt, without thinking, in defense of his friend. Falco grabbed him by the neck and held him out. The strength of his well-fortified body, reinforced with the might of Sentio, allowed him to hold the man inches off the ground, choking him slowly.

"That boy is my son—*my son!* If you are not here to fight *for* me then you are here to fight *me.*" With a mighty toss, he threw the man to the ground. The soldier rolled through the sand, coughing and clutching at his neck.

"You think I haven't heard the whispers? Those who wonder if being reunited with my brothers has perhaps turned me soft? I will not tolerate dissent and there is no room for disloyalty amongst my armies."

Jessop knew his anger, though it had been some time since seeing it. She moved back, and with her, in tow, moved the Kuroi. The soldiers knew how their words had betrayed Falco, and two instantly fell to their knees, their heads bowed low as they offered their loyalty once more. Two others did not. One, with arms made entirely of metal, grabbed mechanically at Falco.

Falco maneuvered out of the machine-like grip, grabbed the leg of the second man, wrenched it up and threw him to the ground. He leapt back and elbowed him in the face—two quick strikes—before reaching down and finding the man's blade on his hip. He unsheathed it and using Sentio, shot it into the chest of the warrior with the metallic limbs.

Falco flipped to his feet and pulled the blade loose before the man hit the ground. Spinning quickly, he crouched down and forced the weapon into the throat of its original owner. He had killed them both within seconds. Before any could speak, Jessop heard the ringing sound, the clear noise made when a knife was being thrown through the air. She froze the blade in the darkness with ease, her hand outstretched in the cool night air. Falco narrowed his eyes on it and then on the soldier who had thrown it—the man he had previously tossed to the ground. He made for the weapon but another got there first.

A strong hand wrapped around the hilt and pulled it from the air, breaking Jessop's mental hold on it. The hand belonged to none other than Kohl. With quick expertise, Kohl forced the blade through the soldier's side, carving through the flesh of his back with ease, throwing him to the desert floor to bleed out.

He approached their fire, bare-chested with his blond hair loose. A splattering of blood painted his strong, scarred chest. Several crimson droplets stained his face. He flipped the blade in his hand and offered the hilt to Falco, who took it with an approving nod.

"Let it be known amongst all of my troops by dawn—you will fight for my sword or you will die on it."

Chapter 17

Haren'dul Daku

Present Day

By dawn, a handful of men had abandoned camp, but only a handful. Falco's men were, for the most part, very loyal. He had offered them refuge in Aranthol in return for their service in battle. Many of them had lived under his rule for years, many had fought at his side before, and were ready to do it again. "It is better that they've left. We don't need the disloyal watching our backs in battle." Jessop reminded him, running her hand across Falco's back.

"They need to die for their treason."

"Falco—"

"You know it's true. It is what would have happened were we still in Aranthol and I was still just the Shadow Lord."

"You are not just a Shadow Lord anymore...You are the leader of Daharia, Lord and Protector. You cannot rule as you ruled Aranthol."

He nodded slowly but Jessop knew she hadn't convinced him of anything. "We can deal with the deserters once we have Jeco back."

He grabbed her hand. "You're right. I just ...it's been a very long time since I've had to kill any of my own soldiers."

"Falco ...maybe the issue is that you lead the Hunters now. Those soldiers, a band of dangerous rebels, they *aren't* truly your men anymore."

He shook his head. "I might not just be the Shadow Lord anymore, but I'm also not going to rule Daharia as all those before me have. These men, those who still remain, they have proven themselves to me time and again. I won't forsake those who are loyal to me now."

"Good to hear," Kohl spoke, his head ducked through the flap of their tent. Jessop and Falco instinctively moved apart as he stepped inside.

Kohl flicked his gaze between them. "We have news—Korend'a has already found a Voyager."

Jessop felt her heart quicken. "So quick! When will they return?"

He turned his amber eyes to her, a small smile pulling at his face. "They think they can return by tomorrow evening, perhaps the morning after—they do have the fastest Soar-Craft in the fleet."

As quickly as the elation came, it disappeared. She didn't know what she had expected. She knew how long it took to travel *Haren'dul Daku*, she knew the treachery her friend faced. The fact that they had somehow found a Voyager so quickly was incredible ...and yet she was not pleased. "A day—perhaps two? That's too long. We need to get to Bakoran."

"Jessop."

"It's too long."

Falco and Kohl both stared at her, concern filling their eyes. She couldn't stand it. She couldn't stand to feel their pain as she so keenly suffered her own. She couldn't stand to be so close to reclaiming her son and having to wait still. She pushed around them and ducked out of the tent.

The desert was unforgiving. She moved past groups of Kuroi and Falco's men training and working, some making food while others organized weapons and provisions. She walked on, leaving them all behind her. The portal wall rippled and waved, a world of darkness on the other side that she so longed to enter. She walked towards it, knowing better than to touch it. The Voyagers were a certain type of being—they could create travel portals where they needed to, they could navigate dark space, and they could touch such walls without suffering grave harm. Jessop was not a Voyager.

Nonetheless, she walked as close to the wall as she could. She walked in the heat, past the Voyager hut, past the burial site, leaving the camp far behind her. She walked and walked until she could no longer hear the warriors training, until her camp was nothing but a small speck in her periphery. She walked as the sweat trailed down her neck, prickling her thirsty flesh. She walked as her throat dried and her eyes itched. She walked until she finally came across something she had not seen in the longest time—a tree.

It was lush, with thick foliage, wide-brimmed green leaves, and cool, brown bark. She didn't know how it existed in such a place, but there it was, tucked against the galaxy wall with roots disappearing straight into the sand. She fell at its welcoming base before turning and resting her back against the trunk.

She had needed the space. She had needed to put distance between herself, Falco, and Kohl. She knew that only Korend'a could have somehow crossed the desert and found a Voyager in one night. She knew that only he could return so quickly. But she was impatient ...Nothing was quick enough. She thought of Jeco and her heart broke again and again.

"Your boy is fine." The foreign voice startled her.

Calis stood before her. He wore all white, his whip secured to his hip, his glowing eyes fixed on her. She scrambled to her feet. "How did you get here?"

He smiled, taking a step closer. "Where exactly is *here*?"

"Don't toy with me—I'll kill you where you stand."

"Have you fallen asleep, all on your lonesome, so far away from that mighty husband of yours?"

Jessop opened her mouth, ready to argue, when she realized that she didn't know. Had she fallen asleep? Was this a dream or was he truly standing before her? Did it matter, if their actions were just as lethal in their dream world as in their waking?

"Where is my son?"

"With his family."

"He has no family aside from myself and—"

"You're the first person I've seen with eyes that glowed in so many years..." He stood but two feet from her, his glowing eyes fixed on hers, completely ignoring her words as he stared.

She narrowed her gaze at him. "We are both part Kuroi. I was raised with our people—you were not."

He let out a surprised laugh. "Oh, I was raised with *our* people, Jessop. I was raised by family."

She didn't know what he spoke of. She didn't care. She would do whatever was required to get her son. She knew Hydo cared for him—she could hurt him, or take him hostage. Unless it was truly just a dream, in which case, she didn't know if she could do anything but cause him harm.

"This is difficult for me, too, you know. Seeing you like this, seeing this rift that has been caused," he spoke.

"I don't know what you're talking about. You know who I am, you know who Falco is ...Whatever you want, I can get it for you, just help me get my son back."

"I do know who you are. I know who you are better than you do."

Jessop lunged at him, grabbing his white tunic and wrenching him forward. She spun and slammed his body against the tree. "Enough with these games! Where is my son?"

"Safe. With his kin."

Jessop pulled one of her daggers loose from her back, bringing the point to his neck. "Stop saying that."

He smiled at her softly. "Easy, Jessop, you wouldn't want to kill your own brother."

She faltered, the point of her blade accidently nicking his flesh. She stepped away from him. "You lie."

"Can't you see it?"

He smiled. And she instantly recognized the smile as her own, when the rare occasion had called for it. But she knew it was only her mind playing tricks on her for hearing his lies—she had no kin. "I have no brother. I have no siblings."

He took a step towards her. Every move he made was suddenly familiar to her. She knew she must have been imagining it but he moved as she did.

"It's what Hydo wanted to tell you the other night, before we fought, when you saw us."

"Us?"

"Your brothers."

At the word, she thought of Urdo. She thought of the Hunters. She thought of Trax—of the men she had come to know as brothers. It took her a moment to remember the first dream. The dream where Jeco had been playing with other children, the fine setting, the plates of food, and the men ...

"I have no brothers." It was all she could say. She would have remembered. She could recall her entire childhood with ease, she knew her parents had no other children. But then she remembered what Mar'e had said—Hydo had visited her family every year of her life before they died, and Jessop had no memory of that.

"I resisted in the beginning too. You and I, we are siblings born of Kuroi lineage but our brothers are not the same."

"Stop."

"You are not the only one with the Fire and Sentio. Hydo has both. I have both. Our younger brothers have both. Feel free to search my mind and find that you are not alone, Jessop."

She knew that she could be in his mind in an instant. She could see his entire life if she wanted to. But she also knew it could be a trick; a way to distract her from the present, to pull her focus while slipping a blade through her.

"I would have known if either of my parents had had other children."

He cocked his head at her. "Of course, you still don't know ...Jessop, your parents aren't your parents. I had a guardian family too—Octayn and Kezo."

The hilt of her blade was slick with sweat. She tightened her grip. "*What*?"

He moved closer to her. He reached for her hand. She had intended to rip it away from him—but she didn't. She couldn't. He slowly took her wrist, the very wrist that bore a snake-like scar thanks to him, and he raised it to his face. "Just look. I wouldn't lie to you, Sister."

Her hand rested against his smooth skin, her fingertips grazing his temple. She closed her eyes and began to fall into his mind. She soared past memories, beautiful and vivid happenings—a wondrous palace, private tutors, a band of young boys all running around testing the limits of their Fire-Wielding. She flew past these images until she found something more familiar—Beyond the Grey. She recognized the territory instantly. She saw him as a young boy. He seemed happy. He laughed.

Behind him, a man appeared, smiling as he watched over Calis. He was a young man and his eyes did not glow. From their small home, a woman emerged. She stood at his side. For a quick moment, Jessop was certain she was staring at her mother. The woman had long blond hair and bright green eyes. But her eyes, like the man's, did not glow.

Jessop approached the woman. She studied her face. Her movements. She was near identical to her own mother. But she wasn't her. "Octayn," the man called her, as they took Calis inside.

Jessop fell from the memory. She needed to see more, needed to see something more telling. She traveled through the waves of images until she saw a face that she most certainly recognized. Hydo. She dropped into the memory and found him, the young Lord Protector, speaking with Calis's parents.

"You say he's already displayed Fire-Wielding? This will please his mother greatly."

Jessop watched as they called Calis into the room and asked him to show the Hunter what he could do. The small boy outstretched his hand and closed his eyes, squeezing them tight as his fingers suddenly erupted in flames. He smiled as the adults praised him.

"It's time he is returned to his mother now."

Jessop was amazed. None of this made sense. She could see the man and woman were not Kuroi, she understood they might not have been

Calis's biological parents, but he believed they were his mother and father and they had surely raised him and loved him. But they nodded, with understanding, ready to let Hydo take the boy.

Jessop circled Hydo. She wanted to interrupt the memory. She wanted to demand answers. He froze in their doorway before turning back to them. "The girl—she has shown no abilities so far. Octayn has told me to perform the test."

The man and woman looked despondent. "Perhaps some more time? Why risk the child's life?"

He shook his head. "It's been too many years already for both children. She says the child will survive the fire. That when forced, the girl will prevail. Only then will I be able to take her home."

Jessop fell to the ground. Of course, the memory version of Hydo did not see her falter. He just continued to speak with Calis's parents—or guardians. He was speaking about her. He was talking about how he would have to burn her home ...to see if she was a Fire-Wielder or not. He was talking about another Octayn, who was neither her mother nor this woman before her. Octayn Oredan.

Jessop felt as though she would be sick.

She forced herself out of the memory. She fell through Calis's mind. She fell until she was back at the palace. There were younger boys. And they were fawned over by a beautiful woman with long blonde hair and bright green eyes.

She spoke to Calis with a soft voice, introducing him to the smaller children, telling him how he was their oldest brother and he had to care for them. She told him that a sister would be joining them soon.

Jessop let her hand fall from his face. Her knees buckled and she hit the sandy ground beneath her. Calis didn't move. He didn't touch her. She turned to her side and retched. She felt faint, dehydrated and sick. He hadn't been lying.

Calis knelt beside her. He waited in silence as she tried to recover. She dabbed her mouth on the back of her hand and shifted so she could rest against the tree, in the shade, once more. She stared at him. She wanted to call him a liar. She wanted to ask him what he'd been told about why she had never arrived. She wanted to fight him and she wanted to embrace him. But more than anything, despite any news of their supposed relation, she wanted her son back.

"We weren't raised together."

"For safety, as children of Bakora royalty, we were separated to live with our respective guardians as inconspicuously as possible."

"If you are a brother to me, why do you side with my enemy? Why won't you help me get my son?"

Her voice was almost unrecognizable. She was parched. She needed water. He shook his head slowly. "You must know we would never harm your son, he is our kin. But there is more to this all then you know, Sister."

She flinched at the word. There had been a time in her life where all she had wanted was family. And then she'd had Falco. And then they'd had Jeco. And she had forgotten the feeling of ever being cared for or needed by any other.

Calis took a deep breath. "Our brothers who are not part Kuroi—they are Hydo's sons."

Jessop forced herself to her feet; almost certain she had misheard him. "What?"

"You and I, we are the children of Octayn and of the Kuroi...but our brothers, they are the sons of Octayn and Hydo. We cannot kill our brothers' father, Jessop."

Jessop thought she might be sick all over again. She knew that this couldn't all be true ...that he might be lying for Hydo. That despite all she had seen in his mind, he hadn't truly proven anything, despite how compelling the images might have been.

"Do you know who my father is?"

Calis shook his head. "She does not speak of yours, or mine. We have Kuroi blood. That is all I know. Hydo has been a father to me for many years though."

"He is my greatest enemy."

"Jessop, you need to—"

"Help me get my son. Calis, you must help me get Jeco," she yelled, grabbing his tunic once more, shaking him.

He grabbed her hands. He was so strong. "Jessop, you need to wake up."

"What?"

"*Wake up.*"

* * * *

She choked on the water flowing down her throat. She rolled to her side and coughed violently, heaving over the hot sand. Falco held her hair back. She looked around, her heart racing. "Where is he? Where's Calis?"

"Who? Jessop, you collapsed from the heat; you need to drink," he ordered, forcing the flagon back towards her.

She knocked it back. "Falco! Calis. *Calis*. The man you fought in the dream, with Hydo ...He was here."

"There was no man, Jessop. I found you under this tree."

She shook her head. It had been in her head. She had fallen asleep under the tree. Had Calis truly visited her in her dream, or had it *just* been a dream? She grabbed her face. She was dizzy. "I ...He's my brother."

Falco poured water over his hands and slowly touched her neck—cooling her off. "What?"

"Calis is my brother."

Chapter 18

Haren'dul Daku

Present Day

Jessop sat under the tree for a long time beside Falco. As she considered everything she had seen, everything Calis had claimed, she couldn't help but let out a small laugh. Falco turned his gaze to her, his brow raised.

She smiled softly to herself. "When I was a child, after Hydo killed my parents, I vowed to set fire to all he ever loved... And all he ever loved are Bakora—they're fire proof."

She laughed. She laughed loud and hard. She laughed until her chest hurt and her stomach cramped. She laughed until she could hardly breathe. She laughed as the tears fell to the sand. She welcomed Falco's tight embrace, as her laughs simply turned to tears.

She leaned against his strong chest. The irony of her situation—of her life, really—was not lost on her. She had hated the fire since her parents' death, only to become a Fire-Wielder overnight, incapable of using her newfound abilities on those who most deserved it. She thought back through the years, to all the signs she might have been one of them, to all the times it was alluded to that she was somehow different. She had long ago believed it was her Kuroi lineage that made her more receptive to learning Sentio, but what if she had been wrong? She thought on Hydo's presence Beyond the Grey, on the times she had seen him in the village, barking at Falco, from a distance. There was still much left to be answered.

She rolled to her knees and got to her feet. Falco rose with her, keeping her hand in his. "Are you ready to return?"

"I must speak with Dezane."

* * * *

"I didn't know," he answered firmly, seated in his meditation position in the large tent. She believed him—or at least she wanted to. He had known her all her life and she had trusted him. But she also struggled to believe that someone hadn't known.

"Your mother—the woman who raised you, the one we knew as Octayn—she was part Kuroi. Your eyes, like hers, glowed as only *ours* can. It was enough to welcome your family Beyond the Grey."

"But you knew I was different—we spoke of it, before I left with Falco."

He gestured to Falco for his arm, and Falco immediately helped the elder to his feet. Jessop felt uncomfortable. She couldn't stand to see him appear so aged. He moved to a small chair, Falco hovering beside him to help him should he need it.

"Yes, I sensed you were different. But I didn't know how—none of us knew, not then. You had our eyes and we had no reason to think you were of Bakora lineage. I wondered if perhaps you would be like Trax, my own son, born to learn the ways of the Hunter. And when you began to learn so quickly from Falco, I believed that was all there was to it."

She could feel herself slowly calming down. She had no reason to think Dezane would lie about what he did or didn't know of her as a child. He was right—she had shown no Bakora characteristics. She wasn't sure she even knew of any, aside from the Fire-Wielding. "I am a grown woman, Dezane, well over two decades—how is it the Fire didn't come to me until now?"

He sighed heavily, his dark shoulder lowering slowly. "I am not an elder of Bakoran, Jessop. I don't know how these things work."

She was ready to leave him in peace when he spoke again.

"Falco didn't let you burn that day, but I imagine if he had, your Bakoran abilities would have come to life and saved you. Hydo thought you'd died. You two fled to Aranthol ...You associated the flames with the worst day of your life. I imagine you inadvertently suppressed your own abilities for all these years."

Jessop looked between Dezane and Falco. The elder's words, as always, seemed to make the most sense. Part of Jessop felt removed from the situation, as though they discussed another woman's power and history, and not her own. "And do you think the abilities finally came forth because..."

"Yes, because Jeco was taken. A part of you knew you had more power to tap into."

She stared at the elder. She wouldn't lose it now, not again, not when they were so close—she had fought for her sanity tooth and nail as they had crossed *Haren'dul Daku.*

"I cannot use the Fire on Fire-Wielders though; it will not help us kill Hydo," she explained.

"No, but this might."

The voice of Trax DeHawn startled them all. Jessop spun around and saw him standing behind her. He wore his Hunter's leather. His golden eyes glowed with warmth. She should have sensed him. He was the most loyal of Hunters, and her true friend. He had come to her in her time of great need. Like Dezane and Urdo. Like a brother would.

She looked down to see what he held out in his hand—a blade, wrapped in leathers and cloth. He used his spare hand to pull back the material, and revealed the hilt, covered in glistening white stones. She had only ever seen one like it before. She could feel the inverted *F* scar tingling in her palm.

She looked from the weapon to her Hunter brother. "You brought us the Blade of Light."

Jessop outstretched her hand, her fingers hovering over the hilt, when she froze. She recoiled slowly, and stepped away from Trax, turning to Falco. "He who wields the Blade of Light, the weapon of the last Daharian Prince, used to fight back the Fire-Wielders, is the rightful ruler of Daharia."

Falco was leaning against a beam in the tent wall, his arms crossed over his broad chest. His gaze flicked over the blade and returned to Jessop. Before any could speak, the tent flapped open once again.

"Does anyone—*Trax*? Brother, you're here?" Kohl's voice trailed off as he saw what Trax held out. They all knew who the blade belonged to. Jessop knew he had never wielded the weapon—none of them had. They had taken the Glass Blade and secured the sword, but in the time since, Falco had had no opportunity to take the blade in his hand, as was typically done at the ceremony of the new Lord Protector.

Falco crossed the space with easy, confident strides. He kept his eyes on Trax as he clapped his friend on the shoulder. "Brother," he smiled.

Trax inclined his head slightly. "Brother."

Slowly, his gray eyes turned to the brilliant white-stone hilt. Jessop knew what the blade should mean to Falco. It was his rightful weapon and it reflected all that they had worked for, all that he was destined for. Trax moved his hands forward, offering the weapon to Falco. Falco's hand reached for the hilt. Jessop realized suddenly that she was holding her breath. She looked to Kohl, he appeared to be doing the same, with his eyes fixed on Falco.

As Falco's strong hand wrapped around the hilt, Trax pulled the material back, gracefully revealing the shining blade. It glistened beautifully, and while perhaps it was blinding for a moment, it did not illuminate the room as it had the day of her initiation into the Hunters. She watched as Falco took a step forward. He cut through the air with the weapon, carving it around his body, slicing it in crescent formations around him. It moved with him as though it had been made *for* him.

They all watched as he tested the blade, spinning in the confines of the tent, fighting invisible opponents—the weapon sung in his capable grip. It was obvious to them all and it didn't need to be voiced—the Blade of Light was rightfully Falco's.

He made one final swipe through the air, spinning low and turning back to face them all. He rose, straightening his back out, and spun the weapon about, holding the blade instead of the hilt.

"It's just a sword. Perhaps the greatest sword ever made. But still, it is just a sword. And I don't need it to prove I am the rightful Lord Protector. If you wish to fight with it, it's yours." He offered the hilt to Jessop.

She felt their eyes on her, waiting to see how she would respond to his offer. She knew it wasn't *just* a sword. It was *his* sword. And she knew whoever wielded it was seen as the rightful leader of Daharia. And Falco knew that too. He knew that if she fought with the Blade of Light against the Bakoran, many would think she was possibly the true leader. And he didn't care. She smiled at him softly.

She knew what he meant by the gesture. Daharia was hers if she wanted it. And in knowing he would give it up for her, she was more certain than ever that she *didn't* wish for it. She wanted him. She wanted their son.

She turned the hilt away. "The Blade is yours, as is Daharia." She pushed the final thought into his mind: *As am I.*

They all remained silent for a long minute until Kohl cleared his throat. "I don't mean to interrupt but a Bakora messenger just appeared through a portal."

She took a step towards him. "Where is he? What did he say?"

"He said to give this to the Fire-Wielder ...I'm guessing that just means you."

Jessop grabbed the paper quickly and unfolded it. She turned the page over, to ensure she wasn't missing anything.

Jessop, come speak with your family tonight. You know how. Octayn

Jessop handed the letter to Falco. "It's Octayn. Hydo's Octayn ...She wants me to appear in her dreams."

* * * *

The messenger had no further information. Kohl had searched his mind to confirm the man's position and his claims that he was just a guard who knew nothing of Jeco. Jessop had spoken with Falco and the others for several hours, deliberating over Octayn's request.

"There's nothing worth hearing," Urdo had insisted, shaking his head over it. Jessop mostly agreed with him. If what Calis claimed was true, Octayn was only interested in her children if they were Fire-Wielders—she had abandoned Jessop and risked killing her. She had no desire to know the woman.

"But if it *is* all true, you have brothers," Trax had added. She had told them all of Calis visiting her dream and all he had claimed.

"Even if they are your brothers, they helped abduct our son," Falco added.

"What if they offer to return him to you? Or explain why Hanson took him to them in the first place?" Dezane added.

Jessop ran her hands over her face. She didn't know. She didn't know the answers, she didn't understand the motives, and she knew nothing of these people or the validity of their claims. All she knew was that she needed to get Jeco back. And if speaking with Octayn could get her a step closer to that, then it would be done.

"Remember, she can harm you in her dreams, Jessop," Kohl added, his eyes darting over the snake-like scar on her arm.

"I'll go with you," Falco added. They still didn't understand how Falco could dream travel, but he could, and she wouldn't refuse his offer.

"That woman—she's dangerous. More dangerous than Hydo, even. She has no regard for the sanctity of life, Jessop. You mustn't be fooled by her or whatever she says," Urdo warned.

"I have no interest in anything she says except the location of my son. I will not fall for her sentiments, if she offers any."

"Then we go. Tonight," Falco spoke, his voice filled with certainty.

She took his hand in his, refusing to falter from her own claims—she *wouldn't* listen to anything Octayn had to say. As a mother, Jessop knew there was no excuse for abandoning your child. Jeco had great powers already, but if he had none, she would have loved him in the exact same manner and measure. "Tonight."

* * * *

Jessop wasn't afraid. Fear was the emotion she was both least and most familiar with—it had eluded her for so many years only to strike her like a blow to the chest when Jeco had been taken. She did not fear harm to herself, she did not fear harm to Falco, for he was *Falco*, but she felt fear nonetheless. She thought that it was perhaps nerves, entering a dream world once again, preparing to meet Octayn and see Hydo and Calis once more. She truly hoped that she would discover the story Calis had told her had been a lie. She didn't want to have brothers and she didn't want to have any relation to Octayn Oredan. She had never thought she would feel such a way, but she prayed that her parents truly were the man and woman who had perished that day in the fire.

She knew *that* Octayn. She knew Hoda. She knew them as her mother and father, two people who had loved her so greatly that they had died trying to keep her safe. She felt calm at the thought, and however sad it was, it gave her a sense of clarity. The two people who had loved her most, who had raised her, had not wanted her to go to Bakoran or have any connection with the true Octayn. That was information enough. She had trusted her parents. She had loved them, and they her. They had died to protect her from the Fire—they had died keeping her from Octayn Oredan.

"They didn't know you were a Fire-Wielder. It's possible that what they did was out of love for you, not disdain for Octayn Oredan," Falco spoke, listening in on her thoughts.

"Even so. They died for me. *They* were my parents, you and Jeco are my family—that's it."

"Jessop."

"That's it, Falco."

They stared at one another in silence. She knew that as they seemed now they would appear in the dream—their clothing and their weapons. For that, Falco did not take the Blade of Light with them. They had discussed it and worried that, at best, it would detract from the point of the meeting, and, at worst, appear like an act of hostility.

"How exactly is it a weapon against Fire-Wielders?" she had asked him as they stared at the shimmering blade.

"I've never seen it in use," Falco had said.

They would leave the blade in the care of Urdo, as Kohl and Dezane watched over Mar'e. Trax would be waiting for Korend'a and Hode Avay to return. He had said the Blade was being well looked after by young Hunters and those who remained on the Assembly Council. They would return to a secure Azgul, he had promised. Jessop hadn't the time to think about Azgul, the Blade, or how secure they were. She didn't care.

"Shall we?" Falco asked, taking her hands in his. She knew Urdo waited outside the tent, ready to come watch over them and the Blade of Light as soon as they passed into the dream. Jessop held tight to Falco's hand as they rolled to the ground, lying side by side, facing one another.

She stared at his beautiful face, his gray eyes. "I don't know how to enter her dreams ...I don't even know her."

"If what Calis said is true, you share blood with the woman. Focus on that connection," he answered.

Her heart was racing. She closed her eyes, squeezing Falco's hand as tight as she could. She focused on her heartbeat. On Calis and all he had said. On the images of Octayn. She honed in on the woman's face. She pictured her life, Calis's childhood, the palace she had seen, what kind of upbringing she could have had—

Jessop opened her eyes and found she was standing in the same grand room she had found Hydo in during her previous dream travel. Falco was at her side. And they were not alone. She gripped Falco's hand tighter and he opened his eyes slowly. She felt him tense. Standing before them wasn't just Octayn, but Hydo, Calis, and four other young men. All of them had green eyes. All of them stared at Jessop with narrow gazes, as though inspecting her.

Octayn was as beautiful as she had appeared in the memories. She was more beautiful than Jessop, more beautiful than any woman Jessop had ever seen. Her eyes were a brilliant green, though they did not glow, and her long hair cascaded over her perfect form. She was dressed in all white and she smiled warmly at Jessop as she stood, her arms outstretched. "My daughter."

Jessop didn't move. She dug her fingers into Falco's hand, focusing on his presence, on their common goal of retrieving Jeco. "Where is my son?" she demanded.

Octayn lowered her hands slowly, her smile faltering. "Safe. With his cousins—your brothers' children."

At the word, Octayn drew her hand out to gesture to Calis and the four young men with him. Calis stepped forward slowly. "Jessop, I am glad you came."

She remained silent, though she could not help but study the men. The same men from the first dream Hydo had visited her in, they were tall and strong, with broad shoulders and muscular builds. Each of them carried the same silver metallic whip on their hips. One of the men stepped forward, perhaps the one closest in age to Jessop. He had Hydo's dark hair. "Welcome, Sister, I am Taygen Jesuin."

Jessop bristled at the name. Jesuin. He—her potential brother—was a Jesuin. The next gestured to her with a small wave, "I am Mesan, born after Taygen. Welcome, Sister."

"Sister, I am Barone," said the next.

The youngest of the group kept his arms crossed tightly over his chest. "Call me Axis."

Jessop tried to keep her focus on Hydo. She tried to fight her curiosity—but they looked like her. They called her sister and resembled her ...It was overwhelming. She was thankful for Falco when he took a small step forward, keeping her hand in his. "Where is my son, Hydo?"

"So this is him," Octayn spoke, a half-smile playing across her face as she looked Falco up and down. "Falco Bane. My daughter's husband." She took a step closer and Jessop thought her heart might explode if it beat any faster. She continued to look at Falco, as though more interested in him than anything else. "That's quite the scar."

"Where's my son, Octayn Oredan?" he demanded again.

"I told you—safe, with his family."

Jessop couldn't help but study her face. Her eyes. The way her mouth pulled into a reluctant smile when she spoke, giving her a wicked appearance. She stared back at Jessop with eyes so green they appeared supernatural.

"I've wondered all these long years ...And when Hydo had said a woman had appeared in the Blade, with such skill and such beauty, I could barely dare to hope, to wonder, could it be—"

"The child you nearly killed in a fire?" Jessop interrupted her. Her voice was strained and trembled with anger.

"You're one of *us*—the flames wouldn't have killed you."

She resisted taking a step towards the woman. Her heart was pounding. Her skin felt alight. She could feel every set of eyes in the room on her. "You didn't know that. You thought I had died with my parents."

"Those guardians—Essa and Hoda? They were *not* your parents. I paid them to care for you."

Jessop's cheek twitched. Essa. Her name had been Essa. She wanted to fight. She wanted to cry. "Whatever you claim, they loved me. They died for me."

"That's true. They were so certain you hadn't inherited my abilities, they wouldn't let Hydo perform the test. Their deaths were no ones' fault but their own."

Jessop leaned forward, her voice deep. "Do not speak of them further."

"Can't you see? They didn't know you. They never sensed your power. Not as I sense it. Not as we all, here, can sense it. You belonged with *us*."

"She belongs with me," Falco interrupted, his deep voice carrying through the room.

Octayn rounded on him, her blonde hair whipping about. "You. Falco, Falco, *Falco*. More powerful than them all—what do they say? You're the 'best there ever was', correct?"

Falco said nothing.

"When Hydo told me of you ...we thought so many things. You'd be destined to challenge him for the Blade. You were stronger than any had anticipated. We wondered if we could bring you into our family, raise you as our own, but that just wouldn't do, now would it?"

She reached out to him, her hand falling just short of his face, her palm facing the ceiling. A small ball of fire erupted in her hand and danced about her fingers. "You have no Fire."

Falco's face pulled into a small smile. "No, no Fire ...But I have your daughter, and I have Daharia."

Jessop felt her hand slick with sweat in Falco's. She could hardly breathe. She could feel Calis's eyes on her, she sensed he wanted to speak with her, but she couldn't turn her gaze from Octayn and Falco.

Octayn raised her brow sharply. "You have my daughter—I have your son."

It was all Jessop needed to hear in order to move. She ripped her hand from Falco's and locked it around Octayn's neck so quickly she knew she had instantly bruised the woman. Octayn hissed as her body erupted in a brilliant golden fire that traveled from her throat down Jessop's arm.

Her sons leapt forward but Falco had his arm out in an instant and, using the full strength of his Sentio, froze them in place. "Stay out of it, boys."

Jessop stared the woman in the eye. She could not feel the burn of the flames and it seemed to her that this was exactly what Octayn wanted to see. "Return my son to me or I swear I will kill you."

Hydo moved forward, but Jessop was ready for him. She had her anger and she had her focus. She had the greatest grasp on Sentio any had ever known—she froze him in place, mid-stride beside his sons.

"Jeco is yours—on one condition." Octayn answered, her voice strained.

Jessop waited, refusing to loosen her grip. When Octayn realized she wouldn't let up, she continued. "Daharia belongs to Taygen, first son of Hydo. Falco must die and leave the Blade to *us*."

Jessop's own Fire came forth with an alarming fury. It engulfed her and circled around Octayn with a wild force. "You would call me here to threaten Falco?"

Jessop squeezed tighter and tighter, until Octayn's knees buckled and her hands were pulling at Jessop's wrist with futility. Jessop felt strong—her anger gave her power. It had always been a source of great strength to her. This woman had abandoned her, and now, upon first reunion, requested that Falco die to free up his throne for her sons, sons who were not strong enough to fight him. Sons who would not inherit the throne of Daharia over Jeco.

"Where is my son?"

Jessop gasped as the force of the hit sent her flying back. She flew into a wall, her body tensing as it made contact. She landed on her feet and saw Hydo holding Octayn up. She had lost her focus and he had taken advantage of it. And she could instantly see his rage. He drew his Hunter's blade and moved past Octayn with a forceful stride, his gaze stuck on Jessop.

She drew her own blade, a wave of fire rushing over her as she did so. He waved his hand at her, an attempt at Sentio, but she cut through it with her own abilities. She felt a fluttering in her chest. Her last fight with Hydo had not gone as well as she had once anticipated.

"You could have killed her!" He struck at her with the same impressive speed and force she remembered from their last fight.

Jessop spun out of his attack, leaping in the air and connecting a strong hook kick across his jaw. She landed with ease, ready to bring her blade down on him, only to find he had already recovered. He thrust his sword towards her abdomen and she shimmied to the side—but too slowly. She felt the sharp sting as his blade nicked her side.

"You are a master at Sentio, and better with a blade than most, but *I* am not most, girl." He spun in a tight circle before bringing his sword down on her, heavy with the force of all his might. She blocked and kicked him back.

She knew he was right. She was superior in Sentio—and he was better with the blade. She threw her hand out and froze him in place. He fought at her Sentio and his body began to move, as though in slow motion, to break free from her hold. Her wound was impairing her focus. She knew he had cut her in such a place that she was bleeding profusely. She needed Falco.

She turned her gaze to him. He could heal her, but not as he held her brothers in place. They held stares for a long moment, and with a sudden bolt, he leapt through the air, landing at her side. He grabbed her and instantly she felt her body begin to stitch back together—and her brothers begin to move. She felt Hydo moving closer and closer. She squeezed Falco's arm with gratitude as her wound recovered. "Swap!"

They broke free from one another's holds just in time to engage. Instantly, a whip stung around her wrist—but she was ready this time. Before she could be burned, she jerked the weapon forward, stepping on it to wrench it free from one of them—Taygen, perhaps. She rolled to the ground and grabbed the whip handle. She shot the weapon through the air, coiling it around two of the brothers. With a wave of her hand, she sent them flying back into the wall, hitting them with enough force to ensure they struggled to get back to their feet.

The young one leapt at her with a sword and she fought him back with ease. He yelled with each strike, and while he was skilled, he didn't come close to possessing her experience, let alone the abilities of his father. He jabbed forward, his blade crossing her body, and she grabbed the hilt, spun out and pulled his weapon from him. With a forceful back kick, she sent the young man to the ground. She raised the weapon high above him, but froze. She did not wish to kill the boy.

"*Stop!*" Calis leapt before her. He held his hands out. "We are your brothers—we do not need to do this."

"Did you know when she beckoned me here that they would only give me my son back in exchange for my husband?"

His shoulders dropped. He had known. Before they could say anything further, the youngest brother—Axis—lunged past Calis, tackling Jessop to the ground. "You tried to kill my father!" he yelled, his strong body slamming Jessop hard into the stone floor.

He struck her once and her face stung. She could taste the blood. She shot her hand up, grabbed the side of his head, and slammed him to the side, tossing him to the ground beside her. She was on her feet in an instant and kicked him with all her might, the added force of Sentio sending him flying across the room. She could feel her brothers prying at the corners of her mind, but they had no hope of entering it. Their Sentio did not compare to Hydo's, and he could not breach her mind in her waking state.

A whip locked around her waist, and she locked eyes with one of the older brothers who wielded it. "You could rule beside us, sister!" he yelled, as his flame traveled from his hand, over the whip's handle, and down the bright metal.

Jessop kicked her leg out and down, her boot landing firmly on the whip, wrenching it to the floor with her strong leg. The weapon loosened from her body. She had the opportunity to fight him—Barone or Taygen, whichever brother he was—but she wouldn't. She didn't. She couldn't. She turned her gaze instead to Hydo. He fought Falco with all his might. They moved in such a similar manner. Falco was younger, faster and stronger. She knew then more than ever that what Falco had been saying all along was true; he could kill Hydo.

Suddenly, as their blades locked, Hydo grabbed Falco's arm. Jessop knew instantly what he intended. She jumped onto the table and leapt through the air—just as Hydo's flames erupted around Falco. He let out a wild scream as his arm burned. Jessop landed heavily, toppling the men to the floor. She latched onto Hydo with unbridled ferocity, rolling with him until she pinned him to the ground. She outstretched his arm, his hand twisted back unnaturally towards the ceiling, and with all her might, she brought her forearm down on him– breaking his sword arm. The crunching of the bone was drowned out by Octayn's scream.

The woman's voice seemed to temporarily freeze them all. She ran across the room making a beeline for Hydo. Jessop leapt to her feet, her sword instantly outstretched with its point nearly touching one of Octayn's perfect green eyes, forcing her to yield. "Where is my son?"

Octayn stared at her with rage—with hatred. "You would choose Falco over your own flesh and blood?"

"Do not lecture me on the notion of family. The Fire means more to you than I ever have."

"You wouldn't have been allowed to rule without the Fire! We had to know."

"Falco and I rule Daharia now, remember? No Fire was required."

Octayn cocked her head to the side. "I thought you were dead. Had I known otherwise—"

"You would have what? Found me and asked me about Falco's power? Told me how you raised sons who weren't strong enough to take Daharia on their own? Found some other way to manipulate me?"

The older woman shook her head. "I have done everything I needed to for my son Taygen to rule. The son of the Lord Protector of Daharia and Empress of Bakoran could merge our two territories."

"Hydo *isn't* the Lord Protector of Daharia. Falco is."

Falco got to his feet, holding his wounded arm tight against his body. Jessop could see the pain he was in, but he still wielded a sword. He looked past Jessop to the Bakora men. "If you want my Blade, come and take it."

He took a step towards them. Jessop knew he was not fit to fight further, but Calis and the others did not. They knew of Falco by reputation alone. Jessop watched as they exchanged looks, pushing thoughts back and forth. Taygen took a step forward, willing to fight Falco, when Octayn threw her arm out. "Stay where you are, son."

"They cannot fight Falco. They are not fit to rule Daharia," Jessop spoke.

Octayn grimaced at the words. "You could be reunited with your family, Jessop. You would have Jeco and your brothers."

"Give him back to me."

"I wouldn't harm him. The child of Falco Bane and grandchild of the Empress of Bakoran is most impressive indeed."

"I am warning you—"

"*No.* No warning anyone. Falco for Jeco. That is my offer. Decide by dawn or meet my army in battle, daughter."

Jessop flicked her sword, nicking Octayn's beautiful face with the blade, just enough to leave a small cut on the woman. "Were you truly my kin, I would have done anything for you. This could have all been different."

"Jessop—"

"Don't. Don't make it worse."

A tear streaked down Octayn's face, trailing the blood from the cut down her jaw line. With nothing left to be said, the room began to shake, the world around them rumbling as it fell apart. Octayn stared at her as the dream world began to break.

Chapter 19

Present Day

Urdo and Kohl were already cleaning Falco's arm as he and Jessop awoke in the tent. Jessop bolted upright and leaned over him. His forearm, biceps, shoulder, and part of his chest were burned. She knew he could heal himself but they needed to let him.

"Stop—*stop*! Leave him be."

The men froze, bandages and fresh water in their hands. Falco writhed in pain, rolling to his side. She lied back down behind him, forcing her chest tight against his back. "Breathe. Just breathe," she whispered into his ear. He trembled under her hold. "Just breathe, Falco." His body began to slow, the shakes dissipating as he regained a sense of calm. She breathed with slow deliberation, ensuring the rise and fall of her chest moved him, allowing him the time to fall in sync with her.

Slowly, they quieted, and he began to heal his body. Eventually, he rolled over to face her. He kissed her forehead. She kissed his chin. They stayed silent for a long moment. It had been horrendous. Hydo lived, Octayn wanted Falco dead, Jeco was still gone. Her brothers ...The youngest had had such anger. They would die to rule a land they had never stepped foot in.

Falco rolled in to a sitting position, pulling Jessop up with him. "Jessop broke Hydo's sword-wielding arm."

"You fought Hydo again?" Kohl asked, his eyes darting between the two of them.

They told them everything. They told them of Jessop's brothers, of Octayn, of the palace, of Hydo and everything that they had said. Urdo shook his head through listening to it all. "I can't believe it ...All these years," he whispered, sipping from his flask. "I should have known."

Kohl ran a hand through his blond hair. "They want Falco for Jeco?"

Jessop wrung her hands together. "Falco's life for Jeco's safe return—otherwise we meet them in battle at dawn."

"Does that mean they're coming here?"

"I don't know," Jessop said. "Maybe they know we found a Voyager."

"I'll do it." Falco spoke, his voice pulling their gazes.

Jessop rested her hand on his. He sat with his tattered, burned tunic in his lap, his bare chest and arm still a bright red from the wound. "What?"

"I'll do the swap."

It took Jessop a long moment to understand what he was saying. "No. You won't."

"It's what makes the most sense, Jessop."

"That's madness, Falco," Kohl barked, shaking his head at his brother.

Urdo tossed his empty flask down. "We won't let you."

Falco ignored them. "We get Jeco back and we avoid war."

She stared at his perfect, scarred face. She studied his deep gray eyes. She saw no confusion in his gaze. He seemed calm and collected and willing to die. Willing to leave her. "Are you out of your mind?"

He shook his head gently. "It gets our son back safely."

"*We* can get our son back safely—without you dying."

"We don't know that."

"*Yes*—we do!" Her voice was loud, much louder than intended, but she didn't care. She got to her feet, and at the movement, Kohl, Urdo, and Falco mirrored her. Falco reached for her but she hit his hand away. "Don't touch me. You would leave me? I just chose you over those people and without thinking you would throw away everything. You'd just give up?"

"For Jeco? Yes! I'd do anything," he yelled back. He reached for her once more and she slammed her hands into his chest, forcing him away from her. She ducked out of the tent and into the dark night sky. She took off in the sand, her step light. She had her sword. She had her vision. She didn't need anything else. She made her way for the tree.

"*Jessop!*" Falco yelled after her but she didn't turn back. She thought of their lives. She thought of their childhoods, spent together in anger. She thought of their transition into young adults, loving each other with such a youthful intensity that they were wildly volatile. She thought of how she had given her body to him and borne him their son. She thought of all the words they had exchanged—the promises and the vows.

The tears were hot on her cheeks. Her throat was on fire. He would just give it all up, without a fight. Her chest ached. He would rather die than fight for what they had—fight to restore all they had grown together. Her sobs were loud, echoing about her in the dark. She grabbed her heart, willing the tension and fire in her chest to disappear, but it just made it worse. She stumbled, her ankle rolling in the loose sand, and she fell forward.

Strong hands caught her before she hit the ground, spinning her around. She blinked the tears away and saw Kohl's beautiful face in the darkness. He had caught her. She knew that the day had finally come where he knew all her secrets. He had seen her in all her forms. He had tested the limits of their relationship again and again—with rage and fire and with love and loyalty. He held her tight against his body. "Jessop—"

She kissed him. Her hand rested on his face, her thumb tracing the star scar, and their lips moved over one another with a sense of hunger and familiarity—and sadness. Her kiss was wet with tears. He held her in his arms, his body warm as the desert breeze washed over them. He kissed her softly and then pulled away, resting his forehead against hers. "You belong with Falco."

She pulled free from his arms. "He doesn't seem to think so."

"Can't you see? Can't you see what he's offering you if you just let him go?"

She stared at him. His blond hair was loose and catching in the wind. His amber eyes were just as beautiful in the pale light provided by the stars—stars he was so unfamiliar with. Stars that matched his scar. His lips rested just slightly apart as he watched her, waiting for her to see. He was perfect. But he wasn't Falco. She grabbed him into a tight embrace. She held him tightly and hugged him with closed eyes, completely trustful of him in his strong, capable arms.

She understood what he meant. Falco was offering her a life, with her son, with her kin, and with Kohl. He was trying to make the decision for her that he had thought she struggled to make for herself.

Finally, she let go of Kohl, knowing what she was letting go. She wouldn't let Falco decide for her. She chose him. She would always choose him. It had never been, nor would it ever be, Kohl. "Thank you."

* * * *

Jessop found Falco alone in their tent, sitting in the dark, as though he was waiting for her. She crossed the space with ease, her expert eyes navigating the shadows as they had done for so many years. "You think if

you die, I'll just live out my life with Kohl. That I'd raise Jeco with him?"
She knelt before him, locking eyes with him.

"You would be happy. He would keep Jeco safe. And he'd love you, for the rest of his life."

"And I would love you for the rest of mine."

"Jessop—"

"Don't. Just don't. I choose you."

They sat in silence. They stared at one another and remembered everything that had ever come to pass between them. They sat for hours. She thought about him and his offer and about Kohl and their goodbye. For that was what it had been—a goodbye. They had done it all, felt it all, and there was nothing left to say between them. Falco had offered them the chance to be together, without repercussion, and she knew with certainty that she didn't want it.

"I kissed him."

"I know."

"I had to."

"I know."

Dawn approached and so did the threat of battle. Urdo had gone to ready the troops. It seemed the Bakoran army would arrive in *Haren'dul Daku* at first light if Falco did not surrender to Octayn and Hydo. She thought of seeing Calis and the others once again. She thought of their anger and of her own. She thought of what Octayn had said about their children. Her brothers had lives—they were married with children and had been raised to love Hydo and to fight to rule. She was supposed to have been raised as one of them.

She thought of Falco's arm, and of Hydo's, and what the battle would bring. She did not wish to find her brothers in the field, but she knew she likely would. She knew if they tried to fight her or Falco, they would die. She thought of Hanson and wondered who would be the first to find him. Perhaps Urdo? Perhaps Korend'a or Trax, if Korend'a had returned by then. Korend'a had the skill to fight Hanson. She realized as she thought it, he may have had the skill but he did not have the Sentio. She remembered how Aranthol had fallen. Not all possessed Sentio, and it would be their weakness in battle with older Hunters.

"We've spent all our lives fighting," she whispered. They had been silent for so long her voice sounded much louder than it truly was.

"Don't grow weary of it just yet," Falco laughed.

"They have more soldiers than we do?"

"We have more skilled fighters. But yes, I believe they have more."

"Are you afraid?"

"I'm afraid of what I will have to do to get Jeco back."

She knew what he meant. She had hesitated to harm her brothers. For no reason other than the belief that they were kin. Falco would not hesitate. She took his hand in hers. For her son, it didn't matter. "Do what you must."

He squeezed her hand tightly. "Are you afraid?"

She thought of Kohl. His face appeared in her mind and she felt the strain on her heart.

Falco nodded, knowing her thoughts. "I'll do what I can to keep him safe."

She crawled into his lap and her hands wrapped around his face with affection. "People we love will die tomorrow. But not our son and not you."

He wrapped his arms around her tightly. "There's not going to be a person out there capable of killing me. We both know it. Except maybe you…"

She laughed, but he didn't, and she knew he was not speaking in jest. She remembered his voice in childhood—what had first come across as arrogance she had learned was loneliness, isolated by his skill with the sword.

"They had Hanson take Jeco because they knew they couldn't fight me for the Blade."

"I know."

"If I had left you to burn that day, they would have realized you were a Fire-Wielder. You would have been taken to Bakoran. Does it make you wish that you'd never met me?"

She leaned forward and rested fully in his arms. "Not for a single second."

* * * *

When Trax woke them it was still dark out, but Jessop knew dawn was swiftly approaching. All around them, the men readied for battle. Korend'a and Hode Avay had returned. They had a Voyager with them, someone Korend'a knew from Aranthol. "He's a good man. He came without question."

"His services might not be needed after all." She explained as briefly as she could all that had happened.

"We have no time then," he whispered, his gaze falling to Hode Avay. She felt as though she understood his fear, but said nothing. Her gaze fell to Dezane DeHawn, who was sitting with Teck Fay, speaking in hushed voices. They had seemed inseparable for days and she wondered what the two natural enemies could have possibly discussed for so long. "Falco and

I must speak further," she whispered, the darkness somehow cueing her to remain silent, though few slept.

"Let them come to us," Urdo said, his voice loud and carrying over them all. Jessop turned to face him. He was standing on a large crate, with drink in hand. "Let them come. They wish to fight us—let them come. They wish to challenge our Lord Protector? Let them come." His voice was loud and rousing. The soldiers were standing. Kuroi warriors gathered nearer to them in the dark. Trax stood, clapping Urdo on the shoulder.

"*Kasei vande te os, kasei vos far'a harana, kasei vande te os!*" He repeated Urdo's words, his own voice just as stirring. The warriors clapped and banged their shields, chanting after Urdo and Trax.

Urdo took a step forward. "The Golden Death Valley saw the last great battle—it shall see this one too!"

"*Haren'dul Daku had'away ha dei far'a harana, had'away ha hes far'a harana!*"

Falco's soldiers slammed their fists into their chest plates, raising their swords, cheering as they listened. The Kuroi began their battle cries. Urdo moved through the men slowly, approaching Falco. Jessop saw Kohl in the crowd, in the darkness. He kept his eyes on her.

Urdo reached over his shoulder and pulled loose a covered sword. Jessop knew instantly it was the Blade of Light. Urdo had been watching it for them. All of the men, Falco's soldiers and Dezane's warriors, gathered around, forming a large circle. Urdo fell to his knee, bowing his head low as he offered the weapon to Falco. Many had never seen the famed weapon. Jessop was amazed by the energy she felt in their camp. She had never led like Urdo, she had never been in a war like the one they prepared to face. She might have been one of the greatest fighters there, but they had known of this warrior camaraderie much longer than she had.

Falco stepped forward and grabbed the white-stone hilt. With a lavish spin, he freed the blade from its cover, turning it about his body and taking on an attacking stance. The blade emitted a brilliant light that shone over all of their faces for as far back as twenty men watching. "Let them come!" He shouted, his voice eliciting a wild praise from his men.

"*Kasei vande te os!*" Jessop yelled, stepping beside him. The Kuroi clapped and cheered. Light was breaking, the last of the stars still visible in the sky. Battle was before them.

Jessop felt a hand against her shoulder. She turned and found it was Dezane DeHawn. He fixed his glowing eyes on her. "I must speak with you."

Chapter 20

Present Day

The sky was a milky gray, ready for the dawn to fully break. Jessop stood beside Dezane DeHawn and couldn't deny the sense of power she felt emanating from him. She had feared many times that Dezane had lived too many long years and fought too many battles to truly be fit for another, but standing beside him she felt nothing but his strength. He held a spear, his shield on his back and sword on his hip, and his age did nothing to diminish his imposing presence.

"I never thought it would have come to this. Had we talked on it years ago, I wouldn't have seen this future," she spoke.

"This has been a long time coming. So long, perhaps none of us truly foresaw it."

The sky began to lighten, shades of gold and rose warming the desert terrain. She ran her hand over her vest, resting it on her hilt. She wished she could see Falco. She darted her gaze to the side and found Kohl standing, watching her. They all had their places. They all knew the plan. Jessop licked her dried lips. She did not fear battle. She readjusted her hold on her hilt. She did *not* fear battle.

I'm with you. Falco's voice suddenly filled her mind. Her heart slowed and her body calmed. She took a deep breath. They had a plan—they had a plan, and they had more power than any army in any territory. She and Falco were unstoppable. Urdo, Trax, and Kohl were some of the greatest warriors in Daharia. Dezane and Teck had more power between the two of them than any other pairing in Daharia. Falco's army was as vicious as they were triumphant on the field. The Kuroi were born ready for war, training from the moment they could walk. Jessop knew all this ...and yet, she knew the Bakoran army would have Fire.

What could Urdo do in the face of a Fire-Wielder? What could Korend'a do against Sentio, if he came up against Hanson or Hydo? She looked back to Kohl. She trusted him. She trusted him to maintain his focus at the sight of his former mentor. Nonetheless, if he could not do it, she would kill Hanson Knell. Before the battle was over, she would end his life.

It hadn't been very long ago that Falco had been the one insisting Hanson die and Jessop had felt contrary. She could still close her eyes and see his face, that day on the terrace, when he learned that she had betrayed him. He had been devastated. As Kohl had been. As they all, in some way or another, had been. She had felt little for the older man, but she had wronged him once. And in doing so, she realized that she had perhaps become someone she didn't altogether admire, someone who would harm others for her own gain. She knew, more than ever, that her vendetta against Hydo had not been worth the harm she had caused—especially to Kohl. But Hanson's act of revenge against her was too great to ever forgive. If one thing was certain, it was that Hanson Knell would die on the battlefield of *Haren'dul Daku*.

Dezane shifted just slightly beside her. "It's time."

Jessop took a deep breath and raised her gaze to the giant portal wall before them. The desert was silent, save for the breeze pulling at the finest top layer of sand. She longed to have Falco at her side, but if she couldn't have him, she was honored to have Dezane. "You're sure about this?"

Dezane nodded. He was sure. Her heart began to race once more. She longed to free her blade but knew that she, more than anyone, needed to follow the plan. Suddenly, the great, rippling wall began to violently undulate. She tightened her fingers around her hilt. The blade that Kohl had designed for her had been made for a battle such as the one they faced.

The portal wall contorted violently, as if a giant object were trying to pierce it from the dark void. Suddenly, a wild roar of angry yells and chants broke through the air, deafening them all. A gust of wind spun about them, driving sand into the sky, forcing Jessop to turn her gaze away.

When she looked back, there they were. Jessop and Dezane were several hundred paces back from the wall, between the two great Soar-Crafts, but the Bakoran army had filled that space with ease. Her gaze rolled over them all, with their golden shields and spears, their white tunics tucked under gilded armor, their angry expressions and ready stances. There were more men than she had anticipated. Falco had not been wrong about the size of their army—it was immense. She took a deep breath, reminding herself of Dezane's words as she looked out on the army. An army ready to die for a throne they had no right to, for an Empress they had likely never spoken with, for Jessop's brother.

She found the Oredan family with ease—they stood front and center, proud and ready. They wore their golden garb, their Fire-Wielding whips at the ready, and their swords tucked in their gilded sheaths. Hydo dressed in their likeness, though he had his Hunter's blade on him. His sword-wielding arm was bandaged tightly and tucked firmly against his chest in a gilded, armored sling. He scanned the desert before them, clearly confused by the setting. Jessop moved her gaze past him. Her eyes locked on Calis.

"Return my son to me, brother, and I will ensure my Oredan brothers always have a home in the Blade." Her voice silenced the Bakoran army.

He took a small step towards her. "Give us Falco and you, sister, will always have a place in the Blade and the Oredan palace."

Jessop ignored his response. *It doesn't have to be this way,* she pushed into her brothers' minds with ease. She saw the look on all of their faces, the pain that came with a forceful intrusion into the mind. They had Sentio, but they could not stop her from entering their minds and they could not enter hers.

Calis shook his head as though trying to force her voice out, but it was no use—Jessop remained with ease. *How well do you even know Hydo? He has been ruling Daharia all your lives—he didn't raise you.*

"Stop!" Axis yelled, his hand grabbing his head at her words. She retracted, immediately wishing to end his pain. She had lived a life set on showing no mercy, and yet, faced with men who claimed to be her brothers, she resisted harming them.

She suddenly felt a strong push, forcing her to take a step back. It had been Hydo, stepping forward as if to shield his sons from her. "Where's Falco, Jessop?"

"Give me my son, and I'll let yours live."

He laughed at her. Using his free hand, he stretched it out before them, gesturing to the open desert. "What's your plan—you and Dezane DeHawn against the entire Bakoran army?"

"Not quite."

She turned to Kohl, who walked out from behind the Soar-Craft, his sword drawn. He was not alone though—with every step he took, he was using his body to shield Teck Fay. Teck seemed to glide over the desert floor and Jessop could just make out his inky blue eyes from underneath the hood of his cloak. She turned her gaze back to Hydo, who shifted uneasily, unsure what their plan was still.

Jessop fixed her stare on Hydo's dark eyes. Their time had come. *Surrender.*

He answered her with a slight shake of his head. *Never.*

Jessop nodded as Kohl stood beside her. "Dezane, Teck—you're really sure about this?"

Teck looked at her with dark eyes from under the hood of his cloak. "I owe you this, Jessop Bane."

"What do you mean?"

But he did not respond, turning his gaze instead to Dezane. Dezane spoke with a deep, calm voice. "Begin, Jessop."

She nodded and pulled one of her short blades free from the sheath on her back. She turned to Kohl, knowing what they needed to do from Dezane's instruction that morning.

Kohl offered her his arm and she could see clearly the scar from where the tracking device they had once shared had been. She quickly carved the blade against his flesh, careful to not cut deeply. He turned his arm over and let it bleed into the sand at their feet. Jessop was quick to inflict a matching wound on her own forearm, hissing as she placed the blade back in its holster. They were all silent, the eyes of an entire legion watching them. Hydo stared with suspicion. He was whispering something to his sons.

She drew her sword. She could sense Hydo would not wait long. "Dezane," she urged the elder. Teck had started chanting in a language Jessop did not understand, his palms hovering over the bloodied sand, his body swaying rhythmically. Dezane began to whisper quick, tight Kuroi words, speaking to the ground. She could feel the sand moving about them. She could hear the Bakoran army drawing their weapons, archers readying their bows.

"*Dezane*," she whispered again, spiraling her blade about her, readying her body for war.

Teck circled them, his voice getting faster and faster as he spoke the invocation. Dezane knelt to the ground, then picked the bloodied sand up and spoke his words into the earth. Hydo yelled an order and Jessop heard the tension in one thousand bows. The singing of burning arrows soared through the air. With perfect synchronicity, she and Kohl threw their hands up, using their Sentio to form a shield around themselves, Dezane, and Teck. The flaming arrows diverted all around them, piercing the sand a mere stride away.

Hydo called to the Bakora army and the first line of soldiers ignited into flames, their entire bodies, their armor and swords burning menacingly.

She spun her blade about once more, knowing they were running out of time. *"Dezane."*

The line of Fire-Wielders began to march forward. Jessop was quick to note that her brothers stayed in place, not leading their army. Kohl twisted his sword about him quickly, loosening his muscles up. "I'd rather not be burned alive."

Jessop shot him an angry look. The Fire-Wielders picked up their pace. They were running across the desert floor, closing the space between their army and Jessop, Kohl, Teck, and Dezane. Jessop shot her gaze between Dezane and Teck, who wouldn't look at her. She turned to Kohl. "We just need to buy them time!"

Jessop took a deep breath and threw her arm out. A wave of Fire-Wielders flew through the air, their flames extinguishing as they collided into one another. Kohl followed her lead. They kept as many at bay as they could through Sentio alone. But one by one, the first row of Fire-Wielders began to break through their Sentio. Jessop's sword clashed angrily with that of a Bakora—his fire posed no threat to her as she kicked and hit her way through the melee. Kohl kept throwing them back with his Sentio, forcing them back—but they just kept coming.

"Dezane!"

Jessop spun, thrusting her blade back past her, piercing through the flaming abdomen of a warrior. Dezane yelled loudly as he punched his hand into the sand, Teck had one hand resting on the elder's shoulder, his other pointing up at the sky. Thunder suddenly filled the air, startling the Bakora, but not stopping them. Jessop swung her arm and sent another wave of Bakora men back, but she could not keep it up, and neither could Kohl—they would be drained if they had to carry on relying on their abilities.

Blood trailed down Teck's scarred forearm. Jessop didn't know what to expect, though she knew what they had told her would happen. Suddenly, lighting struck the mage. Jessop raised her arm to shield her eyes from the light. The brilliant beam traveled through Teck, through Dezane, into the sand beneath their feet. "Dezane!" She screamed, knowing the power of a storm could kill a man.

But none could hear her as the thunder roared. The ground began to tremble beneath her feet. She stumbled as the sand quaked beneath her. She recovered her footing, just in time to block the assault of another Fire-Wielder. She kicked him once, spun, and back kicked him, forcing him to the ground. She threw her arm out and pushed another group back. She regrouped, standing beside Kohl to ready for the next attack. But it didn't come. The Bakora froze as the rumbling ground continued to alarm them all. "Jessop." Kohl clasped her shoulder.

She looked to him, and then back, following his gaze. The desert behind them had raised up into a giant wave of sand. She looked and saw Teck and Dezane, both with their heads low, both chanting. The wave began to move, shifting in the air, raising and lowering—it was taking on new shapes. Jessop grabbed Kohl's arm as she watched the sand twist and turn. It was breaking into smaller parts and forming familiar shapes.

Kohl took a step forward. "They did it. They've actually done it."

Jessop was unable to turn back and face the Bakoran army, unable to tear her eyes away from Dezane and Teck's creation. Standing before them was an army of soldiers, half of them resembling a version of Kohl, the other half shaped after Jessop—made entirely of sand and stone, hardened by the heat of lightning, powered by the abilities of the desert masters.

"They made us an army," she whispered, her eyes trailing over the hundreds and hundreds of sand creations.

She turned to Kohl, finding a look of amazement on his face. He shook his head slowly as his eyes fell on her.

"Jessop..."

"Don't. Don't say anything." She refused to hear his cautionary goodbye. She spun her sword about her once and turned, her body igniting in a ferocious fire that traveled down her arm, over her blade, as she stormed towards the Bakora army. A wild scream from the desert creatures followed as they charged after her. She didn't know their abilities, she didn't know their skill, she didn't know how long Dezane and Teck could give them life—but she knew this was their only shot.

Kohl ran at her side, his powerful legs leaping over fallen Bakora, his Sentio, like hers, sending Fire-Wielders back. They met the second line with a violent crash—the hiss of the desert creatures was deafening as they cut through the Bakora army. Jessop spun about, cutting and carving, in the mess of fire and sand. She lost Kohl in the madness. As Bakora cut through the desert creatures, they exploded like sand storms. They could kill, but they could also be easily destroyed.

Jessop kicked a soldier back, unsheathed her short blade, and used her abilities to send the weapon flying into his chest before returning to her hand. She spun and ducked, punched and sliced, her ears ringing in resistance to the violent sounds of war. Several paces away, she saw Calis—he was skilled with his blade, fighting back several desert sand versions of Jessop with ease.

Suddenly, she heard Falco in the distance, ordering his assault. She couldn't see him, but she heard the wild calls of his soldiers. Though Jessop could only see several paces surrounding her, the battle rippled back, soldiers falling and sand flying, as a great attack was made at the sides of the fight. Falco and Trax, along with Urdo and Korend'a, had entered the battlefield, leading the Kuroi warriors and Falco's army. Jessop felt a strong hand grab her shoulder and spun, elbowing her attacker firmly in the face, ignoring the pain of her bone connecting with a gilded helmet. She flipped her short blade in her hand, pointing the hilt towards her chest and extending the small weapon out of her fist, ready to strike, when she realized it was one of the brothers.

They both froze. Her flames extinguished as she studied his face. He had no scars but he also did not have a look of fear in his eyes—he had been trained to fight all his life. His hands, wrapped tightly around his hilt, burned with a low blue flame. And without saying a word, they turned from one another, carrying on their battle without engaging each other.

She ducked under the arm of a Fire-Wielder, coming up behind him and cutting him down without hesitation. The sand creatures were beginning to die out. The battle was already, after such brief moments, beginning to ebb. She could see Falco in the distance, fighting several Bakora at once. He fought with the Blade of Light and Jessop froze at the sight. The Bakora screamed at the site of the weapon. Any Fire within the immediate vicinity of the Blade of Light was instantly extinguished. That was what made it a weapon against the Fire-Wielders. Jessop made her way towards him, blocking and parrying, shooting her small blade out and calling it back to her with Sentio, instantly thankful she had decided not to take the weapon from Falco.

She heard the sound of the blade cutting through the thick, sandy air, just in time. She blocked right before it struck her neck, spun, and kicked the attacker in the jaw. She took another step, ready to throw her short blade, when it was pulled from her hand with Sentio. She narrowed her gaze, and as the sand began to settle, her green eyes fixed on him. His long hair tied back, he still wore his Hunter's vest.

"Hanson Knell. I've been waiting for this." She curved her sword about her as she descended on him.

He moved with surprising speed, their swords connecting with a violent force. She roundhouse kicked him with such might she could feel his ribs breaking. He backhanded her, quick to use Sentio to call her discarded short blade from the ground and hurl it at her side. She bent out of its way as fast as she could, but not fast enough, the weapon reopening the side wound Hydo had inflicted on her. They both ignored their injuries, bringing down heavy sword strokes on one another without hesitation, their moves filled with anger.

"You ruined the Blade— you ruined Kohl!"

She bent back, ducking as the blade moved over her. "You took my son!" She threw her hand back and punched through the air, using her Sentio to send him soaring back.

Suddenly, a blade was on her throat. She grabbed the hand that held it and with all her might, lurched it forward, ducking low, her attacker flipping over her strong body. His landing was messy and he turned with one shoulder tucked tightly against his body—Hydo Jesuin.

Jessop could not fight them both. She scanned the fray, her eyes darting over the battle and back to Hydo and Hanson.

"*Falco!*"

Jessop barely got the scream out before Hanson tackled her to the ground. She kicked him off of her, and they rolled over the mess of broken weapons and fallen soldiers. She punched his face and exposed neck, pinning him down with Sentio and using all her might as she hit him again and again. It didn't take long for Hydo to descend on her, kicking her with a violent force. She flew off Hanson, rolling back, but was quick to her feet. She focused and called her sword back to her, having dropped it in the melee.

As the hilt found her hand, she circled the weapon about her, ready for their attack. Hydo and Hanson stood side by side, walking towards her slowly. She saw Falco far behind them, fighting to reach her, facing onslaught after onslaught. Jessop knew Sentio was her best option—she would hold them back for as long as possible.

The fire burned her instantly, the sting of the whip sharp as it wrapped around her arms. She let out a wild scream as the flames licked her arms. She saw Axis in her periphery—the youngest of Hydo's sons. She could see Hydo screaming at him, but she couldn't make out his words. She focused, using her Sentio to pull the whip from her body. The pain was excruciating as the metal recoiled and fell loose to the ground. She fell to her knees, breathing heavily.

"Falco!"

She focused on her breathing, on her sword hand, on her Sentio. Falco would heal her burns. She just needed to hold them off.

She could see them before her. Her arms were burned. It took all her might to tighten her grip around the hilt of her blade. She tried to close her eyes to focus on her Sentio, to hold them back, but every time she shut them she could feel the flames once more. Her side was bleeding heavily now.

"Falco." She wanted it to be a scream, but it was a whisper. She looked down her arm. Her shoulders were burned. Her vest had protected much of her chest, but her forearms were covered in the lines where the whip had wrapped around her and trailed Axis's fire. He had such anger for her.

"You took the Blade from us."

She couldn't tell if it was Hydo speaking or Hanson. She tried to look up to see, but sand and bright sky blinded her. She heard the sword swinging through the air. She had failed. She closed her eyes. She could see, in her mind, Falco and Jeco. He would prevail, she knew. He would rescue their son.

She lowered her head back down. She could hear his heavy swing.

The sword clashed with the blade of another. She fell back, startled. Before her was Urdo. He moved, wild and strong, hitting Hydo's blade back with attack after attack, forcing his former leader and oldest friend back from Jessop. Hydo fought with one arm as best as he could, using his Sentio and speed to evade his friend's assaults. Urdo was a truly gifted fighter, but even with his dominant arm broken, Hydo was masterful with a blade.

She rolled to her side, her hand dropping her blade to clutch her bleeding cut. She glanced back to the fight. Hydo and Hanson both fought Urdo. They yelled at one another with every angry strike and vicious block. Urdo threw his weight around, forcing Hydo and Hanson to stay on the defense best he could. As Jessop fought to sit upright, Hydo threw Urdo to the ground with his mind.

Hanson stepped on Urdo's blade. "You're a traitor. We're your brothers!"

Jessop could feel the blood from her side flowing faster. "Falco!"

Hydo brought his sword down with an angry, sharp cry.

Jessop scrambled to get to her feet, needing to get to Urdo, tears welling in her eyes. Hanson raised his own blade, ready to finish what Hydo had started. "*Falco!*"

She tightened her hand around her blade, using it as a tool to help her stand. She pushed herself up and stumbled forward. Suddenly, a strong body tackled Hanson to the ground—Kohl.

Jessop took step after step towards Hydo, her body burned, her eyes stinging. She saw Axis reappear in her periphery and she flung her arm out violently, sending him flying back. She staggered forward, moving towards Hydo and Urdo fast as she could. She saw Falco, fighting to get there in time. Hydo raised his sword once more, towering over Urdo.

"*No!*" Jessop ignored the blinding pain and ran—she ran and tripped over bodies and weapons. She threw her arms out before her. In that moment, she saw her parents, she saw the fire, she saw Falco as a boy ...She fell at Urdo's side, her Sentio throwing Hydo back.

She watched as he soared through the air. With a second push from Jessop, Hydo fell at the feet of Falco. She looked to her husband, who turned his gaze from her to his mentor, and without hesitation, without final words or grand movements, Falco snapped his neck, dropping Hydo's lifeless body on the desert battlefield. He was finally gone.

Jessop wrapped her arms around Urdo, stroking his face. There was blood everywhere. She held his head tight against her chest, and whatever pain she had felt at her injuries paled in comparison to seeing him suffer.

"Falco!"

Korend'a and Trax had surrounded Falco and fought her brothers back, keeping them at bay so Falco could make his way to Urdo. He knelt at Urdo's side, his hands slipping in blood as he tried to cover the wounds he needed to heal.

She saw Calis. She saw the eldest, staring at her as if she had somehow betrayed them, and the youngest, fighting with a rage that hindered his abilities. Korend'a and Trax held them back, Trax's Sentio superior enough to throw them back if they tried to use their fire, and Korend'a skill with a blade too great for any of them. Calis was pulling Axis back, yelling at them to retreat, shouting that they had lost this war.

Jessop let her gaze fall back to Urdo. His eyes were glossy. He was half smiling at her. She stroked his hair back softly. She thought of how he had trained her—how he had been the only one to teach her how to truly be a Hunter. She thought of the battle in Aranthol, when he had charged ahead to protect her. She had come so close to death and he had thrown his body before her.

"You saved me." Her voice broke on her tears.

Falco focused, his eyes shut as he tried to heal Urdo's wounds. But Jessop knew. Urdo knew. He grabbed Falco's hand, shaking his head just slightly. He was dying. He turned his gaze back to Jessop. His breathing was strained. He reached up with a weak hand and pulled her hand to his face. He kissed the back of her fingers. "I'd do it all over again if I had to."

She felt his final breath, a warm gasp, as it rolled over her fingertips. She buckled forward, her forehead resting on his. She could hear the battle ending in violence all around her. She could hear the sound of death. She could smell it.

She knew that as she held Urdo, Falco healed her wounds. She knew she needed to get up. She needed to let him go. *Don't let my brothers return to Bakoran.* She pushed the thought to Falco. She knew they couldn't leave, not before she had Jeco. Falco hesitated and she leaned up to look at him. He was covered in blood. His hair stood on end. His eyes were swollen with the tears he fought back.

"Go." She knew that Falco would ensure they remained in *Haren'dul Daku*. She clutched Urdo tightly, struggling to let him go when the sound of an agonizing wail froze her heart.

She lurched up, snapping her head around to see Kohl. He had his forearm locked around Hanson's neck. The older man buckled, his knees falling deep in the sand. He hit Kohl's arms, he tried reaching back for his face, but he had no power left—he was bruised and beaten. Jessop watched the tears stream down Kohl's face as he tightened his hold on his mentor. Hanson's hands clung to his arm, pulling with all his remaining might.

Kohl leaned his head against his mentor's, as though he were trying to say goodbye. Hanson's hands finally fell from Kohl's forearms. Kohl sucked sharply on air, tears falling freely, as he released Hanson's lifeless body, letting him fall to the ground. As Hanson collapsed on the sand, Jessop saw what his struggling body had hidden. Hanson's blade stuck in Kohl's body.

She leapt from Urdo's side and grabbed Kohl before he could fall. "Falco!" She screamed as loud as she could. She leaned Kohl back in her arms. All around her bodies were burning. Sand was blackened by the fire of the Bakora army. Kuroi were dead. Falco's soldiers were dead. The sand creatures were gone. The Bakora had lost the war—but few Daharians remained standing.

She looked down to Kohl. He had a large cut down his face, similar to Falco's, and his hands were shaking as they clung to her. She stroked his cheek, smudging blood over his skin. "You'll be fine."

He pulled on her, trembling. "Please let me go. Please." His request was barely audible, his whisper scarcely reaching her.

She shook her head. Her tears fell on his face, streaking the blood. She leaned over and kissed his forehead, rocking back and forth. "Never."

She sensed Falco at her side. She refused to move, knowing that he would need to remove the blade from Kohl's body before healing him, knowing he needed her to hold him still in the process. She tightened her strong body around his, kissing his forehead again and again, as if rocking his pain away. He screamed as Falco pulled Hanson's blade free. His blood and tears felt slick against her.

She continued to rock him, to kiss his face and wipe his blood away, as Falco fixed his wounds. He hadn't heard Kohl's dark request. He didn't know that he was saving his best friend when his best friend no longer wished to live. And Jessop wouldn't ever tell him. She knew Falco both loved and hated Kohl enough that, if given the right opportunity, he would have let him die.

* * * *

Jessop and Falco traveled with the Void-Voyager, who had remained safely hidden away with Mar'e, to Bakoran. By traveling with them, he ensured they would have a secure way to return to Daharia. Jessop couldn't speak. She could barely think clearly. Dezane and Teck had both died—their final act of bravery had drained them. On their bodies there had been no sword marks and no burns; they had simply perished with the sand army they'd created. Hode Avay was burned beyond recognition, though Falco had done what he could to help. Korend'a, who would live the rest of his life half blind from injury and with a bad leg, told him again and again that the scarring was not bad.

Trax had laid Urdo beside his father and Teck. While survivors were being moved into the Soar-Craft and tended to by the fortunate unwounded, he prepared the bodies for a rightful goodbye. Kohl had healed completely under Falco's ability, and said nothing about wishing he could have died. He had moved Hanson and Hydo to a different place—they would not burn with the true Hunters. With a handful of remaining soldiers, Kohl watched over Jessop's brothers, allowing them to mourn their father.

The Voyager had landed them directly at Octayn's palace, but before them was a giant blue wall of fire. She knew it would not harm her. But Falco was not a Fire-Wielder, and she imagined the blue flames had been designed to keep Daharians out.

She took Falco's hand in hers. "Stay here, with the Voyager."

Her voice was different. Strained.

"But—"

"You cannot pass through these flames, Falco."

She turned and made her way up the white stone steps. The palace seemed abandoned. The grand corridors were empty, the gilded doorways devoid of guards. The beautiful retreat was completely silent. She knew nothing of the palace, but somehow she navigated it with confidence. She was covered in ash and sand and blood, and she trekked through a place of pristine white stone and golden accents.

She turned down a hallway, stepping over small streams of water that seemed to travel throughout the palace. She carried on down the hall, walking past golden door after golden door. As she moved past one doorway, she felt an eerie chill seize her. She stopped and immediately entered the room.

The space was completely barren except for a giant golden box centered in the room. She walked to it and let her hand run over its intricate design. It was icy cold to the touch. She could see that the designs told some kind of story. She tried to follow it, to make out the vague, golden images. There was a child and two adults. The adults were lying down in the next image. There was the wild curve of a fire. There was another man and then a woman. In the next carving, there was a man wearing a crown. Then there was the image of a fire with a sword through it. The final carving showed the woman with the crown.

"Emperor Ozea Oredan's tomb." Octayn's voice filled the room. Jessop looked up from the gilded coffin and saw her standing in the doorway, a sleeping Jeco in her arms, his chest rising and falling slowly as he rested peacefully with her.

"My uncle killed Hydo's family. I killed him for Hydo."

"Give me my son," she ordered, locking her eyes on Octayn. She had been crying.

"He's dead, isn't he? Hydo..."

Jessop nodded slowly as Octayn's tears began to fall freely.

"And my sons?"

Jessop felt her anger somehow abate, ever so slightly, seeing the woman in such pain.

"They live. All of them."

Her green eyes widened with shock. "Thank you."

Jessop reached out, opening her arms and cueing Octayn to hand Jeco to her. There would be no fight between them—Octayn knew better than that.

Octayn kissed his head, a final goodbye. "It was never meant to be like this. I thought ...We thought it would be different."

Jessop reached out and took Jeco from her. She pulled him tightly into her chest and felt her heart race. He was heavier. His hair was longer. She was certain his smell was different. He shifted in his sleep, clinging to her as a child only clings to a parent. Jessop stroked his hair back and breathed him in. Her boy. She had her boy once again.

She flicked her gaze to Octayn. "You have sons. You should have known better than to ever come near mine."

She blinked tears away. "I know."

She fell to her knees. Jessop knew the older woman was waiting for Jessop to kill her. But as Jessop let one hand fall to her hilt, she saw not

Octayn before her, but Calis. In her mind, she saw her brothers; she saw their pain. They had seen their father die on the battlefield.

Jessop stepped around Octayn, making her way out the door. She didn't need to live with Octyan's death on her hands. She turned into the corridor, holding Jeco tightly.

"I had a daughter once too."

Octayn's voice trailed after her. It froze Jessop for a moment. She could return. They could speak. They could lament a history long gone, a future tainted by mistakes they could not take back. They could forge some sort of life together, all of them, as a family. Suddenly, Jeco woke, and upon seeing her face, he did not shy away at her wounds but smiled brightly as he kissed and hugged her.

"Mama," he cried out, tightening his hold on her.

"I have you, my love," she whispered, kissing his head as she fought back the tears.

Jessop walked on, leaving Octayn far behind her.

Epilogue

Jessop had done her best to shield Jeco from the charred remains of the battle, but he had seen many things he would remember for the rest of his life. There had been no real goodbye between her brothers and her, though the feeling that their lives had been gravely harmed by the actions of their parents seemed to resonate for them all. She had allowed them to take Hydo's body.

While many parts of their lives resumed according to plan, with Falco leading the Blade, Jeco beginning training, and Jessop even assuming a role as an instructor to the young Hunters, many things changed. Trax offered Korend'a a position leading the Kuroi, to take over the role that would have been rightfully his at the passing of his father. Korend'a had accepted, more than pleased to return to the land he once thought he'd never see again. Hode Avay, who would never fight again, had asked Falco if he could retire from the Blade, to live Beyond the Grey with Korend'a. Falco had let him go, making him the first Lord Protector to allow a Hunter to resign his post, and making Hode the first Hunter to willingly retire his blade.

It had taken Falco many years to discover why Teck had felt as though he owed Jessop that day in battle. She had asked him about it after Teck's burial and he had not known then. When he finally learned of the answer, he had told Jessop it was out of unfortunate circumstances that Teck had felt he needed to make amends with her

"The mage who attacked you, when we were younger ...He was Teck's kin."

Jessop was surprised at the information. She would have never held Teck responsible for the actions of his family. But she looked at all of their lives and realized how greatly they had all been impacted by the actions of those closest to them. She still wished the mage Hunter had survived, for she felt she had never had the opportunity to truly know him.

The greatest change of all of them, perhaps, was Kohl. He had seemed content for many years with Mar'e. Perhaps it was a quiet contentment, living with Falco and Jessop's friendship, but there had been days where he had seemed truly happy. It had seemed both sudden, but also unsurprising, the day he left. Mar'e had found Jessop in the early morning, appearing in her doorway with a parchment in her shaking hands. "He's gone. He just left me."

When Jessop asked Falco if he would go find him, he shook his head. "He had to leave, Jessop."

"Why?"

"Do you really not know?"

Kohl had never proclaimed his love for her again after *Haren'dul Daku*, but he had sworn to her it would never falter. After Kohl left, she did not see him for many years, though she kept close tabs on him. She knew he had found his mother. Mar'e had returned to the Kuroi, to live Beyond the Grey once more.

Jessop had retired the blade Kohl had made her, out of respect to both him and Falco. For the rest of her days, she would fight with Urdo's sword. She used it to train her son, who moved with Fire and grace. Jeco had grown stronger and stronger. His abilities surpassed those of his parents well before his ten and fifth Partus. Not only did he have a masterful sword hand, but he was a Fire-Wielder with a beautiful grasp on Sentio.

"We should reach out to them. I have cousins, cousins who are like *me*," Jeco had argued to his parents on more than one occasion. Jessop had not told him, but she had spoken with Calis a handful of times, in their dreams, over the years. She didn't know what the future held for them. She didn't know if a few conversations were all they would ever have. In turn, Jessop didn't know that Jeco had learned dream-travel in secret, when Taygen's eldest, Kross, visited him in his sleeping hours.

"Our parents did it all wrong, but we could do it better," Jeco told Kross, walking through the Oredan palace in his cousin's dream world.

Kross turned to him, arching his brow over his shimmering green eyes. "You really think we could do it?"

Jeco clapped him on the back, encouraging him. "Cousin! Just imagine it, if we joined territories, we would have a nation of Fire-Wielders, desert mages, and Hunters."

Kross slowly smiled. "Well, we are the next rightful rulers."

Jeco smiled back, igniting a golden flame around his body. "Exactly."

* * * *

Jessop looked the girl over. Her name was Laar and she was young, with flaming red hair and large, dark eyes. She sat opposite Jessop, wedged between her parents, her arms crossed tightly over her chest. She and Falco had listened as the parents, farmers who had traveled days to reach Azgul, described the difficulties they were having with their daughter.

The girl stood, angry. "You heard him, they've never trained a girl. This was a waste of time."

Jessop moved around Falco, standing directly in front of Laar. She studied the girl's frame—she was a small, wiry thing. The parents had told them that she continued to get in fights in their village. Laar had slammed her hand on the table. "I'm defending other children!"

Jessop liked her. She was young and she had an energy that those closest to her didn't understand.

"You really want to be a Hunter?"

She nodded.

"Answer me. Use your voice."

"Yes, I do. I don't fight just to fight ...I fight so others don't have to."

Jessop smiled at the girl's response. She turned to Falco. "We've discussed this for a long time. She could be the first."

He smiled at her, slowly nodding his head in agreement. They had long ago decided they would train all who were willing, male or female, but they had found no families willing to send their daughters, and no women willing to volunteer to be the first students. He turned to the parents. "Jessop has insisted for some time that we begin to train women. It seems the day has come where we can finally make those wishes a reality."

Laar's parents beamed as they stood to shake Falco's hand and embrace Jessop. She hugged them both briefly, still, after all these years, disliking being touched by most. She wasn't interested in the parents. She was interested in the girl. Jessop and Falco had changed many things about the way the Blade trained Hunters. The first change, of course, had been to remove the final rites—mentors would never harm their students as they had in the past. The second change had been to cease the elimination of personal ties—their students in the Blade all maintained relationships with their families, who visited regularly.

Jessop knew she would need to get new clothes and smaller boots organized for Laar, the first female student of the Blade. "We can start today, if you're ready."

Laar smiled at her, the excitement visible in her eyes. "Thank you."

Falco and Jessop escorted the family to a separate space, offering them a private room to say their goodbyes. As they made their way from the room, Jessop stopped, turning back to the parents. "Who told you to bring the girl to us?"

It was Laar who answered. "A man from our village. Kohl O'Hanlon."

Jessop smiled as she took Falco's hand in hers. They left the family, turning down the corridor to go make arrangements for the girl's training to begin.

Acknowledgments

I would like to first thank my agent, Richard Curtis, who has been my patient and kind guide through this entire process. I could have never done it without you and I thank you wholeheartedly. I want to thank my husband and our child, for their patience, love, and support. I love you always. I would like to thank Grey, for always sitting with me. I love you. I also must thank Zorro and Big Duck, Bird, Eddie, Logo, his sister, and my mother for their support. I thank my grandparents for their love and their interest in my writing. And I thank Lara, my dearest friend, who has always supported my work. I love you all and I thank you for the role you have each played in the development of this trilogy. Finally, I would like to thank Martin Biro, James Abbate, and the entire Kensington Rebel Base team who have worked tirelessly on this series.

If you enjoyed *Dawn of the Hunters*, be sure not to miss the first book in Ryan Wieser's epic Hunters of Infinity series,

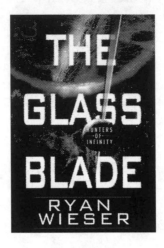

The Hunters of Infinity have been protecting the Daharian galaxy for years, but there has never been a female Hunter—until now.

In a seedy bar in the shadowy corners of Daharia, Jessop comes to the rescue of young Hunter Kohl O'Hanlon. Impressed by her remarkable sword-wielding skills, the Hunters invite her to their training facility, the Glass Blade, though not all are pleased with the intrusion. But they soon discover that Jessop learned to fight from the rogue leader of the Shadow City of Aranthol—and *escaped*. Now they want to use her intimate knowledge of their enemy to destroy him.

As Jessop grows closer to this elite brotherhood, their leader succumbs to a mysterious ailment, and Kohl learns that Jessop is hiding dark secrets, raising suspicions about the enigmatic woman who saved his life. Has the Hunters' security been breached—or do they have a traitor in their ranks?

Allegiances will be questioned.
Loyalties will be betrayed.
Vengeance will be brutal.

A Rebel Base Books e-book on sale now.

CHAPTER 1

The tavern was dark and quiet, barring the muted voices that filled the corners with whispers of quiet corruption and deceit. Hushed sounds traveled on thick smoke to the ceiling and her eyes trailed over the dimly lit corners and over the musty cloaked patrons. Dirty exchanges took place everywhere, too-young girls being offered coins and despair by corrupt travelers, whose lies traveled like fire across the alcohol on their lips. This wasn't a typical bar, this dark, underground dwelling in the heart of Azgul where there were more shadows than light, more smoke than air. It was a seedy, unsafe locale where illegal exchanges could occur. A place favored by those in the city's most important positions, for in this underground dwelling they could act as they truly wished.

From where she sat, with her cloak draped low over her face, she could easily make out the group of Aren. They were more discreet than she had anticipated, but few could go unseen to her well-trained eyes. They were scattered about the bar, donning the civilian attire of common Azgul nomad passer-by. The Aren weren't common travelers though; they were fatalistic believers who waited anxiously for a supposed impending end. A doom and darkness that would swallow the entire Daharian galaxy whole—their belief in some unimagined state of horror for the universe made her certain that not a man amongst them had ever laid eyes on Aranthol.

She scanned the room, counting twelve of the zealots. Without their robes they appeared as normal men, barring their brand, which could be seen on the base of several of their necks. The tender nape of the neck was where all in Azgul had their brands. She knew that their mark was not well-known though, not as well-known as they would have liked it to be. Thinking of the brandings nearly had Jessop reaching for her own neck, certain she could almost feel the hot iron against her still. The smell of burning, blistering flesh unnaturally recoiling from heated metal filled her nostrils. She shivered at the putrid memory and forced it back to the depths of her mind, where she kept all her locked-away thoughts and all her darkness.

Suddenly, the oddest sensation roused her, overcoming her senses. She could feel silk running across her skin, dragging her fine hairs on end, exciting her cells. The energy of the room had completely changed, thickening the air more than any smoke or liquor could do. She had only ever been around one other of her kind, and to feel the changing electromagnetic charge in the room without *him* present was as compelling to her as it was terrifying. The draw was a beast's cry calling her in, feeding her need to find the one like her. It was a pull strong enough to grip her, strong enough to shoot adrenaline through her, to dilate her pupils and ready her muscles and tell her, without question, that Hunters were near.

She closed her eyes and narrowed in on their presence. She could smell the faintest scent of grease on one of them; it had an acidic air to it—like the oil slick found in the Western corner of the city. She could hear his voice though he did not speak. She could see the diminutive smudge of black slick over his boot though she did not open her eyes. Her senses—so refined—ensured she could see most of him without ever glancing his way.

And then she laid eyes on him.

She found herself staring at a silver star-shaped scar, a twisted knot of marred flesh the size of a plum carved into his cheekbone. He had a mess of blond hair that he wore pulled back and dark eyes that he scanned the bar with. His frame was large but he held one shoulder slightly higher—due to recent injury, she imagined. As one of his large hands curled around a drink, the other rested comfortably against the hilt of his blade. His eyes trailed over the room and for a moment she wondered if he sensed her presence too. His gaze returned to his drink, and he smiled with half his mouth, allowing the star-shaped scar to pull and glisten. He was beautifully flawed.

Her gaze fell to the man beside the young Hunter—an older man, another Hunter. The men dressed as she had expected. Their uniform consisted of black breeches and tunic, over which they wore a waist-length black leather vest, bound shut with the belt that carried their blade. The vest had their sigil imprinted over the heart. She watched as the older of the two pulled a stool out from the bar, slowly sitting as his well-trained eyes searched the corners of the establishment with practiced ease. His braid of silver hair rested down his back and as a rare flickering of light caught his face she saw his skin was mapped with the deep lines of worn scars. She had let her gaze hold him for less than a minute when she felt the whirring energy of his keen mind.

His age made him more attuned to the presence of those like him. He turned in his seat, searching the room—he could *sense* her. But Jessop didn't worry—he wouldn't be looking for *her*; he would be searching for a man. Just to be sure, though, she forced her thoughts down, quieting her mind and turning her gaze away.

She concentrated on her hand, on drumming her fingers on the table before her. She could feel her blood coursing, warm and rapid, through her veins, and her heart quickening, all for feeling the presence of those so like her so near. Her foot bounced against the floor, pumping adrenaline through her long legs. The silent room seemed to be getting louder and louder, she could hear her beating heart, swelling under her breast, her green eyes straining to stay down as anticipation welled inside her...

Through her periphery she could make out the lone Aren, moving swiftly towards the Hunters. He held a blade. He needed to be quick. Her beating heart was pulsing rhythmically, deafening her thoughts. Someone—a girl—seeing the knife, screamed, a shriek that set the room into motion. Jessop finally let herself look up. The Hunters moved quickly in the shadows, swift to unsheathe their weapons. The Aren formed their pack quickly; there were thirteen, not twelve. For a brief moment, she was surprised at how one could have passed under her sight. She threw her hood back, finally able to watch the scene unfold. As the zealots formed a semi-circle around the Hunters, backing them up against the bar, the tavern crumbled into pandemonium.

The young girls cried with an adolescent fear that nearly overwhelmed Jessop. But she had learnt long ago how to ignore pain—hers and theirs. Her eyes stayed set on the Hunters as the travelers and girls and workers all fought for the exits. The dark space that had offered them such safety from prying eyes minutes before now offered them danger and isolation from help. Quick to come for pleasure and quick to escape pain—Jessop had many criticisms for those who came to be in this part of Azgul.

The sound of a man dying refocused her attention. An Aren fell to the ground before the Hunters. Jessop watched the young fair one, his strong arm wielding his blade about him like an extension of himself. Something about his flesh appeared silvery to her, somehow reflective. She couldn't quite make it out. He spun low and struck with ease. He *was* good. Despite his well-rehearsed steps, he was still exciting to watch. The older Hunter had his fight memorized, a veteran warrior with a trusted blade, faster than one would have prepared for—*he* was exactly as Jessop had expected.

They were good—better than most she had ever seen. But there were simply too many Aren and she was uncertain what odds the Hunters, especially the young one, had fought against before. With every deflection and assault a new attack came down upon them. It seemed two against thirteen was an impossible fight for them to win without suffering serious harm.

The young Hunter was flung back against the bar as two Aren wrestled his strong arms back, a third moving towards him with a blade. Jessop knew she had little time to make her move.

She leaped from her seat, charging swiftly toward the Aren set on impaling the young Hunter. To the cloaked disciple's shock, she hooked her arm under his neck and kicked his feet out from underneath him. As he stumbled, she wrenched the blade from his grip. With a heavy throw, she lodged the small weapon expertly into the chest of one of the assailants holding the young Hunter's arm back.

The Hunter tore his surprised gaze from her to the dying Aren clinging to him, gargling blood. He shoved his attacker to the ground before gruffly elbowing the other man holding him, bloodying the Aren's nose before striking him in the chest. The Aren fell forward as the Hunter grabbed a bottle from the bar and beat it over the man's head. As glass shattered and liquor spurted across the bloodied floor, Jessop couldn't help but think him resourceful.

He shot Jessop a grateful, if not confused, glance, before grabbing his blade from the ground and continuing his fight. She watched him as he clashed with the fanatics—he moved with skill and grace, his star glass blade travelling silently through the air. The Hunters' blades were forged with the pressurized sediment left over from star formations. The blades appeared as glass, each slightly different in color, but were harder than any material found in Daharia. The young Hunter's sword was entirely transparent, crystal clear from base to deadly tip. It was beautiful.

She kept her eyes on him, while still easily deflecting any attack against her. Thirteen Aren against two Hunters was too many, thirteen against two Hunters and *her,* was just fine. She grabbed the shoulder of one Aren and quickly spun him around. He stared at her with shock.

"*What* are you doing?"

She didn't answer him. To see a woman intervene in an Azgul fight would be a surprise to any. She grabbed his wrist and disarmed him with a forceful twist of his hand. He lashed out with anger, hurling his spare fist towards her small face. She ducked and caught his arm with both hands, twisted at the hip, and kicked him viciously in the abdomen. He fell from her, winded. She knelt beside him and offered a vicious strike to his temple, leaving him unconscious.

She was on her feet instantly, turning just in time to grab the neck of the next Aren. She grabbed his wrist, holding his hand back, and then, quickly, released her hold on his neck, recoiled her hand, twisted her fingers into a fist, and struck back at the exposed flesh forcefully, punching him in the throat. The Aren coughed for air, grabbing at his windpipe. She took a step towards him, darted her arm past his face, and jerked it back, hitting him with her elbow. He fell to the ground.

She stepped over his writhing body and caught the eye of the young Hunter. He too had been watching her. A look of distinct admiration was in his eyes, despite being embroiled in his own fight; it was clear she had impressed him. She turned from him and found the hands of an Aren grabbing at her, coiling tightly around her neck. He lifted her off the ground and slammed her back against the bar. She could hear glasses shattering behind her, stools knocking against her legs and falling to the side.

She brought her arm up and over his hands, jerking downward until she leveraged his grip off of her. She kneed him in the abdomen, and as he buckled forward, she kneed him again, breaking his nose. He stumbled back and she crouched to the ground, spiraling with one leg extended and kicking his legs out from underneath him. She was standing, already in mid-motion for her next assault before he hit the ground. She kicked him swiftly and leapt over his body, her hands landing on the shoulders of one of the three Aren surrounding the older Hunter.

She spun him around and struck. She got his throat and elbowed his cheekbone. Holding his collar as she struck at him again, she looked to the old Hunter. "Get out of here—I've got this!" she yelled to him.

His aged cobalt eyes widened with suspicion. "Who are *you*?" He kicked one of the Aren back, seeming more concerned about Jessop than he was about his attacker.

The guttural cry of the young Hunter drew their attention—the young man was wounded. An Aren fell fatally from the Hunter's sword, but he had left a dagger stuck in the fair Hunter's side. The fight had gone on long enough. As the older Hunter ran past her to his wounded comrade, Jessop took a deep breath and closed her eyes; she concentrated on the feeling of electricity running through her, deep within her. The unadulterated power that she had long since learnt how to lose herself in—how to stay safe within the boundaries of.

She slowly exhaled. And with expert skill, she snapped the neck of the Aren before her, opening her eyes as he hit the ground.

She flicked her cloak to the side and found the hilt of her weapon. She drew the blade from its sheath and spun about, skillfully wielding the sword. The lethal piece was beautiful. Made of star glass, it was the only one of its kind—forged to be entirely onyx in color; the blade was black as night. She ducked low and spun on her knee, moving the sword around her in a circle, and came up behind an Aren attacker. She struck him down and stood as he fell from her weapon's lethal edge, slicking the sword with his crimson blood. She bent her knees and quickly jumped atop the bar, dancing over glasses as she made her way towards the Hunters.

She flipped from the edge, curving her blade out as she spun in the air.

She landed on one knee, the Hunters safely behind her, the Aren before her. She remained crouched down as she brought her weapon's point up into the diaphragm of the next assailant. He stumbled towards her and she spun on her knee out to the side, liberating her weapon from his dying body as she stood. The two remaining Aren descended upon her swiftly. She twirled, her cloak flying about her as she landed a roundhouse kick against one. He fell to the ground as the other, with surprising might, grabbed her from behind. His strong forearm locked around her neck and pulled her back tightly. Her leather boot slipped in a thick pool of blood and she struggled to regain her footing as the other Aren recovered, steadying himself before her.

She backed into the man holding her and thrust her sword outward, connecting with the second Aren's side just enough to sting. He lunged at her, snarling wildly. She leaned back into her captor and kicked at the wounded man. She got his chin and forcefully sent him flying onto his back.

The silvery glint of the dagger caught her eye just in time.

The Aren holding her held his weapon high above her; ready to bring it down on her chest. She closed her eyes, concentrating on the energy between them—on her *power*—and, just as she had anticipated, the Aren shrieked in agony, dropping his blade to the ground, loosening his hold on her neck. Jessop snaked her sword about in her expert fingers, curved her body to the side, and thrust her sword inward, past her hip, into his abdomen.

She spun out of his grip, pulling her blade loose. He coughed, blood dripping from his lip, pooling in his gut. She remained in position with her sword extended out, perfectly parallel to the ground, her feet steadying themselves in the still-warm blood of her slain victims. She stood at the ready in a circle of the dead or dying. None of the attackers moved and she took a cautious breath, mentally assessing her body for injuries—she was mostly unharmed and the battle was over.

She cleaned her blade swiftly on her cloak and sheathed it before turning to the Hunters. The older was supporting the younger, applying pressure to his wound and they both stared at her with wild-eyed confusion, though the young one looked on through fluttering eyelashes.

The blue eyes of the old Hunter narrowed on her. "Tell me who you are," he ordered.

She looked away from him to his wounded companion. She could see the blood shining over his leather. His paling face and slowing breaths were poor signs. "Your friend needs treatment," she advised.

The silver-haired Hunter nodded, more concerned with his young friend than her identity. "Then help me get him some, girl."

Jessop flinched at the word, but nodded. She took a step towards the Hunters, and eased the young one's arm over her shoulder, slowly pulling him away from the bar. It was only once she was close enough to support his weight did she understand why his skin seemed to shimmer like silver to her—he was covered in hundreds of scars.

"You saved us," he whispered, his hazel eyes studying her. She smiled tightly at him, uncertain of how to respond, and then watched as he lost consciousness; his heart slowing caused her own to speed up.

* * * *

"This one," the old Hunter barked, practically dragging them towards what Jessop believed could quite possibly have been the oldest Soar-Craft she had ever seen. She had no time to question the safety of the ship, as the silver-haired Hunter had already begun to push his wounded comrade into the vehicle.

She crawled over the door and into the back, trying to avoid the precarious metal prongs poking through the old vinyl seat cover as she awkwardly continued to help support the weight of the Hunter. The older man pushed his unconscious body at her gruffly, and she coughed as his young heavy frame collapsed against her, pinning her down. She freed her arms from underneath him, readjusting her sheath before fixing his head against her shoulder and pressing one hand against his wound. His hair had fallen loose from its knot and covered his face like a veil of gold. Without thinking, she stroked it back, smoothing it away from his soft skin. And then quickly retracted her hand.

She forced her attention onto the older Hunter as he leapt into the control seat. He fiddled with a compartment door and when it wouldn't give under his rough grab, he let his hand hover slightly above it, and then—like *magic*—it popped open.

Jessop took a deep, controlled breath; this was her cue to confirm her beliefs about the Hunters. "You're one of *them*?"

"Yes, I'm one of the Hunters of Infinity, girl. Can't you see our sigil? Now here, take these," he barked, tossing a pair of worn out leather goggles at her. She pulled the goggles over the young Hunter's head, securing them over his closed eyes. The older man handed her a second set, and despite their frayed leather and browned screens, she pulled them on. She studied the sigil on the leather vest of the unconscious Hunter—she had seen the mark, she knew it well.

The older Hunter hit a button on the dash several times before another compartment opened up and a yoke ascended from it. As he grabbed hold of the yoke, a blue light emitted, scanning his hands.

"Welcome back, Hanson Knell," the automated Soar-Craft voice crackled.

Jessop had heard the name many times before and she was actually somewhat shocked that of all the Hunters for her to have found, it was Hanson Knell. And if *he* was Hanson Knell, she could be certain that the fair, scarred young man lying unconscious in her lap was his mentee Kohl O'Hanlon. She could have mused over the knowledge further, but now was not the time—she was a nervous flyer in the safest of ships. She anxiously looked the vehicle over, and squeezed against Kohl O'Hanlon a bit tighter under the sputtering of revving engines.

"Is this thing sky-worthy?" she yelled up to Hanson Knell.

"It's been safely navigating the Daharian skies since before you were born," the old Hunter called back. He pulled on the yoke and the Soar-Craft began to shakily hover off the ground.

"That's what I'm worried about," she grumbled, closing her eyes as they took off at a surprisingly quick speed for the old machine.

Hanson Knell navigated the Soar-Craft through the underground maze, where those who wished to go to such a bar had to park their ships. It didn't take long for the old machine to gain a terrifying break-neck speed and soon they were whirring through the dark space, taking sharp corners and diving down steep descents. Jessop held the young Hunter tightly, pushing her cloak against his wound.

As they finally emerged from the labyrinth, the unmistakably red sky, where hundreds of other Soar-Craft zipped around them, blinded Jessop. It took a minute for her eyes to adjust to the unfamiliar crimson atmosphere of Azgul.

She wasn't from Azgul, though she had been there for several days, preparing for *this* moment, where she would find the ones like her. She couldn't help but think, as she looked down at the young Hunter's blood, staining rivers into the lines of skin on her hand, that with all the violence that had already ensued, she was exactly where she was supposed to be.

As quickly as the sense of certainty materialized it had disappeared, wrenching from her gut as the Soar-Craft dropped some sixty-feet in the sky to undertake a row of oncoming ships. Hanson Knell was either a brilliant or superbly dangerous pilot. He tore the old machine through the skies, weaving through organized lines of Soar-Craft, cutting off other pilots, making unsanctioned cuts and dives around Levi-Hubs, where other pilots, busy recharging their ships, yelled and cursed at them. Jessop didn't care about the dangerous flying, the precarious Soar-Craft or the angry slurs of other pilots—all she cared about was the direction they were travelling in. She had confirmed who they were and she knew they were going to a place she had envisioned entering for many years.

Jessop could see it nearing in the red horizon, the building that mirrored the crimson light of the city, refracting red rays in every direction. The building that appeared like a needle in the skyline; slender, tall and reflective. The Glass Blade was the training center and home to all the Hunters of Infinity there had ever been, and all the Hunters of Infinity there ever would be. She narrowed her eyes at the architectural spectacle that she had only ever known through the thoughts of others and she wished she could remove her stained goggles to get a clearer look. The sickly sensation of fluid slicking her fingers drew her attention away from the nearing Glass Blade and back to the wounded Hunter.

She cautiously drew her cloak back and pulled at his leather vest. His tunic was saturated with dark blood. She pulled the hem up, narrowing her eyes on the injury as the wind whipped around his garments. The sheer amount of blood made it difficult to assess the actual injury, but with focus, she could see the small pocket of a wound, tucked in between the mounds of his red-stained muscular ridges. It amazed her how humans, Hunters or otherwise, were kept safe by the integrity of this fine skin, and one small slice was all it took…

The wound was bad, the blood loss potentially fatal. She covered the injury back up, pushing a handful of material hard against it. The abilities of the medical team at the Glass Blade were renowned, known of even where she came from. If anyone could save the young Hunter, it was the team residing within his own home. As if on cue, the gleaming reflection of the red sky against the glass-paneled building nearly blinded her and she looked down to the pale face of the Hunter, silently willing him to hold on just a little bit longer.

She looked ahead as they sped towards the glass, with no signs of slowing down, and no visible entrance. She knew the Hunter trick, but she could not pretend she was not put somewhat on edge by the nearing building. As her heart sped up, the old Hunter threw his hand, fingers extended and palm out, in front of him, making the mystical mark in his palm visible to the glass walls. And just like that, the glass seemed to melt, rippling as though burning, and a black hole, barely large enough for the Soar-Craft to fit through, opened up to them.

With a sudden sickening drop, the Soar-Craft ducked into the mystical entrance, enveloping them in darkness. The preternatural mark, burnt into the hand of the Infinity Hunters, was the only way to gain entrance into the Glass Blade. A building that housed the protectors of Daharia, and the Blade of Prince Daharian, or the Blade of Light, as they called it, needed such security measures. Although, Jessop knew, such measures had only been put in place after what had happened with Falco Bane all those years ago.

They soared down a pitch-black tunnel and it was clear that Hanson navigated the ship through such darkness by memory alone. Jessop, on the other hand, pulled her goggles off, able to see in the darkness just fine. She had been raised in darkness. It was more soothing to her than any source of light could ever be. Just as she thought it though, a light did appear. A white glow in the distance illuminated a docking bay. Hanson zipped the Soar-Craft forward, bringing them in for an abrupt landing on the parking zone. Almost immediately, a team of white uniformed techs and engineers began yelling, angry, as they circled the ship.

"Knell, if we've told you once we've—" one began, but froze, his voice caught in his throat, as he saw Jessop and the fallen Hunter.

Hanson leaped from the craft, wrenching open a side door so that Jessop nearly fell out onto the hard floor. "Help me get him inside!"

Hanson and a group of the white uniformed men lifted the young Hunter from Jessop and quickly began to haul his unconscious body down the bay, leaving her, bloodstained, in the back seat. She quickly leapt out of the ship and ran after them, barely getting through the sliding automatic glass doors in time. She stared as Hanson Knell watched over his young mentee with fear, applying pressure to his wound and whispering under his breath to him. She could feel the combined concern of all of them, who clearly knew the wounded man and feared for his life. The second thing for her to learn about the young Hunter was that he was clearly beloved. The first had been that he was a half-decent fighter.

But her attention was torn as she lurched forward, unsteady on her feet as the floor beneath her began to rise. The steel metal platform on which they stood flew up a transparent chute, travelling through the Glass Blade, like a bead in a crystal clear tube. While she dug her heels in, the surrounding men seemed quite accustomed to the force.

They passed floor after floor of training rooms, engineer docks, labs, and workplaces, each one containing groups of men, all in the same uniform—black if they were a Hunter, white if they were not—all conducting different business. After several more levels were passed in which Jessop had seen a handful of young boys, some barely old enough to talk, undergoing martial training, the glass bullet came to a sudden halt, opening its doors to a medical floor.

Jessop nearly fell out, stumbling to the side as the white uniformed men and Hanson Knell carried the young Hunter out. "Let's get some help over here!" Hanson yelled, and immediately, under his vicious growl, a flock of medics and nurses swarmed them. Jessop stepped back and watched the team as they moved like an efficient flight of birds, swooping in, opening the young Hunter's vest, removing his blade, and carrying him away, disappearing down the corridor without any hesitation or questions.

The room fell quiet as all of them stared at the slow swinging doors the medics had taken Kohl O'Hanlon through. Jessop took a deep breath, looking around slowly, amazed by the building she found herself in.

One of the men from the docking bay turned to Hanson Knell. "Do you want us to wait with you, Sir?"

Hanson shook his head, staring down at the young Hunter's sword in his hands. "No, go on."

The man nodded, slowly clapping Hanson Knell on the shoulder as he walked past, leading his group of techs back into the glass chute. Jessop studied the old Hunter's face, the smattering of blood flecked across his cheek, the way his cool eyes fixated on the blade in his hand. He was old and he was weary, and likely in need of a medical inspection. She knew better than to suggest it though. Instead, she let her gaze fall from him, slowly taking in the brilliant opal lights that surrounded her, the pristine ivory floors and glass furniture. It was the brightest and cleanest room she had ever been in.

Suddenly, Jessop was choking. Without warning, a terrifying grip had locked around her small throat, closing around her jugular and flinging her body against the glass doors. Hanson Knell's grizzled fingers tightened around her windpipe and in his spare hand was the blade of his comrade, pointed directly at her face. She was pinned between the blade and the door behind her, his rough fingers grinding at her neck.

She didn't stir, her startled heart slowing as she studied the hardened eyes of Hanson Knell. Being startled was not the same as being afraid— true fear was something that had long since been beaten out of her. She took shallow breaths between his vice grip. "*What?*"

"Who are you, girl?" he growled.

She slowly raised her hand to his and pulled gently at his wrist, willing him to release her throat, but he resisted, inching the blade closer to her eye.

"I don't know what answer you want," she spoke hoarsely, her voice straining against his hold.

"Don't toy with me, *girl*," he barked, jerking her by her throat and slamming her body hard against the glass door again.

"Do not call me girl, *old man*," she growled back, narrowing her eyes on him.

He brought his angry face closer to her. "I want a name, *girl*. And once we have that, then perhaps you'll tell me why you fight with Falco Bane's sword?"

She slapped at his hand, urging him to loosen his grip on her throat... before she forced it loose. Slowly, he acquiesced.

She coughed, swallowing hard against her bruised windpipe. She held his gaze as she ran her fingers slowly up and down her neck. "Because I took it from him when I escaped Aranthol."

Printed in the United States
by Baker & Taylor Publisher Services